Boon

TJ SULLIVAN

Boon

ONE REDBEETLE
PRESS LLC

- Los Angeles -

BOON

ONE RED BEETLE PRESS, LLC
10573 W. Pico Blvd. #348, Los Angeles, CA 90064
www.OneRedBeetle.com

Back cover author photograph by
Juan Carlo/*Ventura County (CA) Star*. Used with permission.
All other photographs and cover design © 2010 ONE RED BEETLE PRESS, LLC.

Library of Congress Control Number: 2009909910
ISBN-13: 978-0-615-32527-9
ISBN-10: 0-615-32527-0

Printed in the United States of America

First edition
Published in 2010
ONE RED BEETLE PRESS, LLC

To Faith
I believe

CHAPTER 1 – BREADWINNER

Even strapped into the passenger seat of her Corolla, sandwiched between a Geo Metro and a Chevy pickup, Jake believed in the power of the radio weatherman on KOPF 1020AM. She didn't just want the salvation of his voice, she needed it. Without his help, her Monday morning crawl to work seemed insurmountable. Absent his encouragement, she doubted her ability to wash away the gray of another weekend wasted house shopping in the suburbs of Los Angeles.

> *"— this light morning fog is sure to burn off*
> *by noon ... sunny skies ... a high of 75 ... and*
> *a low of 69 —"*

Her husband, Keith, slipped one hand across the top of the steering wheel and the other out the window, slapping at the sun-beaten side of his door, sending tremors through the shock absorbers and the springs in Jake's seat. He whispered curses and socked the horn, but his frustration registered only as a faint buzz in Jake's ears so long as the weatherman commanded the airwaves. Worries and concerns dispersed as Jake floated out the window, over the westbound lanes of Highway 101, beyond the curtains of car exhaust and tar-kettle smoke, all the way to the true-blue heaven of her imagination.

> *"— Positive ions will blanket the passes and canyons this afternoon ... delicate breezes will pet the shores until the sandy beaches drift off to sleep ... and that brilliant, blue moon I've been talking about for so long will finally rise to light the night —"*

The weatherman's words were Jake's emotional helium, a cosmic transfusion of optimism when she needed it most, right at the dark start, when the day wasn't bright enough for shadows and anything could go any way. Jake's AM radio weatherman always promised an eventual end to bad air, and, in time, was always proved right. When it rained, which it hadn't done in so long, he reminded Jake of the necessity of precipitation. He pumped up even the worst downpours as celebrations, with the guarantee of a limited stay for every cloud. The weatherman's baritone went down warm as whiskey and, before long, every word became something she needed to hear.

> *"— The long-range outlook calls for the approval of a hearty salary increase at midweek, followed by an extended period of appreciation and lingering respect along the Buckwalter front —"*

Buckwalter was the new section editor, whose anticipated arrival that morning had become a low-pressure event. Change was inevitable, but whatever kind he might effect had yet to be determined. The name — Buckwalter — sounded bad, though not the way Jake's weatherman said it. That voice equalized even the most acute consonants. It neutralized conflicts and balanced fears with the assurance that no ill wind could blow forever. In Jake's daydream, her radio weatherman took the form of a disembodied genie who indulged her every wish and made her feel so high that she forgot gravity, at least until the traffic girl came on all curt and to the point, so sharp a contrast that it popped Jake out of her fantasy and back into the grim actuality of Highway 101.

TJ SULLIVAN

She felt as though she'd had her wind knocked out, all puffs and jitters as traffic jams trebled out the speakers — tie-ups and snarls and stalls and Sig-Alerts. She reached for the tuner dial to seek out a sports station, or the one that played nothing but Mozart. Even the misguided rants of a talk show host like Chad Habit would be better than one more word about how many commuters were headed nowhere in a hurry. She gripped the knob so hard it came off in her hand.

"What the boon!" Keith spit and made Jake jerk for having forgotten he was there. "We can't afford another car," he said. "Stop tearing this one apart."

What little sense of weightlessness was left in Jake's arms and legs dissolved as a motorcycle blasted past, splitting the lane on her side of the car. By the time she realized her cell phone was ringing the call had nearly jumped to voicemail. She fumbled for it in her bag.

The air was dead when she answered. The phosphorescent display identified the caller as "Undetermined."

Keith looked over as she folded the phone closed. "That's almost every day for two weeks," he said.

"My number's not exactly secret. It's on the Web. Maybe it got into some telemarketing machine."

"Or maybe it's a stalker — some perv with a lukewarm washcloth and a bottle of *Jerk*ins."

Jake laughed. "People call with story tips," she said. "And it's Jergens, not *Jerk*ins."

"Whatever it is, it's messed up."

"It's static."

"Panting sounds like static."

"People prank at night, not the morning."

"I did it in the morning," Keith told her.

"You didn't."

"We were dating. You could have been playing me. How could I be sure you weren't with some other dude?"

"So you decided to play games with me instead?" she said. "And since when do you call anyone 'dude?'"

Keith slammed the brakes and stiff-armed the horn, an abrupt stop that threw Jake forward and snapped the shoulder strap straight.

"It's getting worse," Keith said.

"You just think that," Jake replied. "You always think that. But it's the same. It's always the same."

At 50 minutes, Jake figured their daily drive was typical by LA standards, certainly shorter than it would have been if they'd purchased one of the two-bedroom pre-fab houses 90 miles out in the desert suburb of Glencaster. They might have been able to manage one of those. For DINKs — Double Income No Kids — the monthly payment was doable, but it would have meant the elimination of what little disposable income they possessed. There'd be no more Starbucks coffee at breakfast, no more Jamba Juice smoothies on Friday afternoons, not even those crisp, cold salads from Mickey Dee's that Jake sometimes drowned in creamy dressings. Jake and Keith could have handled a house in the desert if they brown-bagged it every day, cooked for themselves each night, and kept the Corolla on the road another decade or so. They'd already gone without vacations and eschewed most forms of entertainment. Jake had never been on a plane, couldn't recall the last movie she'd seen in a cinema, and hadn't been to a music concert of any kind since the summer fiestas she enjoyed as a teenager back home in Española. But, just because the house in Glencaster was possible, that didn't mean it was a home. Most of the men out there looked like corpses in recovery, and only the women had bothered to engaged Jake in conversation — their questions all about children and whether Jake planned to keep the job once she was a mother.

They'd all responded in kind when Jake declared her intent to keep her career.

"That's what I said," they'd told her.

Sleep, Jake concluded, was the only promise in a place like that, because sleep would have been all that time permitted. No barbecues. No gardening. No kids. She thought it wiser to keep up the hunt while toughing it out in Reseda, a borough she'd only ever thought of as a song lyric by Tom Petty, the one that immortalized the place as the freeway-adjacent home of a girl who loved her boyfriend, America and Jesus. For Jake, Reseda was a rental unit, temporary shelter — though not even the dictionary defined the duration of "temporary." Rather than dwell on uncertainty, Jake invested her energy in the establishment of momentum. She was determined not to just request a raise, but to get it. She'd already set up an appointment with a new real estate agent. She told herself this one wasn't like the others, that this agent would help them find a way. Waters End was the suburb where she and Keith worked. Soon they'd live there too.

Jake grinned as the Corolla passed Plum Street, the whole system of street names in Waters End so delightfully silly. Nectarine and Mango streets followed Lime and Kiwi, each block in the grid another alphabetical step closer to the heart of town at Apple and Main. It all sounded so wonderfully American. Except for exceptions like Main Street, most every road in the Los Angeles suburb of Waters End reflected the region's agricultural roots, though most of what the signs commemorated had never been cultivated locally. From city hall east to the base of the Santa Monica Mountains, the routes were named for fruits. To the west, vegetables and flowers. To the south, trees and nuts. North was livestock, fish and fowl. The theme continued throughout the valley floor and up into the curly ribbons of concrete that climbed the hills, where "streets" were transmuted into palm-lined "lanes" and "ways," "courts" and "circles." The Mayor's house sat up there, somewhere on Pearmain Way. *The Pendulum's* Editor-in-Chief had a hillside address too, on Quince Circle, or maybe Quince Court. Jake had yet to receive an invite.

Archival and aerial photographs from the 1940s bore no resemblance to what the place had become. Even the slope of the hills had changed. Jake had seen the pictures, though her knowledge of local history was hardly encyclopedic. She knew only enough to be sure that a man named Calvin Waters was to blame.

It started in the 1950s, when Calvin Waters bought the bulk of the valley floor from the U.S. military, blasted a crater in the center and created a recreational lake ringed by weekend bungalows. A decade after that, he bought all the bungalows back, drained the lake down to a mosquito-infested pit of muck and threatened to leave it that way unless the Covalop County Commission let him redevelop it his way. The commission capitulated and Calvin Waters proceeded to pave the place over. He ripped apart hills and bounced his great concrete echo off the back of the sacred Santa Monica Mountains. Whenever Jake passed a farm not yet consumed by the hungry roar of backhoes, she considered the fields that had gone before. The rest would be sucked under all the same. Few people wept for farmers. What mattered to most were the fields. Homeowners in the hills liked having something to look down upon.

A billboard owned by Pinston-Schilling Realty summed up the rarefied air of Waters End in six simple words. From its perch on a grassy hillside out by Highway 101, near the 13th fairway of the Waters End Country Club, the sign proclaimed:

"If you live here you've arrived."

The move to Southern California had been Keith's idea, a go-west mission that he'd rambled on about almost from the moment they first met. They worked for different dailies back then, in the Sawtooth Mountains of Central Idaho, each at the start of their careers. Keith was behind before he began, easily Jake's senior by seven years of age, yet only an entry-level writer, just like her. Jake was fresh out of college at the time and eager to succeed, old enough to drink but too young to rent a car. She'd been hired at the paper in Ketchum not long after Keith joined the one a few miles south, in Hailey. Looking back, Jake considered the circumstances too consequential to have been coincidence, more likely it had been kismet.

Competition had put them side-by-side in the Blaine County Courthouse on Jake's first workday in Idaho. Her assignment — the arraignment of a burglary suspect — took all of nine minutes. The only words uttered by the defendant were "not guilty," but Jake stayed after to make sure she understood all the legalese uttered by the attorneys. That's when she saw Keith for the first time. He arrived in a wrinkled shirt with his hair mussed, so late that he'd missed the entire hearing. Besides that, he took the seat beside Jake without so much as a "hello," or a "hi," then proceeded to test her dedication to principle by insisting that she share her notes. When she refused, he launched appeal after appeal — first came simple kindness, then a so-called spirit of camaraderie, then his best effort to incite fear. "*Just wait 'til you screw up*," he'd told her. Jake denied each request, but he'd gotten to her all the same. Their romance began that day, like some old movie with Keith cast as the most contemptible man she'd ever met. They married two years later in that same Blaine County courtroom, the ceremony witnessed by a pimple-faced deputy prosecutor and a janitor who stank of cleanser. Two months after that, Jake and Keith departed for *The Pendulum* in Waters End, California, which welcomed the couple as a two-for-one package. The Editor-in-Chief told Jake her smile was as much an asset as her considerable collection of awards, which she'd earned just two years into her career. She was given *The Pendulum's* top reporter slot, and The Chief himself had promised that his middle managers would *"find something for Keith."*

Jake had never considered her husband an accessory, nor had she ever encouraged the characterization. She'd learned early on that it was best to let Keith take control most of the time — the checkbook, the keys, the side of the bed closest to the phone. She'd always considered herself *so lucky* to be with him. Seven years they'd been together, five as husband and wife. She didn't care which of them was the "breadwinner." As far as she was concerned, without each other, they had only crumbs.

Once they reached the parking lot of *The Pendulum*, Keith zipped the Corolla into the first available space, cut the engine and turned so hard in his seat that it shook the car and bounced Jake out of another daydream.

"Is today the day?" he asked.

"I can't push. He'll point to the door and tell me: 'The last time I checked, the sign on my door says —'"

Keith waved his hands and cut her off. "Just treat The Chief like he's your boss, not your —"

Jake threw a fist into his bicep and climbed out of the car.

"What do you guess she baked?" Keith shouted after and laughed. "First day ... The new guy has to get something special from Maxine."

Jake stopped to scan the parking lot, her mood suddenly serious. Maxine Lugner was a fellow reporter, as entitled as anyone else to arrive early to work. But, unlike everyone else in the newsroom, Maxine possessed the uncanny ability to devour entire mornings with gossip from her dermatologist, or expressions of envy about whatever new toy her neighbors bought that weekend. Jake's eyes jumped from space to space in search of that green SUV. Nothing came close, but

Jake's heart raced anyway. Her balance went wobbly and her throat seemed to swell. She threw a hand in Keith's direction, her mouth and eyes wide open as she tried to hack out his name. "Kuh —"

Keith pulled back and said what sounded like "not this time."

In the absence of support, Jake danced backward and bounced her butt against the grill of a black BMW. Her hands hit the hood flat, then scrambled to resist the slip of warm wax on sweaty palms.

"What now?" Keith complained.

Jake steadied herself, then pressed a hand between her smallish breasts. "Maybe too much caffeine," she said.

"You'd better hope that's not the new guy's Beemer," Keith told her and pointed to the hood.

Jake managed one uninterrupted hour of concentration at her desk before Maxine Lugner's round, spandex-encased form arrived in the newsroom bearing a platter up on one hand.

All up and down the aisles, from the design desk to the photo department, heads perked from desks covered with overstuffed files, empty burrito wrappers and dog-eared books. Eyes opened wide and smiles dug deep into the chubbiest of cheeks, all in response to that bouncing body and whatever that plate contained. Abbie Dalton, the mousse-matted editor of *The Pendulum's* Feature section, wiggled her nose and waved with all five of her Press On Nails. Ferrell Meisel, a copy editor with cotton balls in his ears, looked up long before he could have heard the hard footsteps, a reaction that seemed to confirm Ferrell's claim to heightened olfactory sensitivity, an attribute he ascribed to tinnitus, which he blamed on an accidental aspirin overdose, for which a workers-comp claim was rumored as pending. Next came the pale face of Perl Nance, the squat, blue-haired librarian. Perl peeked around the stairwell door, behind which she kept order in the basement morgue, a windowless room that secured 30 years of back issues on spools of microfilm and in paper clip files. Perl put one hand on her head, the other on her belly, and proceeded to pat and rub respectively. Maxine waved and picked up the pace of her strut until she reached Jake and the nearby desk of Fletcher Buckwalter.

Upon seeing that Buckwalter's desk was vacant, Maxine's over-plucked eyebrows collapsed and her big lips constricted as she dropped the plate beside the keyboard. The new editor of the Growth and Development Team — her new boss — was late.

"At least I didn't drive all the way to Santa Monica for the English butter," she said and scooted her chair to Jake's side of the pod. "Corn oil and imitation vanilla extract," Maxine whispered. "They think it's butter every time."

Nick Carlos, the newsroom's cops reporter, arrived at his desk one pod away. "Good God! Doughnuts!" he said.

"Scones," Maxine explained. "His wife arrives today. These are for him and her, from *all* of us."

Nick stepped around and tugged at the plastic wrap on top of the plate. "Not everybody likes doughnuts."

Maxine shooed him away. "I can make doughnuts if you want," she said. "Your cop friends would love my crullers."

Nick smiled big and chuckled. "Cops love big busts."

"Maybe you should send them mine," Maxine said absently, half standing between her desk and chair, eyes painting the newsroom from end to end, seemingly deaf to the snickers that sputtered out of Nick and Keith.

"Maybe we should call to be sure he's OK," she said. "You think he got lost?"

Jake straightened the papers and file folders on her desk, attempting to refocus on work, determined to skip the distraction of *another* Buckwalter discussion. All the critical biographical data had already been circulated, including gossip that his compensation had been augmented by the purchase of a house on his behalf by the corporation that owned *The Pendulum*. In addition, an e-mail from corporate had gone out that morning to all employees. It called Buckwalter "an agent of tomorrow in an industry of yesterday," and advised the staff that they were "no longer in the 'news' business" but rather in "the 'NEW' business."

An instant message popped onto Jake's computer screen. It was Keith, whose desk was flush with hers. He wanted to know if she'd seen the e-mail, the part that professed Buckwalter would *"prove the journalistic wisdom imparted in the mantra 'follow the money.'"*

> KEITH: Why would someone who
> follows money end up in journalism?

Jake reminded him of their meeting with the new realty agent.

JAKE: We leave at 11:45.

Maxine stretched her neck toward Keith's monitor as Jake's response popped up. "What's at 11:45?"

Keith collapsed the window with a slap to his mouse. "Jake has a doctor's appointment at lunch," he said. "She's been getting a little dizzy."

Maxine cooed and cupped a hand to her cheek. "Are you guys pregnant?" she whispered.

Jake snorted and pressed her middle finger into the bridge of her catty eyeglasses. Nick peeked around the side of his monitor. Others within earshot turned too.

"You'd make a great mommy and daddy," Maxine said.

Keith slammed his fist on his desktop. "What the boon!" he spit. "Don't you think we need a house first?"

There it was — *house* — out in the open.

"You should use the agent that found a place for me and Stan," Maxine said.

"Here it comes," Nick interjected and tucked two spongy, orange-colored earplugs into his ears.

Jake closed her file folder, shut her eyes and gripped a knee in each hand. This was a sore spot with her too. Other people in the newsroom owned homes in Waters End, but most of them were lifers who'd sat behind the same desks since the first issue rolled off the presses. Maxine joined their ranks prematurely, on staff two years and already a member of the Census designation "Owner Occupied Households." Maxine emphasized it daily, directly and indirectly, whether on point or as a tangent, seemingly oblivious to the indignation she incited. *The Pendulum's* under-30 clique of copy editors and clerks dedicated entire lunchtime bitch sessions to rehashing and rebuking it, exchanges that Jake observed as she might a public spat between lovers, her eyes glazed at the candy machines, all her attention covertly focused on the expressions of frustration. Though pessimistic outlooks could be poisonous, in small doses they made Jake's day more bearable. It mattered little how Maxine achieved that most coveted proprietary rank, whether on her own or with the ample income earned by her husband,

Stan, a senior writer at the big paper in Los Angeles. Jake wanted nothing to do with jealousy. But lately, Maxine's every expression of "I got mine" inspired the wish that she *finally* get what she had coming. Jake told herself to be more forgiving, but the impish impulses endured.

Now, all because Keith used the word "house," Maxine prattled anew about homeowner headaches — applesauce on polished white marble … black-bean juice in counter grout … chocolate pudding on beige pile.

"Kids kill a house," Maxine said. "Be sure you buy a fixer because you're going to need to fix it anyway once the little one's done with it."

Jake's phone saved her.

She expected the call, had watched Keith dial from his desk. She answered it quickly, said "hello" and slipped lower in her chair.

Keith spoke as though engaged in an interview, even introduced himself as "a reporter from *The Pendulum*" and asked his make-believe subject to spell her name.

Jake held the receiver tightly, but didn't lie. At worst, she reasoned, she was playing on assumptions, not engaging in deceit. A fake phone call afforded the sole polite means of escape, a way to divert Maxine's pontifications elsewhere, somewhere out of earshot, down to the Sports Department, or around the back in Advertising. Maxine danced through her usual sequence of steps once Jake picked up the phone — shifted her weight from foot to foot, crossed her arms, heaved a sigh, then turned and walked away.

Maxine reappeared as Jake switched off her computer at 11:43 a.m.

"We have that thing," Jake said to Keith and stood to go.

"You going to find out for sure?" Maxine asked.

"It was a joke!" Keith spit.

Jake interrupted and dug in her handbag, her voice up an octave on purpose. "Keith, did you see the keys to the —"

She meant to imply her need for his immediate and undivided attention, to save him, and herself. But Keith did not respond, his mouth and eyes wide open, his focus trained on Maxine.

"You'd never joke about a baby," Maxine told him.

A fragment of inaudible babel came out of Keith, a kind of "omm" with the resonance of a growl.

"You must have the keys," Jake said, though they both knew full well that Keith had them in his pocket. She expected him to get the hint and follow her out. But, he stood there and continued to stare at Maxine. Jake had traversed the entire Sports Department before Keith finally snapped back to life and jogged to catch up.

"I have a baby-name book you can borrow," Maxine yelled after them. "I'll bring it tomorrow."

———————

After lunch, Jake stopped in the shade of a parking-lot palm tree and asked Keith to go on into the building without her. "I need to decompress," she said.

Keith turned to comply, then stopped and spun back around. "I'm just saying, this agent sucks as bad as that other one."

"They can't all be bad. You're frustrated is all."

"Great, if you like her so much, then we'll —"

"I didn't say that. But, it's not the agent's fault that we don't make enough to qualify. At least she was honest."

"She was a ffffuh—"

"Keith!"

"I still think it when I say 'boon,' so what difference does it make? Nobody's around. Let me say the real word."

"It's the principle."

"How principled is it not to say what I mean?"

"Keith? Not now. OK?"

"Principles are the reason we're still looking. Five *boonin'* years, Jake. We could have had that place on Cassava if you'd have —"

"Not that way," she said.

"It was one extra zero. And like the guy said, everybody's —"

"A lie is a lie."

"Oh really? I thought it was a principle."

Jake huffed and started for the building. "Never mind," she said. "The Chief is going to give me this raise. He has to. We deserve it."

"Everybody lies," Keith said, following close behind.

"I can't be late."

"How do you think all these other people got their —"

TJ SULLIVAN

"We make what we make," she said.

"We're reporters," Keith replied. "We don't *make* anything."

Jake reminded herself to smile as she strutted through the cafeteria to the newsroom and right up to The Chief's office door. She lifted her fist to knock, then paused to take a deep breath, her eyes stuck on the slim plastic nameplate before her.

Editor-in-Chief.

It was more than a title. It was a promise, and a threat too. All the most serious discussions at *The Pendulum* ended with a nod in that door's direction: "*This was suggested by The Chief ... just ask The Chief ... take it to The Chief —*"

Just as coaches, congressmen and priests were referred to by titles for life, The Chief's identity emanated from that brown piece of plastic. *Editor-in-Chief.* It turned heads. It got results. The Chief did not wait in lines, but was seated in a flurry of handshakes and back pats regardless of where he went. Though he didn't complain the times Jake had seen him reach for his wallet upon entry to prayer breakfasts or business luncheons, his look of innocent surprise at being asked to pay often hinted that such was rarely required. The Chief rushed for no one, but walked slowly with his chin up. Everything from executive club dinners to black-tie political fundraisers lined the pages of his pocket calendar and desktop daily planner, which he routinely left on display at the edge of his desk. Each year he attended the World Series, the NCAA basketball tournament, and The Oscars. The Chief even kept a tuxedo wrapped in dry-cleaner plastic on a coat rack in his office, one hook away from the fishing waders he took on his regular river trips.

From Jake's first day on staff, she needed The Chief. Same as a bullet required gunpowder to be effective, or a rocket needed fuel to fly, Jake's belief in The Chief powered her forward. Had he been most anyone else — just another big boss in the world outside the newsroom — proof of his propriety would have been required. Had he been the subject of a story, she'd have run his social security number, birthdate and mother's maiden name through every accessible Internet database and courthouse computer. But, The Chief wasn't her subject, she was his. What good was a god unworthy of trust?

Her tap on The Chief's door seemed to knock the entire newsroom silent. The Chief replied with a brisk "yep," but did not look up as Jake stepped inside. *"Yep"* was how he said *"good to see you,"* the opposite of *"what!"* which meant *"this better be damned important."*

Jake sat in the chair closest the door, then looked to his taupe shirt and the dark slivers of dampness at its armpits. The Chief's head remained down as he instructed her to wait. Even seated at a desk, he looked barrel-chested, overweight in a burly sort of way, with suspenders that hiked his pants around the base of his rib cage, same as those fishing waders. The Chief was nothing like the editors that formed Jake's first impressions of newspaper management. He was rounder and moved more slowly, more of what made a tugboat skipper. There was no word for what he was. He was *vanvulgarboyant.*

Jake got right to the purpose of her visit.

"I'm up for my review and I'd like more than the two percent we've all received the past three years," she said.

The Chief launched into his reply as if he'd rehearsed it. "There's plenty of people making less," he said. "I'd do it, but we had that salary analysis done and ... Jake, you're at the highest step."

His words were identical to those he'd used every other time.

"But —" Jake stopped to think.

The Chief tossed his thumb toward the newsroom without raising his elbow off the desk. "A lot of people would be damned angry to find out what you make," he said. "I know you want to be fair, so go make them see you're worth it."

Jake sat up straight. "I always do my best," she said. "I earn my way."

"I'm not so sure they're aware of that. All some of them see is that pretty face of yours."

"I'm not ... I mean ... So, no raise until everyone makes what I do?"

The Chief's head appeared to sink lower between his shoulders, as if preparing to charge straight out of his chair and right through the desk. "I didn't say I was going to raise *their* pay," he said.

Jake stifled the reflex to apologize, to stutter the one word she'd heard too many other women use too often, to say "sorry ... sorry." *For what?* She swallowed hard and held it down.

"If I give *them* more, they won't work as hard as you," The Chief said. "So, make me look smart when I tell this guy Buckwalter you're the best I got, and then maybe you and I will talk again in a few months."

"You told him that?" Jake asked.

"You've got to be patient."

She straightened again and felt the cool steel of the chair back through her blouse.

"We want to buy a house," she told him. "You know what you say. Everybody is nobody until they have a house."

"Great."

"But we're still priced out."

"Ah, c'mon. Can't you smell what you're shoveling?"

Jake dug in, explained that she and Keith had found nothing within their price range, neither in Waters End, nor the Valley. She emphasized the need to pre-qualify with a reputable bank, and that the promise of a pay raise, however sincere, wasn't enough to convince any reliable loan officers. Proof was required in the form of cancelled checks, receipts, or tax returns. Promises couldn't be cashed. Explanations couldn't buy pity.

"I don't want to lie about what I make," she said. "Of course, we *could* do that, but —"

Two thumps sounded from beneath The Chief's desk, the unmistakably deep resonance of big shoes being dropped from sock-covered toes.

"Look harder," he said. "People who make less are buying up entire towns. Maxine makes less than you and she's got a house … in the hills. They're giving it away out there. You know all this."

"But Maxine's husband's —" Jake stopped herself, ashamed that she'd even thought to disqualify someone else's worthiness. "This isn't about anyone else," she said. "It's about me."

The Chief returned his elbows to the desktop. "You're flip-flopping and you can't even see it," he said. "You want a pay increase based on need, but a minute ago you cited merit. Which is it?"

Jake looked to the black Mary Janes on her feet. "Both?" she said. "It's both. Yes, both."

The Chief laughed and embarked on another of his monologues about the company budget. He said revenue concerns expressed by the corporate suits had all but resulted in a salary freeze. He claimed to have been rejected for a raise himself, that money was so tight he'd been forced to neglect necessary maintenance on the paper's fleet of delivery pickups and vans.

"Get out there and give me something to hang a raise on," he said. "Help us sell more papers. Go get us a Pulitzer. You need a Pulitzer. If anyone can get us a Pulitzer, it's you."

One, two, three — Jake counted the "P" words as The Chief said them, the first time in her experience that he'd ever referenced the venerable awards program without dropping the F-bomb.

"But you said awards aren't what we do," she said. "You said we —"

"Listen," The Chief said and shot a finger above her head. "You see that sign on my door?"

Jake drummed her lips and fumbled for an explanation. Words tumbled out suffix over prefix, all to fill the void of uncomfortable quiet. "— ing … pre … re —"

Salvation arrived in the form of Maxine Lugner's scones.

The plate crossed the threshold first, followed by what had to be Fletcher Buckwalter, a chainsaw of a man in a wrinkled, white dress shirt. He was slim and tanned with short brown hair, smallish sideburns, a belt that missed half the loops and eyeglasses with polarized lenses that gave the whites of his eyes a yellowish tint. Rather than a wristwatch he sported a copper chain bracelet. He was wearing cowboy boots — so obviously a newcomer to Southern California.

The rim of Jake's catty eyeglasses came so close to the plate of sweets that the two clicked together. She cleared her throat and readjusted the frames on the cocoa-brown bridge of her nose. Still, Buckwalter held the sweets right in front of her, as though she were invisible.

"We good to go for the three-o'clock?" Fletcher Buckwalter said.

"Gotcha," The Chief replied and jerked his jaw toward the plate. "What's that then?"

Buckwalter grabbed one of the scones in his free hand. "That Lugner woman made 'em," he said.

"Don't believe everything you hear," The Chief said and stretched to grab one. "Only the best in my shop."

Buckwalter kept the plate steady as The Chief's fingertips scrambled over a scone. Jake's eyelashes fluttered as the golden pastries hovered a sickening-sweet breath away. The plate trapped her in the chair, and Buckwalter's position in the doorway robbed her of an escape route.

"I don't usually eat this crap," Buckwalter said and raised the pastry as though it were a cocktail. "You can taste the goddamn butter."

The Chief collapsed into his chair, scone in hand, crumbs across his necktie before he'd taken a single bite. "She's a keeper, ain't she, Jake?"

TJ SULLIVAN

"Who? I mean, Maxine, yes," Jake said into the plate. "We need her. We should keep her. Don't get rid of her."

The Chief mumbled through the mush of half-chewed scone. "I'll say … We're done now, right?"

"Oh, right," Jake said. "Sure."

"You're my highest-paid reporter," The Chief said. "Go show Buckwalter here that I'm not just a sucker for a pretty face."

Jake struggled to smile, then hated herself for the effort. She thanked The Chief, then stood to leave, the plate still in her way. She ducked around it and danced her way back to a sense of balance. "Butter" was the last word she heard out of The Chief before she bumped hips with Buckwalter and returned to her desk.

"Homemade f---ing scones," she hissed, leaving out the three most unprincipled letters.

Her head felt full and warm as a wad of dough, as though her skull would squish and skew if she pressed her palms to her ears.

Maxine started up before Jake had time to settle in her seat. "Did he say anything?" she asked.

Jake focused on the air between them. *Said what? What was said?*

"About the scones," Maxine continued. "Does Fletch like my scones? Did you know his wife's a vegan? Did you know a vegan's different from a vegetarian? No butter. Isn't that weird? It's like I knew not to use butter, but, oh, I forgot to tell —"

Jake grabbed her phone and dialed her apartment in Reseda. The answering machine picked up and she was greeted by her recorded self at the other end, five years younger and so much happier than she now felt. "*We may be away,*" the recording said, "*but we always return, so please wait for …*" At the beep, Jake told herself what she wished was true, all the words she longed to say. It was everything she believed.

"He said 'yes,'" she whispered through the lump in her throat. "We can start our life now … We did right. We waited. We made it through the dip … It all fell into place exactly like it's supposed to … Good things come to those who —"

Maxine scooped a hand to her ear and Jake curled away, still talking to herself on the phone.

By the time the machine cut off, the newsroom had melted into a watery blur. Precipitation had not been expected.

Enviro Group Disputes Claim It Caused Crisis

By Jake LaMotta
Pendulum Staff Writer

Planning Director Vic Vident warned the Waters End City Council Tuesday that a housing crisis could result if growth-control laws are permitted to remain in effect.

"It's 'BANANA planning,'" Vident said. "It's 'Build Absolutely Nothing Anywhere Near Anything,' and it's unsustainable."

He said the laws promoted by the non-profit group Save The Open Places have eliminated new construction and artificially inflated the values of existing houses.

Kendrick Hindern, founder of STOP, called the comments "a pathetic attempt at self preservation."

"STOP makes city planners obsolete," Hindern said. "House values should go up. Otherwise, why own one?"

Please turn to page A3

CHAPTER 2 – RESOLED

Jake was alone, drifting deep in thought between the faint blue lines of her legal pad when Fletcher Buckwalter bounded into the conference room and took the high-backed executive chair at the far end. No eye contact was made. No greeting was offered. If he'd been a stranger, she'd have flashed a smile, but Buckwalter was an in-betweener, neither unknown, nor known, and Jake was still slightly miffed at having been ignored the time before. A faint "thunk" sounded out the air ducts as the AC kicked on and sent a steady stream of cool air down the nape of her neck. She wiggled out of the vent's reach and repositioned her pad in her lap. Newsroom meetings rarely started on time, but at least none had ever been delayed because she was late. Two minutes left until eight o'clock and half the group had yet to arrive. It was best to look busy.

Buckwalter pulled several file folders out of his satchel and removed its leather shoulder strap before dropping the bag to the floor. He sighed and rocked back, bumped the armrests against the beveled edge of the table and thumped the seat back into the wall. He stayed balanced like that for several seconds, gripping the leather strap in one hand

and wrapping it around the other. He stretched it from the crook of his thumb down, up the back and around again, doubling it over the meat of his palm. He flexed his knuckles and gently slapped the lump of the overlap. He held it like that for several seconds, his leather-fettered fist flush with the vinyl seat between his knees. Jake half expected him to ride the chair, to throw his free hand up and give a "yee-haw." Common sense kept her from giggling as he undid the wrap and repeated the procedure. It was as though she wasn't there at all.

The fidgeting almost made Buckwalter seem sweet — almost — the wrapping and slapping a trigger for thoughts of Jake's first crush, a 15-year-old boy with the compulsive tendency to ride imaginary bulls on wooden fences and arena bleacher seats. That boy spent one whole summer strapping himself to things and fussing with his Stetson, never quite content with the shape of that hat. Last she heard the boy had become a lawyer in Albuquerque, nowhere near the future she'd figured.

Jake continued to feign interest in her legal pad as she sized up Buckwalter out the corner of her eye. The red-and-white lid of a cigarette pack peeked at her from inside his breast pocket. That, and his boots, suggested an urban-cowboy wannabe, but the rest of his outfit was typical office attire for a middle-aged member of management, complete with short shirtsleeves so lengthy they made his arms look stingy.

Buckwalter's sideburns, insignificant as they'd been before, had since disappeared completely; the nose fuzz too. The hair on his head stood straight up in one of those tight clipper cuts, the kind that made barber poles famous, infamous, and nearly extinct. He'd found a shop somewhere, out in Chatsworth probably, or down in Woodland Hills, one of those places with squeaky ceiling fans, dog-eared Playboys, and a staticky TV tuned to a baseball game, or the news. Jake's father favored a barbershop exactly like that, and, as a child, she'd begged to tag along every time he went, though he usually said "no."

Jake dropped her pen on purpose and bent beneath the table to inspect those boots close up. The decorative stitching across the toes said more than the hair, the cigarettes and shirt combined. These weren't mere boots, not simply another mass-produced pair of Lorne Kings or Chap Waddies, not that there was anything wrong with footwear made by machines. But these were Luccheses. Handcrafted. The best.

These were the kind of boots the boys back home saved to purchase, the brand most fathers, including Jake's, wore all week to work and again on through the weekend. Back home in Española, Sunday suits lasted only as long as it took to make an appearance at church, but the Luccheses stayed on all day. These were boots worth polishing, and repairing. Buckwalter's looked to have been resoled a couple times. He'd obviously had them for years.

Before Jake returned to the tabletop, Maxine's clogs clomped to the seat directly across. Jake watched her hold a file folder tight to the bulge of her belly, then, once Jake emerged, Maxine's eyes popped wide open. The wall clock showed it was two minutes past eight o'clock, and still no sign of Keith. Jake pulled her legal pad into her lap again and scribbled some more in the margins, resisting the desire to congratulate Buckwalter's good taste. She wanted to tell him how she hadn't worn her boots in years, that they were just outside in the trunk of her Corolla, that they'd been there for years, since before California and Idaho, since she left Española. But, she didn't say any of it. The last thing she wanted was to be taken for a suck-up. He was the new boss, and she was nobody, as far as he knew.

Buckwalter dropped his heels hard from the rungs of his chair to the carpet as Keith took the seat nearest the door, at the other end of the table. No introductions were offered, or requested. Unlike most management types, Buckwalter did not engage his little group in any pointless pleasantries, no sharing of names or histories. They'd been told to bring story ideas and to be prepared to pitch. Buckwalter looked to Jake before he spoke, the whites of his eyes yellow in those polarized tints. "Our goal ought to be obvious," he said.

Keith gave the tabletop a hearty smack. "A Pulitzer," he said.

"Come off that shit and tell me what you got," Buckwalter snapped. "Bring me something I can use. I want dogs that bite, not puppies that wag and piddle every time I shout 'jump!'"

Maxine stretched her fingers across the cherry wood veneer, each fingernail tipped with the opaque white polish of a fresh, French manicure.

"Jacqueline!" Buckwalter barked.

It hit Jake like a punch and sent her hands scrambling to hide the margins of her legal pad and the hollow bunny silhouettes she'd doodled there.

"I'm Jake," she said. "Just Jake."

"Uh huh … Yeah, so … What you got for me?"

Jake tripped into her unprepared pitch — an investigative report she'd been researching for weeks. "There's evidence of discriminatory lending practices," she said. "It's solid. Home loan applications in Waters End are three times more likely to be rejected if the applicant is a racial minority, and besides that we —"

Buckwalter waved his hands madly. "And, and, and … Twenty different newspapers have done that 20 times already," he said. "I want news, Jackie, as in 'new.' Make *them* copy *us*."

His face and neck turned chestnut red as he detailed his ideal mix of scandal and injustice. He wanted it above the fold, out front, on as many days as possible. He cited the latest exhaustive readership analysis, which declared that the average subscriber in Waters End had a six-figure income, an Ivy League education, a five-bedroom residence, four vehicles, a three-car garage and took prescription medication for high cholesterol, high blood pressure, Attention Deficit Disorder and erectile dysfunction. Happiness was an illness and bad news its only cure.

"These people have positively everything," he said. "And people like that need negatives to give their lives balance. I couldn't care less whether Joe Six-Pack can get a loan. Joe doesn't live here. And nothing Joe does is 'new.' We're here to sell papers."

A stinging sensation ran through Jake's lungs, and her tongue seemed to swell. Her heart was beating so hard it felt like it might burst. Everything she'd said and left unsaid was none of what Buckwalter wanted. Suddenly *she* was a source of disappointment. It couldn't be. Her story was real. The voiceless were being oppressed. Buckwalter was supposed to care. He was supposed to say "Sic 'em," not scold her like a child.

"No," Jake said. "This is news because it's new *here*."

Buckwalter ran his tongue around inside his cheeks. "No, Jaye Girl. It's news because it's news to you," he said.

Before Jake could bite back, Buckwalter cast his next question to Maxine, who was still rubbing that file folder into her belly.

"Fresh," Maxine said and tapped one of those garish fingernails on the documents covering her abdomen. "This isn't about Joe Six-Pack. This is about Jose Cuervo."

Maxine insisted that her source would only speak to her, which qualified the story as "an exclusive," though no piece in *The Pendulum* had ever been labeled as such in print in the five years Jake had been there.

"You won't believe what some people do to get a house," Maxine said.

Buckwalter raised his head slowly, as if about to nod.

Maxine continued: "It's an illegal alien story. A real scandal. And … Well, maybe you and I should talk alone after. I mean … It's sensitive and —"

"Illegal '*immigrants*,'" Jake interrupted. "We don't say 'aliens' at this paper. We say 'immigrants.'"

"Or maybe 'illegal homeowners,'" Keith offered.

Maxine's eyes rolled. "OK," she said. "They're not legal people. But, that's the point. They're getting loans, borrowing money, buying our houses, and *they're* not even from here."

Buckwalter scribbled a note and mumbled out the corner of his mouth. "Illegal aliens," he said.

Maxine gave a sly wink. "I know. Right?" she said. "It sounds so wrong."

"What could possibly be wrong?" Jake argued, suddenly unable to keep quiet. "Americans buy summerhouses in Mexico. Americans buy land everywhere. Is that wrong too? Are we going to do stories about that?"

"C'mon," Buckwalter said. "Tell me what kind of suck this story's got. Why do I goddamn care who wins this fight?"

"Because the illegals aren't even supposed to be in it," Maxine said. "They're playing *our* game. They're taking advantage of *our* system. And the city doesn't do anything fast enough. This stuff has to go through the courts."

Maxine portrayed the situation as an organized invasion of the residential real estate market. She said four families buy one house at a time and split the place up by installing deadbolts on each bedroom door, one room for each family. Vehicles end up parked on lawns. Garbage-bag stacks become walls at the curb. Lights burn behind closed blinds all night, every night.

"And their music … pish," Maxine said. "This is Waters End, not Juarez."

Buckwalter pulled the red-and-white box of cigarettes from his shirt pocket and picked at the cellophane wrapper. "That's what I'm talking about," he said. "That's good guy versus bad. I don't want to live next to that. Do you?"

"Not for a second," Maxine said. "No way."

Jake seethed as Buckwalter not only took control of the pitch, but mentored Maxine on how to make it more sensational. He theorized that four families in one house would flush toilets four times more often, that traffic would quadruple and the skies would go brown with bad emissions. He foretold a future of four families in every house, of packs of feral dogs and herds of unwashed cats. Underground pipes swelled and spurted greasy sewage out the seams. Income levels and tax revenues dropped. Divorce and dropout rates skyrocketed. City layoffs of police officers and firefighters followed unhappy budget battles, and the streets became unsafe to walk at midday. Hospital emergency rooms were flooded with domestic violence cases and drug overdoses. By the time Buckwalter was done, the city landfill — which wasn't even located within the city limits — had grown to such a height that it blocked all but the sun from view.

"They cook with lard, too," Maxine said. "Pure lard!"

Buckwalter pointed his right thumb to Jake, then to Keith. "You two get it now?"

Jake piped up so fast her voice cracked. "No! No … I don't. I just told you that minorities were being discriminated against. That's the real issue. This story … This *thing* … It's a distraction. It's an anomaly. It's gossip. It's —"

"It's our Sunday package," Buckwalter declared. "It's a headline that screams 'Hometown Invasion.' This is 'Illegals Next Door' in 72-point type. If there's so much discrimination, then you explain to me how migrant workers are getting home loans."

"Immigrants aren't all *migrant workers*," Jake said. "Some work in Circulation and deliver this newspaper. Some are nannies for people in this newsroom."

"Doesn't make it right," Buckwalter shot back. "We give our readers information and we let our readers decide how they feel about it. We magnify their world. Nobody's worried about a nanny invasion. Nobody cares about the guy they never see delivering their paper. But, they give a good goddamn about the encampment next door."

Jake stared at her legal pad and curled her toes in her black Mary Janes. She'd seen how stories like this misrepresented facts and painted victims as suspects. Aspersions could be crafted to come across as fair, to look justifiable when they were anything but. The sting of one recent report still made Jake seethe. It was intended to be a simple budget piece highlighting how strapped local hospitals were for finances. But when the design desk decided to highlight a Congressman's inflammatory quote in the 72-point headline, it transformed her evenhanded analysis into an indictment. The local pol had called Mexican immigrants "*Chupacabras* of Medicaid," characterized them as a collection of soulless non-citizens who crept across borders by dark and sucked public services dry by day. Despite the lack of supporting facts, the Congressman collected accolades in the letters readers wrote to the newspaper's opinion page. In missive after missive they demanded medical care be flat out refused to non-citizens. Never mind that not one townsperson acknowledged the wounds and illnesses that hospital staff were being asked to ignore. Forget that these nonnatives were human beings. Supporters of the Congressman hailed him as a crusader and even presented him with a ceremonial pitchfork and torch, implements of encouragement for his drive to turn back the invaders. Jake grew up hearing her father rant about such mindsets, said it was the same with him and his Italian ancestors as it was with Jake's mother, a native New Mexican whose family tree stretched all the way to Spain. Jake's father blamed it on greed and fear. Together they made people stupid.

"They're taking advantage," Maxine said and thumped the tabletop with her fist.

Jake refused to lay down. She'd seen too much of it and had stayed silent too long. Ever since the move to LA she regularly encountered brown people peddling oranges or cherries at busy intersections, while white people 100 feet away hawked for handouts with cardboard signs that said "smile," "God bless," and "no lie, I need beer." No one wrote stories about that. The double standard used to confound Jake, but there in the conference room with Buckwalter she saw that the standard wasn't double at all. It wasn't hateful or xenophobic, not on the part of *The Pendulum* anyway. The standard was, in fact, chronological. Lazy white people weren't news because white people weren't "new." Immigrants were "new" by definition — the new arrivals — and that was distinction enough to warrant front-page play.

Buckwalter merely meant to make more stories like that. Forget context or perspective, the pursuit mattered less than the result. This was athlete logic, a never-look-back approach that equated every assignment to a race for the finish line — run, run, run and get it done and go again.

"We have a duty to tell readers what things mean," Jake said. "We provide analysis. We show where this might lead."

"Brainstorm with Max," Buckwalter told her.

"We always work together," Maxine chirped.

Jake hoped Keith would join her defense of principle, but he said nothing, his faraway look an implication that only his body remained in the room.

Just then Buckwalter slapped the table so hard the copper chain on his wrist took a chunk out of the veneer. "Corporate wouldn't send me to fix this place unless it was headed in the wrong direction," he said.

Jake's heart was pounding hard again as her ears went all funny and full, every sound muffled, as if underwater.

"I don't make or keep other people's promises," Buckwalter said. "Yesterday is over. All that matters is what you do for me today."

Jake took slow breaths and trained her attention on the scribbled bunnies in the margins of her legal pad, her focus more difficult to maintain the more Buckwalter spoke. Behind her eyelids, the scribbled bunnies flopped into inverse outlines, like neon force fields of calm that faded quickly against the onslaught of her electrified angst. She grabbed the seat of her chair with both hands as all the shapes began to swirl together in a counterclockwise turn. A familiar voice cut through the mush after that, a voice she hadn't heard in years, so clear it felt as though it was coming from deep inside herself.

It said: *Tell me 'bout the rabbits.*

It had to be him, always full of those slow, hopeful words. She'd met him in middle school, yet, despite the distance of years, hearing his voice again elicited that same sense of joy and sorrow, as close to a bittersweet emotion as she was capable at the age of 13. It was her oafish friend who first taught her that even good people could go wrong.

He said it again: *Tell me 'bout the rabbits.*

Friends as big as her unrefined pal were not so numerous that she could ever forget. Rabbits were his *raison d'être*. The promise of bunnies was what kept him going. And so, it seemed, it was with Jake. But this voice in her head, in this place, had to be insanity. In a girl it qualified as imagination, but in a woman it was surely serious sickness.

Her lungs filled and her brain reeled. The bunnies were lies, all lies. Her simple childhood chum had no friends, couldn't even trust his partner, a well-meaning sort, who nonetheless bummed off the bigger one's brawn, all under the pretext that someday there would be rabbits. Rabbits! Bunnies! Lies! Jake recalled The Chief repeating his promises of pay raises that would come next year, next year, next year. Next year! Rabbits!

One day there will be rabbits.

Whatever the form, it was all the same, every promise of prosperity as empty as the first one fed from childhood onward. Even the red wonder cloaked in the goodness of Santa Claus was a lie. "Yes, Virginia, there is a Santa Claus," or so the headline said year after year for more than a century. Newspapers. Lies. Santa Claus was just another bunny, a promise that even the most skeptical children curled up with on cold nights, only to grow up and slip into the whole cloth coats of bigger bunnies, potential promotions, guaranteed savings, no money down, the opportunity of a lifetime, *but only if you act now*. Jake felt duped, like a good country churchgoer who staked her life on a pastor's truth, only to lose hope watching him led away in handcuffs. American icons washed into the blurry tornado of her dizzy spell and sucked her heart hollow. She felt strung along on a daisy chain of cute and fuzzy bunnies — the house, the picket fence, the backyard, the kids — more kids to feed more lies about Easter bunnies and fairies. Clap your hands if you believe in fairies? Fairies take the teeth and leave the money. Lies. All lies. No fairies. No bunnies. No cheering in the press box. Her brain looped and splashed with ripples of remembered passages, of pledges to live off "*the fat of the land*" someday, someday, someday. Jake had a vision of a white wand linked by a long cord to a machine that sucked at her belly and pumped wide-eyed rabbits out of her and into a rose-colored plastic pouch.

There are no bunnies. There are no bunnies.

The swirl stopped and Jake fell forward, bumped her forehead on the table and shot up straight with her eyes open wide. She was still in the conference room, still drunk on aftereffects, still determined to defend her point of view. Keith's lips were parted and his finger was pointed at Maxine. He was saying something and it seemed even he hadn't noticed Jake's dizzy thump. But, this was her moment and she wanted it back.

"The plume," she said, as though introducing the title of a book, or poem.

Keith coughed and sputtered into a fit of hacks that sent him out the door with wet eyes. Jake continued, unfazed and unfiltered, her emotions in control, her ideals transcended by outrage.

"The plume," she repeated.

"Yeah? And?" Buckwalter said.

"Poison …" she said. "Corruption —"

Jake proceeded from there to further embellish and enhance the folklore of "the plume." At best, it was a ghost story whispered around City Hall and outside the City Council chambers during evening smoke breaks, nothing anybody took seriously. The plume was gossip fodder, propaganda perpetuated for dubious purposes by members of the local anti-growth group "Save The Open Places," or STOP, a band of residents whose charge was exclusivity, to close the gates on Waters End by stopping the construction of additional housing. On the record, the plume didn't exist. Off the record, it was unlikely, unsubstantiated nonsense — a ghastly bubble of poison hidden deep in the city's water supply. Jake had heard it described in various forms — a forgotten fuel spill from a long-gone WWII military base, or maybe the result of a secret experiment gone wrong up in the hills at the old lab, which hadn't been occupied since the end of the Korean War. No one had ever proved the lack of proof, though that hardly quelled the whispers. Prior to her present predicament, Jake had seen no reasonable reason to mention it. Any effort to confirm the plume's existence or nonexistence would not only have been onerous, but as unpopular as betting the paper's credibility on some crackpot's panic-inducing earthquake prediction. If false … *what an irresponsible boondoggle*! If true … *what to do? Rope the city off? Walk away?* Only chaos could result. Waters End was dominated by homeowners, which meant everyone had a stake in the city's future and no desire to see that stake driven through their hearts. In the context of Buckwalter's pitch session, however, the plume provided a sharp way for Jake to prove her point.

She presented it as though she believed, emphasizing the potential threat to health, as well as the damage it could do to the value of homes.

"A complete and total crash," she said.

She implied injuries and slights, but kept it all vague enough to pique interest. Both Buckwalter and Maxine stretched and pivoted their chairs in Jake's direction as she laid out her unplanned plan. It made Jake feel euphoric, vital and superior, those rapt facial expressions like puffs of pure oxygen. They were following her every word. Shallow as her pitch was, she'd managed to make it appear deep and promising as a wildcat well.

"My source says we could be seeing cancer clusters already," Jake said. "Rich people know how to sink a story. If we do this, we'll face extreme resistance."

The sting of guilt that might otherwise have restored her senses became a pleasurable piercing pain as her imagination continued to manufacture facts.

Buckwalter's mouth was on the cusp of a smile. "Anonymous whistleblowers get attention," he said. "Scandal sells."

Keith returned to the room with red eyes, but Buckwalter seemed not to notice, his butt at the edge of his seat. "You'll have more?" he said.

Jake nodded.

"Corroboration?" he said.

"All anonymous," she replied.

Keith mouthed the word "anonymous" at Jake and raised his fingertips off the table.

She bulled forward: "Sometimes proof gets lost on purpose, so we may lack the usual verifiable facts. And with everyone anonymous, well, that's no concern. We're trustworthy and —"

Maxine cleared her throat.

"Anonymous is good," Buckwalter said. "Anonymous gives it zing. Anonymous means a bigger headline."

It was time for Jake to pull her punch, but Buckwalter had yet to flinch. He just sat there, soaking in satisfaction, smiling his ass off, as though waiting to be hit, as if defying her to do it. This wasn't the reaction she sought. He was supposed to see the idea as shallow and unjournalistic. He was supposed to let himself in on the joke and learn from his own hypocrisy. But that look on his face — it mocked her. Here she was, bearing down on him behind the wheel of the most horrendous lie she could engineer, and he sat there docile as a Hindu cow in the center of the road. She couldn't stop. She plowed the rest of the way through.

"It'll go national," she said. "EPA, FEMA, USDA — The follow-up stories will fill the front page for weeks. And the opinion page ... They'll be turning letters away by the hundreds."

Buckwalter pinched a cigarette from his pack and grinned. "You should have told me that one first, Jackie."

"It's Jake," she said and felt her left eye twitch. "Just Jake."

Buckwalter closed the meeting with an assignment for Keith, a minor bit of reportage billed as "an idea passed along by The Chief," which meant "*do it and don't ask questions.*" It was elementary enough, an explainer about where property taxes went and who got how much, the type of report that ended up in the bottom right corner of A-1 on Sunday with no photo and no reason for anyone to pay any attention.

"Make it a fun read," Buckwalter said and twirled the unlit cigarette between his fingers. "Can you handle that kind of shit?"

"I'm all over that kind of shit," Keith said. "That kind of shit is what I love. Not the old kind of shit, but this new kind of shit."

Buckwalter was up and out of the room before Keith finished.

The moment the three reporters were back in the pod, Maxine wheeled her desk chair around to Jake and whispered with her hands cupped to her mouth. "Fletch's wife got here yesterday. I hear she hates the house."

Jake maintained her smile but said nothing to encourage further conversation. Maxine lingered anyway, straightened Jake's mouse pad, ran a finger down the cracked spine of Jake's dictionary and untangled the cord on Jake's telephone. After two uncomfortable minutes, Maxine smoothed her silk blouse down her belly and excused herself to the restroom.

"Busy, busy," she said.

Keith called Jake's desk phone as soon as Maxine disappeared.

"What did I just do?" Jake whispered into the receiver.

"I couldn't believe it," Keith said, his words punchy and quick. "I couldn't —"

"She just made me so ... And he called me Jacqueline ... But, I didn't mean to ... I wasn't serious ... I just wanted to show how shallow they were and ... What did I do? Why did I do it? Why didn't I stop?"

"A total surprise," Keith said. "Almost perfect."

"I have to tell him," she said and pushed back from her desk, preparing to stand.

Keith ducked down and lowered his voice to a rasp. "You can't!" he said. "He'll fire us, *both* of us."

"I shouldn't have to explain," Jake said. "You should understand."

"I understand what's coming. Are you blind?"

"He might get mad, but he'll see my reasons were good. Won't he? Shouldn't he?"

"He doesn't need a *good* reason. Go ahead, give him one. He'll make you his own personal fabulist. You want to be the next one of those?"

Jake bounced a fist nervously on her knee as she considered it. In the space of seconds, she tried, convicted and sentenced herself to ruin. She wiggled her chair back up to her desk.

"It's scary," Keith said. "You're scared."

His voice came out so warm that Jake wanted only to hear more of it. She peeked around her monitor and into his blue-eyed squint, the phone receiver hanging from her fingertips, the mouthpiece hooked under her chin. This was why people got married.

"I was worried at first," Keith said.

Jake's shoulders melted. "You're my strength," she whispered. "I don't know what I'd do without —"

"I didn't do it on purpose," he continued. "I was tired and … it seemed real enough."

"Wait. What?"

Keith rambled on about something from years before, said he hadn't planned "it," some uproar over a column he'd written at his college paper. It was flagged the following day as something close enough to plagiarism to cause serious concern. Several suit-clad representatives of the university administration had gotten involved. The consensus was that the consequences should be dire. Readers expected ramifications for contemptible acts. The cancellation of all future columns was spun as "equitable retribution."

"They fired me," he said.

"Oh Keith," Jake replied and slipped her fingers across the divide between their desks, but Keith pulled back.

"Exhaustion," he said. "I was tired. I thought I was making it up. I plagiarized on accident."

Jake's shoulders retightened. "But … You lied? 'Making it up' is the same as saying you lied."

"I forgot. I'd read it in somebody else's story."

Jake closed her eyes and tried to speak calmly. "You plagiarized on accident … but you lied on purpose."

"No. I 'pretended' it was real. Everybody does it. Nobody knows when I do it now."

Jake was only half listening, suddenly struck dumb. *Secrets? He kept this secret for seven years?*

Keith went on muttering. "They're stupid man-on-the-street stories, walk-and-talks."

"What?" Jake said. "Now? You do this now? Still?"

"Yeah. Now. When I do it now I do it for the walk-and-talks."

"You're making them up *now*?"

"You never hear what I say. I just told you that."

"But —"

"No one at the county fair wants to be quoted about deep-fried Twinkies," Keith said. "Only editors think about deep-fried Twinkies. I'm better than that. I make up the names. I make up the quotes. I go bowling. They think I'm out reporting. But, usually, I'm bowling."

"You can't," Jake said. "You're supposed to —"

"Nobody bowls here. Nobody will catch me."

"Nobody expects you to lie either."

"Exactly. That's what's so flawless. It's perfect. Even if they get suspicious and try to check up, they can't. Everybody in this town is unlisted. Everybody's hiding something. There's no easy way to confirm anyone's existence. They all have to take what I give them, or leave it."

Jake pulled at her ring finger; still no ring. *After the house. After the house.* "Why are you telling me this now?" she asked.

"Cause now we're in this … together."

"This isn't a game," Jake insisted.

"Whatever it is, we're in it. You've got to follow through with this. You've got to give Buckwalter what you promised. If you don't —"

Jake told herself it couldn't be, that her mistake was all a side effect of searching so long and finding nothing. It was hard to stay upright beneath the weight of so much waiting. Together she and Keith would survive. There was a way out, a way to fix this. She'd find it.

"Think of it like Halloween," Keith said. "All those needles in candy? Some urban myth got reported as fact and now nobody lets their kids go door to door. A lie killed an American tradition. The media killed Halloween. Poof! So … you just do that with this."

"No way," Jake said.

"You do it right and this plume thing could put homeowners in a panic. It could crash the market and we'll get a —"

"No! I won't lie."

"C'mon Jake. We print lies everyday. We just put quote marks around them."

She set the phone receiver down next to her keyboard and left it to sit off the hook.

Maxine tossed a copy of *The Pendulum* in front of Keith, who jumped back as though startled.

"What the boon!" he spit and slapped her hand away.

"Jake should do that," Maxine said and pointed to the story up top. "She's such a good writer, I bet she could win."

Jake peeked across to see. It was a story about an essay contest for which the prize was a five-bedroom house in New Hampshire. The headline read: "Write Your Way to the American Dream."

"New Hampshire?" Keith said. "You expect us to move to New Hampshire?"

Maxine huffed, took back the paper and tossed it on Jake's desk. "You just write," Maxine said. "Tell them why you don't have a house. Write how you're going to have a baby and that you can't get a raise. Even if you write the truth, you win."

"We're not having a baby!" Keith spit.

"Who told you that?" Jake asked.

Maxine pointed to Keith. "He did," she said.

"No, who told you about the money, the pay raise?"

Maxine flipped her hair across her shoulder. "Duh. It's a newsroom, Jake. People talk. But, the way I hear it, The Chief still respects you … same as me. Same as everybody. You're good, not *pretty*."

Jake pulled her purse from the bottom drawer of her desk and stood in a rush. "People talk?" she said. "Really? People talk?"

Buckwalter arrived back in the pod, followed by an invisible stink of cigarette smoke. He dropped behind his desk and thrust his chin in Jake's direction. "Why are you leaving?"

She had to recoup, to regain control, to keep herself from saying what her heart ached to say. She had to put one foot in front of the other before she put another one into her mouth. She had no end of reasons, though none she could share.

The ring of her cell phone saved her. She glanced to Keith's desk, to be sure it wasn't him again. The faceplate said "Undetermined." The sound at the other end was static. Jake glanced around as she listened. Maxine was smirking. Buckwalter was staring, so obviously impatient.

Jake began to speak into the dead air. "We need to get this out in the open," she said. "We have to deal with it. The sooner the better … yep … OK."

She clapped the phone closed, motioned to Keith for the car keys and rose up on the round toes of her black Mary Janes. "I have to go right away," she announced. "I need to do this."

Keith passed the keys over without complaint, but Buckwalter blocked her retreat with his boots crossed at the ankles, halfway into the aisle. "That your source?" he asked. "On the phone?"

Jake repositioned her purse strap on her shoulder and stared at his feet. "You like Luccheses?" she said.

Buckwalter gave her a snobbish look. "Luke who?"

"The boots," Jake said. "Luccheses."

Buckwalter gave his feet a look, then pulled them back and tucked them beneath his chair. "Hell, I don't pay attention to that shit," he said. "That's the wife's department. Half our closet's from a goddamn vintage store."

New Flipper Trend A Flop For Upscale Neighborhoods

By Maxine Lugner
Pendulum Staff Writer

Two weeks after Whitney Oates met the new owners of the house next door, she began begging Waters End Police to put them out.

"It was like living next to Grand Central Station," said Oates, of Glen Archer Estates. "Eight cars were parked on the lawn."

The police passed the matter to city code inspectors, who found four immigrant families in the house, each of which shared legal ownership of the property.

Real estate agents say it's part of a disturbing new trend. Upscale homes are being transformed into mini-motels until they can be flipped for a profit.

Please turn to page A4

CHAPTER 3 – SMOKE

Homemade flippin' scones.

Maxine tossed a plate of them on the passenger seat of her jade-green Land Rover, slammed the door and peeled out of *The Pendulum's* parking lot so fast her tires spat gravel onto her coworkers' cars.

Those people!

They'd ignored all her work, left the whole plate of freshly baked delights to go dry all day, and without so much as an apology, or a smile. Couldn't they see that she'd gone to the extra trouble of drizzling imitation orange-flavored frosting on top? Didn't they care?

She glanced at the plastic wrap, the way it flapped off the far edge of the plate, like a baby waving bye-bye. She hit the brakes hard at the next stop sign and all 14 pastries flew from the seat to the floor.

Homemade flippin' scones.

Over the years, Maxine's oven had launched a thousand sweets into the bellies of her bosses — chocolate cupcakes, lemon bars, snickerdoodles. All she'd ever taken home every time before was a crumb-covered, empty plate. But then came *that damn diet.*

Everyone at the paper was on it, all thanks to that editor in the Sports Department, the one with that damn East Coast accent, the one who rambled *ad nauseam* for weeks about how many pounds he was losing. *Nah-tin but meat. Nah-tin!*

Even the temps jumped on board. Maxine tried to dissuade the biggest bosses from buying into it. She doubled her efforts in the kitchen and focused on their favorites. But, in the end, all she really doubled was their resolve. As Buckwalter's weight increased, so did the attraction of *that damn diet*. The proof lay beneath that upside-down plate on the carpet of her SUV.

Buckwalter told her it was all about a new tuxedo and a pair of press credentials to the Academy Awards, but to Maxine's ears that was all so much tripe. She ground her teeth all the way home.

"Now what?" she yelled at the windshield. "What?"

Her cookbook arsenal offered no new options. No culinary combat technique existed that could defeat a dream diet that involved no strenuous exercise and allowed all the meat anyone could eat. Hot dogs. Spam. Bologna. Lunchtime in the newsroom was awash in wet sandwich bags full of pink nitrates. The Hostess cupcakes in the vending machine had begun to gather dust. Spider webs stretched between bags of potato chips and pouches of Corn Nuts. At least Maxine could say her scones survived long enough to be the last temptation — a victory that warranted no celebration.

Maxine looked to the mess of pastries on the floor of her Land Rover, the frosting in the carpet, the shattered pieces of crust all around. She cried her first tear since the last time she lost anything important, and that was just an old earring, probably still beneath the backseat of that boy's car in Texas. He was easy — sugar cookies was all it took and she was off to the Sadie Hawkins dance with a wrist corsage and a pint of peppermint schnapps. Everyone had a weakness. All Maxine had to do was figure out Buckwalter's.

She sped up her driveway at 5:35 p.m., her 10-minute drive reduced by half in the rush to get home. Frosting stuck to the floorboard carpet as she turned over the mess of scones and took her plateful of problems up the back steps and into the kitchen. She looked to the refrigerator first, then to the stove. *A cooked meal? With everything else going on? Not a chance.* There was no time for dinner. Maxine's impending loss of clout was a level-red threat. About all she could still count on was that Stan's arrival would be delayed by the usual LA traffic jams, which meant she had at least another 90 minutes or so alone. That was serious thinking time. Stan could fend for himself.

The kitchen table was clean of all but the plate of busted scones and several blank sheets of white paper. No sifter or mixer was necessary. Not even egg substitutes or artificial sweeteners could help Maxine now. She scrawled the first thought that came to mind, then scratched it out so hard she cut through to the tabletop.

~~Carb free.~~

Baked goods without flour were as pointless as jelly doughnuts without jelly. The specialty bakery at the corner of Main and Peach might have considered it "a confectionary coup," as proclaimed by a sign in its window, but Maxine gave the place six months before it went the way of wheat germ and bean sprouts. Only matters of the mind could be denied forever. The gut governed itself. Cravings could only be resisted so long before the mouth reclaimed control. The body always fought the brain. Maxine knew enough alcoholics to understand that. The Friends of Bill W were no different than eaters, and plenty of people were both. Hard as some worked to climb aboard the latest waistband wagon, reality regularly bounced them out and back to where they'd been before, each fall more forceful than the last. Maxine's flock would return, but she wasn't about to practice patience. She had to force herself to properly preheat an oven, never mind waiting for people to warm to her way of thinking. This situation was beyond Betty Crocker. This required something more powerful than raw sugar, and more artery clogging than real cream. Maxine needed to tap the very essence of longing, the source of the ache that accompanied man's worst wants. She had to harness harm itself, with zero calories and no carbohydrates, but all the guilt of warm shortbread and cold buttermilk. Her weapon had to be lighter than the best meringue — virtually weightless — a provision capable of such euphoria that even trendsetting, anorexic ingénues would be powerless against it.

Ingénues. Accessories.

Ingénues loved accessories — little dogs and sparkly bags and colorful little cupcake boutiques that wrapped all purchases in beautiful cardboard boxes tied up with string. Maxine would have to have some of that — the appeal of an accessory. What could be better than an addictive consumable that said something about the consumer as it was being consumed? Maxine stared so long and hard at the page that the surface of her eyes seemed to dance with liquid smoke. And then all was clear again.

Smoke!

Buckwalter was a smoker.

The craving! Smoke!

Maxine dashed off a quick note to Stan, suggested he seek out the eggplant parmesan leftovers and some store-brand, crinkle-cut fries in the freezer, then she added a little PS and propped the paper beside the plate of broken scones.

"PS Sweets 4 U! N-joy!"

————

Maxine arrived at the Memorial Promenade shopping mall with two hours left until sunset. It was the only shopping mall in Waters End and the only place Maxine had ever seen so many elegant smokers gather all at once. She parked in the lot outside the PasPourVous Day Spa and remained behind the wheel to spy and take notes:

> *Inhale* — pinky extended.

> *Exhale* — head up, hair back.

> *Laugh* — never with cigarette in mouth.

> *Sway hips* — gently.

> *Repeat*.

The Land Rover's window tints concealed her as she mimicked the movements, an imaginary cigarette between her fingers, the rearview mirror turned down to reflect her face. These women weren't so pretty. She got good sense and they got good fortune. No other difference.

Once the last two women climbed into their Bentleys to depart, Maxine slipped into the well-lit lot. With quick steps in her clogs, she scooted to the knee-high ash container, skimmed the surface debris into a sandwich baggie, then clip-clopped back to her Land Rover. With a pair of eyebrow tweezers beneath the vehicle's dome light, she picked through the cache of lipstick-stained filters, chewing gum and torn foil pill packets. She inspected each butt as a detective might, assigning each to one of four rows of similarity set up on the passenger seat. There were 20 cigarettes in all, but one brand dominated the bunch. She bundled a sample of that one into a tissue, dumped the remains out the door, and raced south on Highway 101. She knew exactly where to go. The Los Angeles community of Woodland Hills had a 24-hour tobacco shop located in the same strip mall as a designer factory outlet for women's shoes.

The cashier didn't speak when Maxine entered to the ding of a motion detector. Neither did he say a word as she slipped one of the used butts through the slot of his glass enclosure and inquired about the brand. He spun to face the wall of tobacco behind him, then slapped two packs on the countertop — a red one and a blue one.

The label on each box read "Dunhill."

Maxine pointed to the blue one, said it was "pretty," and raised her eyebrows at the clerk.

"International Mild," he said in an accent Maxine guessed was Greek. Greeks, she often said, could run any kind of store or restaurant.

She tossed a credit card through the slot.

"Give me a case of that, Zorba," she said.

"A case?" the man said. "Twenty cigarette packs to a carton. No cases. You buy a carton."

"Carton," Maxine said as she picked through what little cash she had in her pink, quilted, imitation leather wallet.

"I need ID," the man told her.

"Do I look that young?" Maxine said and pulled out her license. "I'm married. See?"

"For the credit card," he said. "For security."

Maxine smoked four cigarettes on the drive home and swore she already felt some significant benefits. Aside from a slight lightheadedness, her appetite disappeared despite missing dinner. That alone made these almost as good as the white, 20 mg Ritalin LA capsules she secretly obtained from her husband's 13-year-old nephew — a bimonthly brownies-for-medication barter agreement set up two Christmases prior to the last. Ritalin killed her appetite in the daytime, but was no help at night. Taking it in the evening made sleep impossible. Cigarettes were the perfect complement.

"Meaty Schmeaty," she said and punched in the electric cigarette lighter to smoke fag number five.

Fags. Maxine loved that the Brits call them fags.

The next morning, Maxine joined Buckwalter on the loading dock. It was his first smoke of the day. Maxine was on her third.

"You a secret smoker?" Buckwalter asked.

Maxine sprayed smoke up and away with a swan-like dip and swoop of her neck.

"They hate us here," she told him. "But when I saw you weren't afraid of … I decided I'm sick of sneaking around. No more secrets. I'm with you. We'll show them what's what."

Property Taxes Feed Dubious Special District

By Keith Torrance
Pendulum Staff Writer

Skyrocketing home sales have been a boon to government agencies at all levels in recent years, especially for one little-known special district in the City of Waters End.

Created and quickly forgotten by city residents more than 30 years ago, the Waters End Mosquito Abatement District was formed to combat a persistent bug infestation at a man-made lake once located in the city center. Not long after the district was established, however, the lake was filled in and downtown Waters End was built on top of it.

Although WEMAD lost its purpose, it continues to employ a full-time staff and to collect property tax revenue — $3 million last year alone — all despite the city's virtually bug-free environs.

Burton Brand, who has served as president of WEMAD since its inception, did not respond to calls seeking comment.

Please turn to page A5

CHAPTER 4 – THE SHOES

Burton Brand's feet went hot inside his black, leather Florsheim wingtips as he waited for the "fasten seatbelts" sign to go dark. He counted the tiny fingers on the sign from left to right and back, and still the little, airplane light held him hostage. He felt choked, not just by the belt across his lap, but by every other little insult and inconvenience. Even his urgent need to pee reminded him of what he planned to forget — his birthday. He was 70.

Seventy years old.

The day had begun back in New York City with the same breakfast he'd requested each morning of his weeklong stay — egg whites, lite salt, wheat toast (no butter), decaf (no cream), and imitation sweetener in the pink packets. He'd made the desk clerk write it down — *"Pink, not blue, not yellow."* The kitchen complied, right down to straining the yolks from his whites instead of using the usual egg substitute.

But that morning, as Burton had stared at the odd shape of his yolkless eggs, he saw more than what was there. Ten years of bland breakfasts flashed before his eyes. He was 70 and, despite all his expectations, he felt it.

The day was doomed from that point on. After breakfast it took him two hours to get from the middle of Manhattan to John F. Kennedy International Airport, during which time half a dozen strangers had shot him with the same word.

Don't trip, said the cabbie.

Don't strain yourself, said the skycap.

Don't be shy about getting up to use the bathroom,
said the yuppie on the aisle.

Burton had responded to each admonition with spite. The cabbie was told to "work for tips rather than offer them." The skycap was directed to check his attitude "along with the suit bag." And the young man on the aisle was advised to keep his head "out of other people's pants." But now, there on the plane, Burton had to go.

He was home, back in LA, but still the "fasten seatbelts" sign refused to let him leave his seat.

"What the hell?" he mumbled and turned to look out the window. He stuffed his face into the crook of his elbow, then inhaled through the wool sleeve of his sport coat. He knew what old people smelled like, that mix of vinegar, talc and French-milled soap. He never intended to get like that. Never. But, Christ, he had to pee. He refused to excuse himself, would not give the guy on the aisle the satisfaction. He would not. Would not. Not!

And then came the ding.

Burton was the first to unbuckle himself once the little lighted sign went out. He brushed past the young man, raced through the jetway and hurried into the nearest men's room, his pants undone before he hit porcelain. He cursed and cocked his head back as he settled in. And then it wouldn't come.

"Son of a bitch," he spit.

"Shy bladder, huh?" said some guy behind him.

Burton closed his eyes and counted backward from 100.

By the time he got to baggage claim, everyone else had already grabbed their luggage and hurried out onto World Way. Only a lady security officer remained as Burton stood at the carousel and waited for his suit bag to come around. He searched his pockets for his claim check and sorted through a week's worth of unanswered pink, hotel message slips. One name was repeated on every other pink sheet — "Chick" … "Chick" … "Chick."

Burton switched on his cell phone and checked the time. It was after midnight. Monday morning. The day after the day he turned 70.

"Happy birthday, honey!" someone shouted.

His head snapped up.

It was his wife, Jenny, waving and clicking her way across baggage claim in a pair of fuchsia slingback sandals. Twenty years since the last time she'd met him at the airport, and there she was without warning, dressed in one of his favorites, that simple yellow dress with the hem that stopped right at the knees. Jenny had "gams," legs more shapely than women half her age. She was slim too, five-foot three-inches tall and never a pound over 105 before, or after, she had the kids. She was five years his junior, but still moved as easy as when they got married. Her hair had started to go gray, but she'd done something to keep it as blonde as ever. Happy as Burton was to see her, she didn't belong. She was supposed to be waiting at home.

"Jenny," he said as she stood on her toes to kiss his cheek.

"I know, but … you get tired," she whined and tugged at the lapels of his sport coat. "It's getting harder for you to see at night, and you deserve a chauffeur."

He shifted his suit bag strap from one shoulder to the other, heaved a sigh, then looked her up and down. "Every time I'm out of town it's another $800 hairdo and a new pair of shoes!"

Jenny gave his arm a slap.

"Oh Burt, I've never spent $800 on a hairdo. And I bought these shoes on special, so don't pop a stitch. You ought to be glad you've got a gal who can still move in heels. It's the bowling. I'm one fit chick."

Chick.

Burton felt for the phone messages in his pocket again.

"I know why you're here," he said. "And, if you hired a town car, I'm going to have a —"

"I drove the Chrysler. Myself. It's your birthday. I called and called. I talked to the hotel manager, to make sure you checked out. You turned your phone off again, didn't you? I hate when you do that."

"So now you check up on me?"

"What if something happened, Burt? Did you ever think of that?"

"I'm fine!"

"Not just you," she said. "I'm talking about me, too. What if something were to happen to me?"

"I've provided for you since day one! Don't you worry. Nothing's going to change because of one goddamn birthday."

Jenny responded with one of those indulgent looks of hers — arms crossed, eyes wide, grin tight.

Burton left her like that, turned to the double doors, stepped out onto World Way, and caught the shuttle to the long-term parking lot.

Once behind the wheel of his Hummer, Burton sped out to Interstate 405 and punched the accelerator to the floor. He opened all the windows, turned up the heater and grabbed his BlackBerry.

1:15 AM

He was determined to beat Jenny home.

As the Hummer's all-terrain radials ripped through the early morning dark of LA's Westside, he punched up his voicemail to check his messages. The first four calls were from a reporter at *The Pendulum*, someone named "Keith Torrance."

"It's about the Mosquito Abatement District nest egg," the reporter said in the first one.

"*Nest egg.*" It made Burton bristle. Depression-era talk. Code for "old," as if he stuffed money in mattresses, or buried coffee cans of cash in the backyard.

The reporter's second message said he needed to "talk about how the district uses tax revenue."

"It's a routine story," said the third message.

"It'll publish Sunday," went the fourth.

The fifth call was from Mayor Chick Nimbus, who'd shouted so loudly that it made Burton jerk the BlackBerry away from his ear: "Call that boy back and set him right before this gets away from us. He'll get curious. Our friend hates headlines."

The message from Mayor Nimbus was the last Burton heard before his hairpiece began to flap loose. The glue had lost its grip, a combined result of having both windows open, the heater on high, and a forehead soaked by beads of sweat. He tried to tamp the flap back into place, but forgot the BlackBerry still clutched in his fist. He saw sparks as it bonked him in the head. After that, he threw the phone, chucked it at the Hummer's dashboard and grinned as shards of broken plastic chattered into the windshield seam at the far end. It felt good to break something, at least until he remembered the memory card — his call logs and address book — all his work info was still inside that damn phone. He strained to snatch it, stretched his knobby fingers as straight as he could, but he only ended up thumping the temperature controls, switching them from hot to cold. On the next attempt, he leaned so far forward that his chest blasted the horn. Finally, he gave a grunt and punched his foot down on the gas pedal. The speedometer flew from 30 to 50 mph as he banked into the transition loop of Highway 101, the most traveled interchange in the country and he had it all to himself, which made it way too easy to take too fast. His foot reached the brake late, the force of the turn already sucking the busted shell of the BlackBerry across the dashboard. He watched the phone hit the frame of the passenger door and flip end over end out the open window and into the dark.

"Goddamn piece of shit!" Burton shouted, his eyes searching the rearview mirror for a sign of it. It was back there somewhere, in the weeds … on the asphalt … "That goddamn piece of —"

Jenny would beat him home if he stopped.

He swiped his hand down his face and gunned it through Sherman Oaks, Reseda, Woodland Hills and Calabasas, so alone on the road that he started to yawn. The trembling of the tires felt like a massage to his tired body. White lines went by and by and by and before long his eyelids were heavy. He slapped his face as hard as he could.

"'Nest egg' my ass," he said. "No-account bastard."

Once he was within four miles of Waters End, he let up on the gas, laughed at himself in the mirror, then spun the radio dial through classical music, rock and rap in search of a public radio station. He was sure it was there somewhere, but as his bumpy fingers worked the knob it occurred to him that it might have signed off for the night.

Finally, the waves of static snapped to a clear, crisp signal. He'd found it. The station. At the same time, he realized the Hummer had coasted to a dead stop.

The radio flew away before he looked up to the road.

Burton felt like he was under water as the back of his head sank into the cushion of the Hummer's headrest. His arms went rubbery and his fingers splayed. He could sense the Hummer fishtailing, his guts sloshing like a tether ball around the shank of his spine. Then everything went black. The smell of soil filled his nostrils.

Burton sat upright and motionless in the idle seconds that followed. He gulped air and slapped his scalp to find his hairpiece was gone. He took hold of the wheel and marveled at how elastic the joints of his fingers felt.

"Goddamn airbags!" he spit.

They hadn't deployed.

He pushed buttons and pulled knobs — the headlights, the hazards, the cigarette lighter. Nothing. He spied another car out the window on the passenger side, the only window not covered with dirt. That car was stopped too, and looked like it had spun a full 180 degrees before coming to rest in the fast lane, the same place Burton's Hummer had been prior to the crash. Its taillights were lit, but the headlights were out. Burton pushed his door open and stepped down to grass. He was in the median. He ran his hands up and down his rib cage, over his bony hips and down his thighs, feeling for injuries that weren't there. He untucked the tails of his shirt, loosened his necktie, and pulled off his sport coat.

"You crazy son of a bitch!" he shouted and stomped toward the other car.

The closer he got, the more familiar that car became. It was a Chrysler 300C with Magnesium Pearl paint and forged-aluminum wheels, almost identical to one he'd purchased a few weeks earlier as a gift for Jenny. Even the dealer plate frame was the same, its name offset in black letters on chrome. The difference was the plate. Jenny's car didn't have one yet. Hers was overdue from the DMV. One more pain he had to deal with, and now this too.

His shoes stuttered to a stop.

A small pair of bowling shoes lay in the back window, behind the back seat.

Jenny?

Burton jerked into a sprint and yelled as he ran.

"Jenny!"

At the driver's door, he leaned to look inside. The airbag hid the driver's face, but the blonde hairdo was unmistakable. He wrenched the door open and pulled her body back.

"Jenny?"

She sobbed and slumped forward into the scratchy weave of the airbag. A syrupy red ooze stretched in a string from her nose to her hand as she reached under the steering column as if in search of the ignition.

"It won't start," she said. "Burt, it won't start. Burt?"

He bent down, unfastened her seatbelt, and slowly slipped his hands beneath her arms. He pulled her from the vehicle in a careful hug, and stood her up in the road to perform the same inspection of her that he'd performed on himself. He ran his palms up and down her torso, checked her ribs, then her hips and legs.

"Anything broken?" he asked. "You seem OK. Are you OK?"

The feel of Jenny's body reminded him of how fragile she was. It had been years since he touched her this much all at once.

"Your legs are good," he said and guided her to the front of the car. "Your gams still got it."

She smiled.

Burton surveyed the smashed-in grill of the Chrysler as Jenny turned to look back at the Hummer in the median.

"We're OK," Burton said.

The Hummer made a sound like a drip from somewhere beneath it.

"These cars were both stolen at the airport," Burton said. "They're insured. That's the way it happened. They were stolen and we got a ride home from … I have to figure this out. How did they steal both cars?"

He slipped his right hand up Jenny's back and caressed the nape of her neck.

"No, Burt. We —"

"Hell, either way, I have to call Benny over at the yard. He can come pick us up in the truck and —"

Burton patted his pockets for his BlackBerry as a pair of headlights crested the horizon. The driver did not appear to see them. He was not slowing down. By the time Burton kicked into motion, the car was

20 yards away and roaring. He scooped up Jenny. His black, leather Florsheim wingtips were pulled off his feet. His toes went cold.

Nick Carlos walked faster and faster the closer he got to Lily Frink. She was bent over in the fast lane, on the other side of the police tape, and she looked to be shooting a pair of men's shoes.

"Oh hell!" he huffed and moved as quickly as he could, careful not to break into a full-on run.

She was shooting shoes. That was the last thing Nick needed. He'd never get access to anything if the cops saw his photographer doing *that* again.

"Jesus, Lily!" Nick rasped. "You know better!"

"Frink," she shot back. "It's Frink."

Nick cupped his fingers over her lens and reached to pull Frink upright. "They'll crucify me if they see my shooter doing that," he said.

Frink snatched her camera away. "Fingerprints!" she said. "And I'm not your shooter. I'm a photographer."

Nick followed her up the road, her equipment clunking and clinking as she went. She had three Nikon camera bodies and two lenses the size of deluxe Thermoses. One lens bounced off a breast while the other dangled like a lame appendage beneath her arm.

"Two in the meat wagon, one in ICU," she said. "Been here since dark. I heard it on my scanner. Got spaghetti shots, but … The Chief —"

Nick motioned to the chins lined up along the chain link fence 50 feet away. "One of them could be family," he said.

"Lookie-lous," Frink said. "Family don't stand with lookie-lous."

"Whatever. Just shoot the plates."

"But the shoes fell funny, backwards and side-by-side. Look —"

"The plates. I need names," Nick said. "The watch commander will make me wait all day, way longer than DMV. I told you last time. Just do it. I can't see from here."

"So walk over there and do it yourself."

"And piss off the sergeant? No. Use your big lens. I don't want him to know what I'm doing. OK?"

Frink trained her camera on the Hummer and Nick punched up the newsroom on his cell. He waited through 10 rings before a slap between his shoulder blades made him jump.

"Fucking hell!" he said and shot around to see who it was.

Keith laughed. "Boonin' Valley," he said. "Took us an hour from Reseda and we still haven't made the office. What's going on?"

Jake stepped up as Nick repeated what little he knew so far.

"I tried the newsroom," he said. "Fifty people and nobody answers."

"Morning meeting," Jake explained. "Every day at nine o'clock."

———

Maxine Lugner slapped a file folder shut as soon as Jake got close enough to glimpse it. "Where you been?" Maxine said and shoved the file inside her desk.

"It's LA," Jake said. "Never less than 20 minutes from traffic."

"You poor thing," Maxine replied. "I wouldn't know. It takes me 10 minutes. Streets all the way. But Stan ... We should put the radio on in the morning for him. Isn't that funny? I'm so local I don't even pay attention."

Fletcher Buckwalter threw his leather satchel at his chair the second he arrived.

"Fucking freeways," he spit.

Maxine perked and pulled a blue pack of Dunhill cigarettes from her purse.

"You got that number?" Keith said to Jake.

Maxine leaned toward Keith's desk. "What number?"

"DMV."

"Oh. You guys on an accident? I thought we weren't supposed to have to do that stuff anymore. Right, Fletch?"

Buckwalter's eyes lit on the Dunhill pack as he patted his empty shirt pocket.

"I'm helping Nick," Keith explained. "He's at the scene. Besides, he's taking my next weekend shift."

"Oh, you're so good," Maxine said. "But ... We're not supposed to be in the weekend shift rotation anymore. I thought our team was excused from that regular-reporter stuff. Right, Fletch?"

Buckwalter pulled a cigarette from Maxine's pack and pointed it butt first at Keith. "Accidents don't take two," he said. "Leave Nick to that. Do your tax series. And, Jake? The water thing? When?"

Jake stared back as he pinched the cigarette filter down to a chisel point.

"We always do this," Keith said.

"Then why am I here?" Buckwalter said and turned to walk toward the dock.

Maxine followed him out with a Dunhill in her hand.

"Yeah," Keith whispered once they were gone. "Why *are* you here?"

"He just doesn't know," Jake said. "It's good that you're helping Nick."

Once the pileup achieved the rank of "daily" on *The Pendulum's* news budget, assistant city editor Neil Thrumming appeared at Keith's desk. Keith was on the phone, but Thrumming kept eye contact and whispered the same question three times in a row.

"Any locals?"

Keith pressed the phone receiver tighter to his ear each time he waved Thrumming away. The DMV kept people on hold forever, all for nothing more than a name to go with a plate. Two hours later he got his answer.

"BN," he said as he ripped through the phone book. "Brand Name Real Estate. Generic real estate agents."

Jake held her fingers to her lips as she watched Keith dial the first number he found.

"Nick didn't ask you to do that," she whispered. "You don't even know what happened."

Keith turned away. "Excuse me," he said into the phone. "Was that 'District office?'"

He ran his hand across the back of his neck.

"Keith Torrance. I'm a reporter for the —"

He spun around to face his desk again.

"You do?" he said and straightened in his chair. "I did?"

His ballpoint scratched something into his notebook, though Jake couldn't see what.

"Burton Brand?" he said. "This is *that* Burton Brand?"

He slammed the receiver down and gave Jake a grin.

"It's Burton," he said. "My tax story. The bug thing. This is that guy. It's the same number I called last week, the same office. My Burton Brand is the 'Brand Name.' Is that sweet or what?"

"He does real estate too?" Jake said.

"He had to be one of the bodies."

"Wait. You don't know. At least one person was alive. Nick told you. Maybe somebody borrowed this guy's car. Maybe an employee was driving. You don't know. It could be anyone. It could have been stolen."

"Don't you have a *water* story to write?"

Neil Thrumming appeared again at Keith's desk.

"I'm still working," Keith told him.

"And?" Thrumming said.

"If I break the news, I own the story."

"I own you," Thrumming said. "It's a double-byline, you and Nick."

Keith sucked his lips. "We got a local," he said.

"Two hours to deadline," Thrumming told him. "Don't bust it."

Keith kicked the underside of his desk.

"Buckwalter and buck you," he hissed once Thrumming was gone.

Jake pulled her legs up onto her chair, tucked the heels of her Mary Janes underneath her, and looked over the top of her catty eyeglasses at Keith. He was dialing again, his eyes blank.

"This is the reporter you never called back," Keith said into the phone after a long pause. "This is another story. It's about the accident you were in last night. Call me."

Jake snapped at him the moment he hung up. "What are you doing? What if his wife or kids or somebody gets that? You could get them all panicked for nothing."

Keith glowed. "Boonin' moron," he said. "All that money just sitting there. Saving for what? Locusts? Old people are crazy. This Brand dude's dead. Definitely dead. And it's *my* story, so back off."

Mayor Wants To Put Brakes On STOP Laws

By Maxine Lugner
Pendulum Staff Writer

Bitter waitress giving you a bad attitude? Cranky cashier too slow?

Mayor Chick Nimbus blames bad service in Waters End restaurants on the open-space preservation laws promoted by the non-profit organization Save The Open Places.

Nimbus said this week that he regrets supporting the STOP laws five years ago and will now campaign to abolish them.

"Service workers can't afford to live here," Nimbus said. "A waitress who lives two hours away doesn't care about how cold your coffee is.

"STOP made developers out to be the enemy. But, the enemy was all of us. We did this to ourselves."

Please turn to page A6

CHAPTER 5 – NONDELIVERY

The last carrier was supposed to be gone by five, yet there they were, still lined up when Jake arrived at half past.

Even from a block away it was obvious, the papers stacked along the loading dock in lopsided columns of three and four bundles apiece. *The Pendulum's* fleet of pickup trucks were there too, headlights out, tailgates backed against the big rubber bumpers along the concrete platform. Jake cranked her window down to see.

Keith cut the turn into the parking lot so close it made the car bounce hard off the curb. Jake gripped the door handle on reflex, but still grazed her head on the ceiling. Keith thumped the wheel with his fist and fumed.

"I told you," he said and jerked the car into the space farthest from the building. "Those gang bangers are going to be blaring that Mexican polka crap for another hour. You're not going to get anything done. I could have slept in."

"Don't call them that," Jake said.

"Gang bangers?"

"If you were in a gang, would you deliver newspapers?"

"Just lock your door. Trust me."

Jake pulled her cell phone from her pocket, then looked to the long morning shadows that stretched across the pavement. Home delivery was guaranteed by seven. It was 5:33.

"They should be done," she said.

"*You* should be done," Keith shot. "It doesn't take five weeks to make up a story. Why the hell are we getting up early? So you can write a story you never finish? All I ever see you doing is taking notes. What good are notes? The whole thing is a lie anyway."

Jake patted her lap in a fret, twisted to check the back, climbed out of the car and bent to feel beneath her seat. "My bag," she said.

Most of what Jake needed to do her work — the news clippings and photocopied records — were kept in her newsroom desk. The draft versions of her water story were securely stored in her computer's hard drive, password-protected and hidden from prying eyes, ready for another day of tinkering. Her notebook, however, was too crucial to trust to an office drawer. She kept it beside her at all times, zipped inside her bag, same as her wallet and press credentials. Losing her wallet was bad enough, but at least she could cancel and replace credit cards and IDs. Her notebook, however, was unlike any of that. The threat her notebook posed to her security was bigger. In the wrong hands it could imply she was a liar, a conspirator, a fabulist. It could destroy her — the very thing she was trying to avoid.

Jake's cheek twitched and the corner of her mouth contorted. Sure as she was that she'd left the bag on the kitchen counter, her sureness had lately been very unreliable. She was sure the city's water wasn't contaminated, until she tried to verify it. She was sure city officials weren't corrupt, until she searched for evidence. She was sure she'd do the right thing, until the day she didn't.

"We have to go back," she insisted. "I need my ... I can't do the —"

"What now?" Keith said.

"Buckwalter. He wants this thing and ... I forgot my bag and ... My notebook is in my bag."

"You're doing this on purpose," Keith said and looked to the boots on her feet. "What's with those?"

Jake had pulled them from the trunk the night before, the leather still supple and undistressed despite seven years of car heat. The fit was perfect, such a long-lost sensation. The turquoise color would not have been her choice, but in the current context of her life the boots alone were a comfort.

"I wanted something different," she said. "I don't know."

"You remembered boots you never wear, but you forgot your bag? You forgot on purpose, to have an excuse."

"No, I —"

"Fine," he said. "But I go alone. You do what you promised. Go in there and work. I'll be back."

Jake forced herself to smile as she waved him away, then turned toward the building behind her. Lately she'd gained a greater appreciation for time spent away from Keith.

The carriers stood shoulder to shoulder on the dock as Jake approached. Together they made a wall of plaid, all of them dressed in flannel shirts and ball caps and paper-thin windbreakers. Every eye was downcast. No grins. No chewing gum. No cigarettes. Jake blushed as she passed, never quite comfortable with the way the men watched her. To most anyone else in her office, she likely looked as though she could have been their cousin, or sister. But to her the drivers were barely coworkers. She relied on them, and, the way she figured it, they relied on her. She respected them. Without them her words would reach no one. But, much as she might have wished otherwise, they were still strangers, phantoms who worked in the shadows, not a one known to her by face or name. She reached instinctively for her purse and blushed. Not only was there no good reason to hold it close, it wasn't there anyway.

"*La Migra,*" one of the men whispered.

"*Gringa!*" said another.

Jake stopped short when a woman in uniform stepped sideways to cut her off.

"*Identificación,*" the woman said, her Mexican accent so forced it almost made Jake snicker, until she caught sight of the piece.

"Excuse me?" Jake said.

The woman wore a sidearm on her hip, but appeared barely old enough to drink. Her cheeks were puffed with baby fat and her shiny black hair was cut schoolboy short.

One of the woman's hands flew forward as the other slapped her holster.

"*Identificación*," she repeated louder than before.

Jake patted her pockets, the BlackBerry in her hip pocket all she currently possessed to prove her identity. "I'm from here," she said. "I have a phone."

The woman's hands twitched and her feet shot out, widening her stance. Jake froze.

"No," the woman said. "That's right. Nice and easy. Don't move. Answer my question. Do you have identification?"

Jake stuttered: "I ... have ... a phone."

"Do you have ID?"

"I work here. What are you —"

Another uniform — a man with a mustache — approached from behind the woman. "Did you get a name?" he said and looked to the clipboard in his hands.

"Negative, sir."

Jake jumped at the sound of the carriers' feet as they moved in unison toward the stairs at the end of the dock, their hands restrained behind their backs with plastic ties, the same sort that the pressmen used to bind newspaper bundles.

Jake jerked her chin toward the restraints. "What is this all about?" she said.

The male officer tapped a ballpoint to the badge on his chest. "Immigration and Naturalization Service," he said. "Your name, please?"

"These people ..." Jake said. "They're my coworkers. I mean we —"

"OK. Tell me a name," he said. "Any name."

"No. I don't *know* them, but I know them. They're the delivery guys. They don't ... We don't ... They're usually gone when I get here. I —"

"You know them, but you don't know them," the woman said flatly, one hand still on the butt of her holstered pistol.

Jake nodded to a pair of vans, into which the carriers were being led. "Where are you taking them?"

"Depends," the man in uniform said and laughed out his nose. "Voluntary returns get a free ride to Tijuana. The ones who want to fight get to sit in a cell until their court date. Of course, if we find any outstanding warrants, well ... that's where things get complicated. So, your name?"

"Tijuana?" Jake said, one hand squeezing the other, needing her notebook and pen. "What if Tijuana isn't home? What if this is their home? They work here. They probably live here, or near here."

"You don't know a single name," the man said, "but you know where all these people live? I want your name. Now, for the very last time —"

Both officers seemed to smirk at Jake's reply. The man flipped through the pages on his clipboard. The woman drummed her fingers on her hip.

"No 'Jake LaMotta' on the list," the man said.

"What list?" Jake shot. "I work here. I write."

The woman plucked a newspaper off a nearby stack and snapped it open. "Got a story in today's edition?" she said. "Let me guess. 'Jake LaMotta' is a sportswriter."

Jake bit her bottom lip. "I … there's nothing in today, but —"

"Yesterday?" the woman said. "The day before? Last week?"

"What are you, my editor?" Jake said and gave a nervous laugh. This was too ridiculous to be real.

The woman officer finally cracked a grin. "Maybe you meant to say 'Roberto Duran,'" she said. "Or, how about 'Jose Vargas?' C'mon Jose. Show us some footwork."

"Listen," Jake said. "Do I sound like I'm —"

She stopped herself before she finished, closed her mouth and felt her cheeks go warm. She shrank, ashamed of having even considered using her proficiency in English as an indicator of legitimacy. To suggest language skills were evidence of a law-abiding nature was the same as saying all foreign accents were cause for suspicion. It was ignorant. It wasn't what she believed. She refused to save herself that way.

The man with the clipboard stirred the air with his ballpoint pen. "Do you sound like you're what?" he said. "Do you sound … like you're some fighter from the '50s? I've seen the movie *seniorita* and, let me give you the *cuatro uno uno*. He's Italian, not *Mexicano*. Jake es *hombre*. *Comprenda*? He's a man, do you understand?"

A loud thump sounded as a couple uniformed men shut up the last of the carriers in the white vans. Other officers were busy cordoning off the parking lot from the dock with yellow police tape.

"Ask my editors when they get here," she said. "Anyone who works here can tell you. It's early for them to … My husband went to get my —"

The man with the clipboard lowered his voice and bent to Jake's ear, his warm breath flowing down the collar of her blouse. "No ID means you're nobody," he said. "And nobody goes to Mexico tonight, *chica. Su asno el es mío.*"

Much as Jake wanted to be angry, she felt suddenly frightened and violated. There were laws. She was an American. This was a man in authority, an officer who'd pledged to protect and serve. People like that couldn't do this to people like her. Jake's eyes began to water and she raised her hand to her mouth.

The moment she moved, the woman officer sprung forward. In one motion, she took hold of Jake's thumb and twisted it around and behind her back. Less than a second later, Jake's chest thumped against the wall of the building, her legs spread wide apart. Her cheek pressed into the roughness of the imitation stucco as the steel toe of the woman's boot bounced back and forth between the heels of Jake's turquoise-colored Luccheses. Her thumb was on fire with the unrelenting pressure. Another hand was on her too. It went around her shoulders and down her arms, across her breasts and belly. It roamed the insides of her thighs and down to her boot sleeves. As soon as it slipped away the woman officer shouted "clean."

Buckwalter's familiar bark never sounded so welcome as it did after that. Jake turned her head around so fast that she scraped her forehead on the wall.

"Now!" Buckwalter said. "Right now!"

The stress on Jake's thumb let up and she bounced herself off the side of the building, dancing in place to regain her balance.

Buckwalter pointed the butt of his cigarette to the white vans, then to Jake. "You got warrants?" he said. "On what authority are you screwing with these people … my people?"

"No ID," the woman officer said.

"What goddamn cause you got to see anyone's ID?" Buckwalter said. "This isn't some communist cabal. These are goddamn drivers with papers to deliver, and they're late."

"Not one of them had ID," the man with the clipboard said. "With all due respect, you might make the news sir, but you don't make the law."

Buckwalter bit into the filter of his cigarette, sucked almost half of it to ashes, then huffed the smoke out his nose. "That so?" he said. "Well, that lady you got there doesn't write stories that end up framed on office walls, if you get my meaning. And if she isn't at her desk in five minutes I'm going to assign her a first-person report on what it's like to be deported to Mexico by bigots."

The woman officer took a step closer to Buckwalter. "So what's the *lady's* name?" she said.

Buckwalter pinched the tip of his tongue and spit. "LaMotta," he said. "Jacqueline LaMotta."

Jake cleared her throat. "Actually, I've never been that!" she said. "I'm Jake. Just Jake."

Jake sat and stared at her reflection in the dark screen of her computer for two hours before she insisted that Keith give her the keys. She said she had to take the car and go. It was *her* car. But he clutched the keys so tightly and held them so high above his head that she couldn't reach.

"Give me the keys," she said. "You weren't there. You don't know how it is."

When that failed to sway him, she breathed deep and tried again, this time playing to the audience of newsroom eyes around them. She claimed to have an appointment, said she had to meet her source, knowing full well that Keith was aware no such source existed.

"Anonymous sources expect secret meetings, face-to-face," she said.

Keith raised the hand with the keys higher above his head, seemingly oblivious to his coworkers. "You need help," he whispered. "You're psychoanalyzing imaginary friends. You're making up reasons not to keep your word."

Jake stomped one of her turquoise boots. This wasn't a honey-do, but a honey-don't. *Honey, don't argue. Honey, don't be difficult. Honey, don't make me look crazy in the middle of the newsroom.*

The whole situation had become a farce of Shakespearean proportions. Jake no longer recognized her husband, or herself. They'd morphed into one of those restive couples she used to cross the street to avoid, the type of people who bickered loudly in parking lots and on public sidewalks no matter who was around. Their ugliness grew bigger every day, as toxic and amorphous as an oil spill and nearly as difficult to contain. Jake needed to stem the flow, but first she had to get her head above it. Repairing their lives required perspective. Essential as it was, however, she didn't dare make another grab for the fist with the keys, not with everyone watching.

Buckwalter brought the scent of cigarette smoke with him as he bounded back from the dock, marched straight into the pod, slapped his hand to the top of his monitor and kicked the wheeled rungs at the base of his chair.

Keith dropped the fist with the keys in it. Jake sat in her chair beside Keith.

"You familiar with Atwill?" Buckwalter said, as though he'd rushed inside only to seek the answer from the both of them. "At-will," he repeated, enunciating each syllable. "Did you know California is an 'at-will' state?"

Keith cocked his head, and Jake gave a nod. "At-will" meant anyone could be fired for a good reason, a bad reason, or no reason at all. It meant Jake worked at the whim of her boss — The Chief, as far as she was concerned, though Buckwalter surely figured himself more than a figurehead. "At-will" meant statements that began with "I will" were no longer acceptable. It meant Buckwalter wanted to hear "*I did*," as in "*I did the story ... I did what I promised ... I did what you wanted.*" Jake slipped her fingers over Keith's fist.

"Subscribers continue to cancel *at will*," Buckwalter said. "Corporate cuts are coming next quarter. I don't have to wait to start trimming fat."

"Cuts?" Keith said. "This newspaper makes money every year."

Buckwalter scoffed. "You're an accountant now?"

Jake tried to change the subject.

"I will be nearly done —"

"Nearly done?" Buckwalter said and pointed to The Chief's office door. "After that fiasco this morning I'd say the sign on that door says 'Nearly Done.'"

"But, wait, what do you mean?" Jake said. "That wasn't The Chief's fault. You were on my side on this one. I thought we were a —"

"Why would I want you on my side?" he said. "I want my story. That's it. I want the story you promised me weeks ago."

"But, what you said out there … The stuff about me writing a first-person piece on deportation. That's the story. That's the one I want to —"

"That," Buckwalter said, "was bullshit. That was *me* trying to get *you* back to work. Do you really believe our readers give a shit about what happens to a deportee? Get real. You're working in Waters End, not Juarez."

"Quit!" Keith hissed and jerked his hand away from Jake as soon as Buckwalter departed to attend an emergency meeting about the sudden lack of delivery drivers. "You should be done with your story anyway."

"A walk-and-talk," Jake whispered and jumped for the keys. "That's what you said I should do. I have to at least *look* like I'm out there interviewing people. Isn't that how you told me to do it?"

Keith kept up the fight, reached higher and kept the keys away. "You should be done," he repeated.

"I *am* done," Jake said finally and dropped her arms to her sides. "I'm done with all four of them."

"Four what?" Keith said and slipped into his desk chair.

"Quotes are all I need."

"Four what?" he said again.

"Stories. Four stories. I wrote four stories."

Keith immediately scooted his chair around to Jake's desk, bumped her chair with his, and seized control of her keyboard.

"Which one is it?" he said and stared at a computer queue containing four separate story files.

"The password is 'pop.' It's the same for each of them. Just type 'pop.' Each one's a different version of the same story. I don't know which one to use. I don't want to use any of them. But I still need to get quotes and —"

"Four?" Keith whispered as he opened each of the files. "You wrote four?"

Three of the stories said the city's water had been poisoned in the 1950s. One blamed nuclear waste that was dumped in "an undisclosed location" in 1952 (the messy result of a meltdown at the Copper-Sykes Laboratory on the Covalop County side of the Santa Monica Mountains). The second story proposed a perchlorate contamination that occurred sometime after 1955 (a massive dynamite stash never located by law enforcement after all parties of a pact to

BOON

blow up a religious cult in Shadow Canyon were put in jail). The third version regarded a petroleum spill in 1951 (a fantastic crash and fuel-farm fire at the military airport, which used to be located on what later became the lake, and, after that, downtown Waters End). The fourth and final variation was the story Jake considered most sinister, because it suggested the culpability of the least likely of citizens — the farmers. It painted them as rogues who were fully aware of the consequences of their fungicide use. It told of the potential toll — on children, on the elderly, on everyone. Jake's so-called "anonymous sources" suggested a cover-up, blackmail and avarice on the part of certain city officials to be named later. Real-life attempts by the city to curtail the use of such chemicals by farmers were portrayed as politically correct maneuvers, actions intended to create a false sense of security, to cover chemical damage that couldn't be undone. The poison was still down there, somewhere, lying in wait like a devastating cancer.

Jake reeled as she reread her vile words over Keith's shoulder, disturbed that such demons had come out of her.

Keith complained about what wasn't there. "The earthquake?"

"There weren't any earthquakes," she said. "I can't make one up. Besides, it's the shakers to come that ought to scare us."

Dishonorable as the entire exercise might have been, Jake adopted an ethical approach in the making of each monster. She'd dug with the intention of disproving her assertions, only to discover facts to support all the horrors she'd suggested. Waters End had grown too quickly. Critical questions had gone unasked, and, therefore, unanswered. Environmental tests were never done. What data did exist was often improperly filed, or questionably recorded on forms that lacked official signatures and stamps. Some documents had disappeared, quite a convenience for contractors and developers who still did business in town.

"You created a nuclear accident?" Keith said. "What kind of stupid is that?"

"I didn't fake it. It happened."

It was mostly true. There'd been a meltdown in the '50s, at Copper-Sykes, up in the hills. It was a test reactor, an early version of a device later installed on a satellite and launched into space. It was still up in orbit more than three decades later, still loaded with plutonium and ready to switch on, a potential power supply for astronauts in case of emergency. Early testing on the prototype had not inspired confidence.

The data was all public record, including an eyewitness account of how the meltdown occurred and why. Details of the cleanup, however, were supposedly lost. The disposition of the waste remained a mystery — where the contaminated water went … how much spilled on the ground … who was responsible for disposal. The threat to groundwater was real, though no one but Jake seemed to care enough to ask.

"Radioactive particles endure for lifetimes," she said. "Thermonuclear fuels don't disappear. Tritium last longer than love, or hate, or people, or trees."

Keith tapped his finger to the middle of the monitor. "An earthquake could shake it loose," he said. "It could be in the soil and then … plop."

Jake pretended as though she hadn't considered it, let it seem like Keith's idea. "Once it's in the water, it binds instantly to the molecules," she said. "There's no way to filter it. You can't take it back."

"Irreversible," Keith said and smiled. "Awesome."

Just then, Maxine flopped her spandex-clad torso hard into her chair and leaned to have a look. Keith clicked the stories closed, pushed himself back to his desk and reached for his phone.

"You gonna deliver?" Maxine asked.

"Mind your own business," Keith barked.

"Fletch told me … He says everyone except —"

Maxine stopped as Buckwalter drifted back into the pod. "Torrance," he said. "Get your shit and get going."

"What'd I do?" Keith complained and pointed to Jake. "She's the —"

"She's got a story I want. I'm giving you and Maxine to Circulation. They've got papers to get out. Pickups don't drive themselves. Immigration took all our carriers."

"It'll be fun," Maxine chirped. "Papergirl for a day."

"Deliver papers?" Keith said. "You're kidding."

"Now," Buckwalter said. "Teams of two. You two. Together. Now."

Keith tossed the keys to the Corolla on Jake's desk. "It's practically lunch," he said. "Nobody wants what we've got *now*."

Jake stared absently at the ring of keys, the newsroom mostly empty except for a few copy editors and the office assistants taking complaints by phone about missing papers. One of them appeared at Jake's desk and pulled her out of her trance.

"Yes?" Jake said.

The woman could have been Jake's baby sister for the rich cocoa tone of her skin and the shape of her face. The woman's arms were crossed, her eyebrows as square as her shoulders.

"What you got?" Jake said and snatched up the car keys.

"Where you from?" the woman asked, her voice tinged with a hint of a Mexican accent.

"Where? Here. Well, not *here*. New Mexico, but —"

"Mexico?" the woman said and thrust her left hip out. "You from Mexico and you do us like dat?"

"What? I didn't say Mexico, I said 'New—'"

"Nothing new about it. As long as you gets away, it don't matter what *La Migra* do to no cholo, right? Send 'em back. Dump 'em down in TJ. Dey ain't no people no how, not nobody worth no headline to tells it like it is, right? Right?"

Jake tried to formulate a response, only to confuse herself. She thought to tell the woman that they were both on the same side, but realized she'd have to clarify that she meant the side of fairness. Of course, then she'd have to explain that fairness was less of a side than a kind of vantage point for disinterested observers. Not that Jake was disinterested, but rather bound by journalist ethics. Jake was on the side of truth, but the truth could be tricky. Legal wasn't always right, and wrong was sometimes necessary. Nothing sounded right, so nothing was what she said.

The woman stood firm, her brown eyes big and dark and fearless. "If you ain't got no *cojones* to look at me, you ain't never gone see what life like for reals. You don't even know where you from. Alls that matters to Chicas like you is dat you gets what you wants."

Jake kept her eyes downcast, sat there trapped. Not a single phone rang. The police scanner didn't squawk. The newsroom had never before felt so small.

NOTICE TO ALL SUBSCRIBERS:

Home delivery of today's edition of *The Pendulum* was delayed due to circumstances beyond our control.

The Pendulum apologizes for any inconvenience this caused. All subscribers will be credited the cost of one day's paper.

The Pendulum hopes to return to regular delivery tomorrow. We appreciate your understanding and value you as a reader.

Sincerely,

The Pendulum Staff

CHAPTER 6 – STRIKE

Jake circled the bowling alley parking lot three times before she spotted a lone available space out on the street. She lined up the Corolla, eased it into reverse, then turned the wheels through a slow crunch of gravel, kernels of broken glass and an empty soda can. She steered the whitewalls clear of the curb, cleaned up her alignment with a spin of the wheel, and cut the ignition with a smart twist of her wrist. She smiled and sat back to savor her parallel-parking success, wishing only for a moment that Keith had been there to witness it. She rolled her window closed, the air outside fetid with the sweet scent of antifreeze, its likely source the faded blue Buick up front. It was a model of do-it-yourself ingenuity, with bubble-beaded, smoke-colored film in the back window and a punched-out trunk keyhole strung through with a length of bike chain and a combination lock. The paint was worn on both sides of the rear end, like the seat of every pair of blue jeans Jake had ever owned as a kid. Used to be blue jeans were all she ever wore. But, that was before she left.

Home … Española …

Back home, her preferred means of transportation was a horse, that and her father's pickup. Española probably hadn't changed much since she left. The leaky, old Buick with the punched-out trunk was probably from a place like that. It had to be. Somewhere east of coastal California no doubt, on the opposite side of the fracture at the San Andreas Fault, a town where nobody needed to know how to parallel park.

Jake fished for quarters in her bag on reflex as she got out of the Corolla, but found no meter at the curb. The curiosities continued from there. Oldsmobiles, Fords and Chevys dominated the lot, and what few convertibles there were had weathered vinyl tops, all leprous and flaking in the afternoon sun. One ragtop had been patched with duct tape, another stitched with picture-hanging wire. Jake traced a finger along the yellow fender of a Ford Bronco, its paint chipped by a half dozen pellet dents. *Scatter shot.* Her father's truck had similar blemishes. Jake was 13 when it happened. A turkey hunt up north of Taos. Her father was half awake at sunrise when the sound of wings surprised him at fireside. He'd emptied two barrels at it before Jake had a chance to turn and see. He'd missed the bird, but hit the pickup. They'd sworn to never to tell anyone. She never did.

Jake brushed at the air and turned to check her parking achievement one last time, the only bright spot so far in an otherwise dismal day. She couldn't find it at first glance, her Corolla suddenly so similar to all the other cars that it didn't stand out like usual. Most places in Waters End, her car was the dull exception, always outshined by Land Rovers, Range Rovers, BMWs and Mercedes. But here, fancy chrome-plated grill guards and flat-black fender flares were as rare as valets. There wasn't even a single Ten-One-Hundred license plate frame — those coveted silvery symbols of affluence, indicators that the vehicle's owner was a five-figure donor to causes favored by cops, not that highlighting such charitable acts resulted in preferential police treatment, no matter what Jake's husband thought. The drivers in this particular lot opted for more subtle expressions — black-and-white bumper stickers that declared "Jesus Saves;" rosaries on rearview mirrors; gearshift knobs embedded with the image of The Virgin of Guadalupe. People with the fewest reasons to be optimistic always had faith to spare. Hope was free. Only those who had everything had no use for it.

A cold blast of air hit Jake in the face as she pulled open the bowling alley door, the swoosh of cars on Highway 101 quickly replaced by the thud, roar and crack of balls dropped repeatedly on lane after lane. Some fell harder than others. Some skittered. There were rumbling rolls and thunderous cracks. Women cackled, cheered and clapped their hands. Taken together, it played like a summer rain in Jake's ears — the hissy spray from a can of shoe disinfectant, the sputter of a popcorn cart, and the one woman whose laugh had the reach of an ambulance siren.

The place was 28 individual lanes wide, hundreds of shiny maple-brown planks pieced together in short, reflective canals beneath bright, moodless fluorescent light fixtures. Neon-colored paint in shades of yellow, orange and red streaked the wall at the far end. Automated pin setters whirred and clanked and sent balls barreling back on dark, divisive rails. High above, in the center of it all, hung a mirrored disco ball, though whatever kept it suspended was impossible to detect from below. Jake figured it had to be something of industrial strength. In a building full of balls, it stood out almost as much as Jake did among all those women.

The heels of Jake's turquoise-colored cowboy boots went quiet on the indoor-outdoor carpeting, a sea of blue moons and orange stars that stretched from the sunny brightness of the entrance to the dark din of the video arcade and beyond. The carpet flowed past the shoe-rental kiosk with the antiquated cash register, but stopped at the entrance to a coffee shop on the other side of the building. Jake paced the length of it, and back again.

The lanes were filled with bowlers, at least 200 women, all dressed in shirts of varying pastel shades, each one stitched in cursive with a different name, the sort nobody used anymore — Midge, Hannah, Flossie, Flo. They looked old enough to be grandmothers. If a few had great grandchildren it'd have been no surprise. Yet, despite their fragile frames and advanced years, they dished each other digs that rivaled any Jake had ever heard.

"You couldn't hit your own head with hairspray," said one.

"You're gonna break your hip before you break 100," said another.

Rough as they talked, their elegance proved worthy of appreciation, the way even awkward throws ended with an arm straight in the air and one leg dragging behind. It reminded Jake of the poses her mother struck in the oldest of the black-and-white photographs back home, the ones that were kept in a saltine cracker tin. *Mother. Mother.* Jake's mother used to say good things blew with bad winds. *No hay mal que por bien no venga.* Jake wondered if it worked both ways, if bad things came with good ones.

She slipped into a Naugahyde booth and looked to her reflection in the fingerprint-stained trophy case beside her. She appeared transparent in the glass, a ghost among a collection of statuettes frozen in mid hurl, like an abandoned army of tiny Midas men, an eternal testament to league championships, perfect games and high scores. These were achievements once so important they merited engraved brass plates mounted to marble foundations. But now they served only as supports for spider webs, headstones for dead, dry flies.

How do you know when to start over again?

Jake wished her reflection could stay in the case with the trophies and the flies after she walked away, so she could start over again as someone new, instead of trying to be who she thought she was.

She rolled her ankles and regarded her boots, the turquoise-colored leather such a glaring contrast to the Neapolitan-ice-cream patterns of the bowling shoes all around. She'd hardly looked at the boots in years, not since she received them as a gift for college graduation — the last time she and her mother spoke.

The bowling alley café seemed to Jake like a fortress of solitude, so well insulated from the crashes and booms of the balls and pins that she could barely detect them once the thick glass door closed behind her.

"Whooooooo is that?" said someone in the back, behind the counter, in the kitchen. "*Who* is that? Who *is* that? Who is *that*?"

"Jake," she said, but he kept asking again and again, a different way each time. He wasn't talking to her, she guessed. He wasn't talking to anyone.

She sat on a stool and peeked across the service counter, into the kitchen. The cook's eyes were on papers in his hand. Practicing lines from a script, or one line of a script anyway.

"Who *is that*?" he said.

Jake giggled.

Like the parking lot, the coffee shop had the feel of a relic, from its fake-wood baseboards to the Formica countertops. Sprigs of parsley filled a bowl beside the sink. A dozen trays of single-serving paper butter cups leaned like Towers of Pisa atop a pie case. Three toasters, a soda fountain and several bottled condiments sat in a row. Plastic flower bouquets decorated the tables. A series of sunken ceiling lights lit each and every red, vinyl-upholstered stool. Jake could feel the heat from the one above her.

The waitress gave Jake a start. "You wanna get your order in, hon?" the woman said. "It'd be good to do it before the gals come. Lady bowlers are plain-old bowlers when they're hungry, if you get what I mean."

Jake grinned and grabbed one of the menus balanced between a screw-top jar of mustard, a vial of red sauce and a bottle of ketchup. The soup of the day was listed as split pea, though the waitress advised against it.

"I wouldn't," she said and cocked her chin toward the kitchen. "Mr. DeMille's soup is still *in production* and, hon, you don't want any part of it."

"A cheeseburger with a fried egg on top?" Jake said, a choice that came from so deep a place that the request came out in the form of a question, as though permission was required.

The waitress snapped her gum and peered over the top of her eyeglasses. "You want what hon?"

Jake explained: "Um, the burger goes open-faced, cheese on top, egg on top of that, yolk whole, no tomato, no lettuce, no onion."

"To drink?"

There was no Coke or diet Coke. No Pepsi or Diet Pepsi. Royal Crown, but no Diet Rite.

"Whatever," Jake said and turned to watch a van jiggle to a stop out the window behind her.

The driver was a round, brown-skinned woman with curly hair down to her shoulders, a plaid shirt with the tails out, and blue jeans marked by white handprints on the thighs, the kind of flour stains Jake used to see on her mother's willowy hips every day. The round woman pulled the rear doors of the van open, hiked a plastic bread rack on her hip and waddled out of sight toward the alley entrance.

Four women bowlers rumbled into the café after that, wedging themselves into the U-shaped booth against the windows. All four were involved in conversation. Jake turned away, but watched their reflection in the side of a four-slice toaster.

"She wouldn't tell him *not* to drive."

"The police said he was asleep."

"Isn't that a shame."

"He never seemed like a sleeper."

"Oh Agnes! What's a sleeper seem like anyway?"

"He never seemed sleepy. That's all."

"I'm gonna have pie today."

"What about those cars?"

"Oh, he had the Hummer since forever."

"Those are Maggie Gonzales' pies."

"Jenny had a new Chrysler."

"That gangster car?"

"I don't like the way she does her meringue."

"Alice will you shut up about pie?"

"Jenny couldn't see over the wheel. That's how she hit him."

"Jesus, Mary and Joseph. How does a salesman afford those cars? The paper said —"

"He got his real estate license a couple years ago."

"Oh, Agnes, he did no such thing."

"Yes he did. He went and took the test and everything. You just ask Maggie when she gets in here."

TJ SULLIVAN

"I'm not talking to *that woman*."

"Still?"

"She's a dirty, dirty bird."

"Hi Maggie."

The woman from the van outside knocked against the glass door on her way into the café, the plastic rack of baked goods up on her round belly.

"Like usual?" the waitress said and waved toward the countertop to Jake's left.

The rack went down with a crack. "*Hijole!*" the woman said. "That's a ton."

Jake raised her chin to survey the contents, at least 20 churros bundled in plastic wrap and a dozen assorted muffins. There were packs of tortillas, and half-gallon sized bags of white cookies that resembled biscochitos. *Biscochitos!* Jake's mother used to make them at her bakery once a week, the batter so sickening sweet that just the scent used to give Jake a bellyache. Once baked, however, she never failed to devour them with a glass of cold milk on the side.

The round woman then rested her right buttock against the stool closest to Jake and slipped a liter-sized bottle of water onto the counter.

The group in the booth began to battle again.

"Burt's gonna wish he died if ever that coma ends."

"Oh, Agnes! It's not like he killed her."

"He fell asleep. The police —"

"Oh, the police. Pfft. Police don't know so much. Only God and Burt know for sure and neither one of 'em's much of a talker."

"Lucky he's got medical. My brother-in-law got insurance from —"

"Your brother-in-law is dead."

"Cause he didn't have no medical. Not everybody can get one of them special board appointments to —"

"Oh, be quiet, Agnes."

"Only reason he was on that district thing was the Blue Cross. That newspaper story about all that money and … It made him look so bad. Jenny was gonna ask him to quit and —"

"Oh, that *noose*-paper don't know so much."

"Did you see the paper today?"

"I don't read it, Agnes. I don't read it."

"The both of you oughta hush."

"Both of who?"

"I didn't get my paper today is all."

"Hi Maggie."

The round woman stood and turned to smile and wave, then sat back on her stool as the waitress delivered Jake's burger. It was open-faced, as requested, the yolk perfectly placed on top, the white shiny with melted butter. Jake popped the yolk with her fork, slapped the bun on top and took a hearty bite. The taste pulled her eyes closed — a chewy knot of egg, bun, and red meat. *Bliss*. The round woman, who Jake assumed was named Maggie, pointed at Jake's plate and ordered one of the same.

"Where you from?" she asked. "Nobody here eats like that."

Jake swallowed hard and took a sip of soda before responding.

"We commute from Reseda," she said.

"From Reseda, or *from* Reseda? I never met nobody who was *from* Reseda."

Jake confessed her New Mexico roots, with the emphasis on the "New," and explained what people there did with eggs and burgers. She translated her high-desert geography into California terms, starting with Santa Fe, juxtaposing it to Taos. She said Española was in between — less than half an hour northeast of Los Alamos, "where Oppenheimer built the bomb," and an equal distance southeast of Abiquiu, "where O'Keefe painted pictures of clouds, and bones." No one Jake ever met in California knew Española, but everyone who was anyone knew at least a little about one O or the other.

"Nobody goes there on purpose," Jake said. "Española isn't the sticks, but it's within walking distance."

Maggie erupted with a laugh. "*Hijole!*" she said. *"I spent summers in Truchas and Tres Piedras as a girl. Española from there was like New York City."*

Jake bit through the red middle of the meat patty, felt the slippery juice of it and the sticky trickle of raw yolk drip down her chin. She slapped a napkin to her face and shot Maggie an embarrassed grin. After that, anonymity fell away one word at a time.

"So, what do you do?" Maggie said.

First came the name.

"Jake LaMotta."

"*Mija!*" Maggie replied. "That's no Española name. That's like something out of 'The Godfather.'"

Jake giggled and leaned close. "Wrong movie," she whispered.

They laughed and simmered down as Jake offered more about how her father had picked the name and why. She shared more than she ever had before with a stranger, or anyone else, even told Maggie her mother's maiden name, but only because Maggie seemed the rare sort who could appreciate it. *Ce de Baca.* Spanish. Jake's maternal ancestors had been in North America three hundred years, since before it was known as New Mexico, since before there was a United States.

"If he'd asked my mother I wouldn't be Jake," she said. "You'd be sitting here with '*Emiliana*' instead of me."

"*Macho, macho, muchacho*," Maggie said. "They all know better than to ask about the important questions."

Jake snorted. Nobody ever said that to her father, much as it might have fit.

"My mother was recovering from labor when he did it," Jake said. "But it's not like he wanted a boy. It was a premonition; a sign."

"*Eee*, a sneaky sneaker," Maggie said and blinked. "But you can't ignore no signs. Gotta listen to your ghosts."

The story of Jake's birth slipped out slowly, how she'd been premature by three weeks, nearly born 30 miles from the hospital. It was the middle of the night when her mother woke with the telltale pangs. Her father was surely wide awake despite the hour as he made the drive to the hospital in Santa Fe. They'd lost their first baby, so Jake's birth was serious enough to make her father run red lights and stop signs. He'd passed the bulk of the time in the waiting room alone, not allowed to watch the birth, not that he would have wanted to do so. He read magazines and newspapers and saw somewhere that his hero's birthday was that very day. The boxer! The *other* Jake! She was born on his 50th birthday. Her father used to talk incessantly about it, how it played into his suspicion that they were related — him and the boxer — a theory that not only involved the commonality of their last names, but the fact they both began their lives in the same Italian neighborhood in New York City. The *other* Jake was the first fighter to beat the great Sugar Ray, who most people considered the best until then. That meant a lot to an Italian American like her dad. As far as her father was concerned, only Columbus and Michelangelo came close to that kind of accomplishment. So, when the doctor first appeared outside the delivery room and announced that his daughter was "a fighter," all the cosmic tumblers ticked into place and her identity was set. A girl named "Jake." Her father signed and filed the birth certificate before Jake's mother knew what happened.

"Names are powerful," Maggie said. "They're chosen for you. They can make you."

Jake turned her butter knife end over end in her hands.

"*Mija?*" Maggie said "They must be proud of their girl."

"She never said anything," Jake replied, her eyes still on the knife. "Twenty three years and she never called me anything but 'Jake.' I mean, I knew she could have been happier, but the dancing and that whole Fiesta Queen thing … It wasn't me. I couldn't —"

"Me either," Maggie said. "But, I'm not as —"

Jake winced in anticipation of the word.

"… Pretty."

What Jake didn't say was how it all ended, how she'd driven home for dinner after graduating college, all the things from her apartment in Albuquerque packed into that Corolla, all ready for the trip to her first job as a journalist in Idaho. She'd expected nothing more than another of her mother's meals, and more of her father's stories and advice.

But what she received was a sober recitation of what her mother and father had waited a lifetime to tell her. They'd bitten their tongues and planned their shared speech for so long they seemed to have forgotten how to be angry. In less than 20 minutes, they called into question every word they'd ever said, as well as every expression of affection for each other, and for Jake. Their explanation was academic. They'd confused the impression of desire with the indelibility of devotion. They said it happened all the time, that self-deception was human, that the only difference between them and everyone since Adam and Eve was that divorce was no longer a disgrace. Her father contradicted most every piece of advice he'd ever offered with three words: "Everyone does it." It still took the wind out of Jake's chest to think of it. *Everyone* ... She filled in the blanks from there. Neither of them called her by name that night. Her name. Jake. That was the reason. She was to blame. Sitting at the cafe counter next to Maggie, staring at the handle of that knife, she could almost hear her parents' voices in her head. Her stomach began to flutter. She draped a napkin over the remainder of her burger and pushed the plate forward.

"They still in Española?" Maggie asked.

"They made their choices," Jake said. "He's got the tack-and-feed store and she's practically bricked into the walls of that bakery. They know what they know."

"I haven't been back in 15 years," Maggie said.

"I like my name," Jake said and leaned forward to catch the tip of the bendy straw in her soda.

"Your mama was a *Ce de Baca*?" Maggie said. "*Cabeza de Baca*? Jake's way better, *Mija*. Those crazy Spaniards. Why'd anyone name themselves something that means 'head of cow?'"

The ring of Jake's cell phone interrupted Maggie and Jake pulled it out to whisper "hello" with her hand cupped over her mouth. It was another prank, dead air at the other end. It made her feel even more foolish, already so exposed. Instead of clapping it closed, she did as she'd done in the newsroom, spoke as if someone was there, just to escape the judgment of silence.

"You should have told me sooner," she said into the phone. "This changes everything. I'll have to get back to you."

She forced a smile into her cheeks and glanced at the faceplate before putting the phone away. It said what it always did — another

"Undetermined" caller. She fidgeted, gripped the stem beneath her stool with her ankles and spun the seat back and forth.

"*Mija*, why are you here?" Maggie asked. "What do you do?"

Jake felt embarrassed to identify herself as a reporter, but did it anyway. "I write real estate, mostly about mortgages, housing issues, builder scams —"

Maggie's eyes sparkled. "The paper? The paper! *Bueno*. Oh, but … what are you doing here, at the bowling alley?"

"Water. I need to get reaction from people for a story I'm writing about water. I wanted to go some place local and —"

"Don't get much more *loco* than this," Maggie said.

The women in the booth came back to life, their menus down and their voices up.

"I told you, I can't have anything fried, or with cheese."

"That's everything."

"Not the soup."

"Too much sodium, unless it's homemade. It isn't homemade, is it?"

The waitress advised them against the soup, same as she had Jake.

"I say we go someplace else."

"I don't want to be a bother."

"You're always a bother."

"Let's go across. Hartman's has that 'Healthy-Hart' menu. But, they got no pie. We love your pie, Maggie."

Maggie smiled to the blonde one with the gray roots as all four women squirmed out of the booth, each one holding a pink bowling-ball bag. All four of them thumped the doorframe with their hips on the way out the door.

"Been like that since 4-H," Maggie said as she watched them go.

Jake perked and leaned back. Maggie's burger arrived.

"I was 4-H," Jake said.

"Still a few farmers," Maggie said. "Before there was a Waters End there was farmers and ranchers."

The waitress began to put Maggie's baked goods into the pie case.

"My family's one the *ricos* couldn't buy off," Maggie said. "We've been on our land a hundred years … what's left of our land anyway."

"Before the base?" Jake asked.

"*Hijole!* That base."

The history of Waters End began long before the town's incorporation. Though Jake was more aware than most, she'd yet to hear a version anything like Maggie's. Maggie told how the place was ranches before the base was built during World War II, how the base was what pushed half the ranches out in the first place, before Calvin Waters was even a thought. The government paid market value, "*as though any amount of dollars and cents could replace a sense of home.*" Some of the families remained, mostly because they took jobs on the base. They took jobs at the lake after that, then in the town that followed.

"We're adapters," Maggie said. "Carpenters. Mechanics. Sandwich vendors. Burton Brand's papa was one of us. He printed leaflets to drop on the Japs, to convince them to surrender. But … Burt ain't his papa. Burt went bad, persuading his own side to surrender one farmer at a time. He makes them sell their land. He says he's helping his people, but you watch, he's just helping *ricos* get to be bigger *ricos*."

Jake confirmed that "Burt" was the Burton Brand from the Mosquito Abatement District, the one in the car accident that Keith had written about. Maggie claimed she wouldn't wish an accident like that on anyone, said surviving the death of a wife had to be hard, but that life in a coma had to be worse.

"They say you hear everything in a coma," Maggie said. "But you can't do nothing about it."

Maggie's attention shifted to Jake's left hand.

"No *esposo*?" Maggie said.

"No," Jake mumbled, embarrassed. "I mean, yes. Keith Torrance. I just don't have … a ring, a wedding ring. I mean, he's at the paper. He did the bug district story, and the accident story and —"

Maggie wiggled to the center of her stool. "Oh! I read him," she said. "You tell him to keep digging. There's a whole *escándalo* with that Mayor Nimbus. We got a cemetery district and no cemetery."

Jake's face continued to go warm. She felt as though she ought to know this.

"Old timers run every backhoe and bulldozer in town," Maggie said. "The Memorial Promenade? That's not just a mall."

Jake chuckled and kicked the heels of her boots against the stem of her stool. "Yeah?" she said. "It's fancy."

Maggie grinned. "No, there's bodies under it. They never moved 'em. Just moved 'em deeper. We dig the holes. We know what's buried."

"Tombstones?" Jake said. "Coffins?"

"Ain't none of our folks cocooned in silk-lined caskets. Those were plain pine boxes with wood markers, mostly mulch. The way I figure it, Mama and Papa are at the cinnamon bun place, in the food court."

Jake rambled off a half dozen questions, all about what the newspaper had done at the time.

Maggie claimed not a word had been printed. "What's bad for the *ricos* is bad for us," she said. "Being little people don't always put us on the right side. I got bigger battles. That mayor thinks he's a silver spoon, but he's as plastic as they come."

Maggie finished her burger and mumbled what sounded like: "My poor brother."

Jake plucked a notebook and pen from her bag. "Your brother?"

"Burt got to him," Maggie said. "All these anti-fungicide lawsuits and the STOP laws … Burt made my brother sell, said it was the best thing he could do. Now they're gonna undo the STOP and all that land is gonna be worth 20 times more. *Mija*. If only he'd waited."

Jake kept writing and kept her eyes on the pad.

"You gonna write about Manny?"

"I don't know," Jake said. "This is all new and I'm writing about something else. Water. The plume —"

It slipped out.

"The plume?" Maggie said. "*Hijole!* That's a story."

Jake tried to trivialize it, to change the subject. "I'm still researching," she said. "But this thing with your brother —"

"Oh, *Mija*, you get the plume in the paper and I'm gonna get you the Nobel Prize. You get the *ricos* with that one and you deserve a medal."

"It's not real," Jake whispered. "I just read something about a meltdown and —"

The waitress looked up from her crossword.

Maggie slipped closer. "Copper-Sykes, in the hills, in the '50s," she said. "We call it 'Area-51 West.'"

Maggie's eyes brightened as Jake grinned. Jake bopped her knee with her fist, convinced in an instant that this was the breakthrough she sought, that this was the truth. She had intuition. Her lie wasn't a lie after all.

"Up in the hills?" Jake said. "Did they dump the waste in the hills?"

"No, no," Maggie said. "LA people don't dump nothing in their own yard."

Jake looked hard at Maggie, but didn't say a word.

"My papa talked about it. He was always up early and out walking. He said he saw something out near the base."

Jake wrote some more, bouncing her eyes from the page to Maggie and back.

"He definitely saw something," Maggie continued. "He saw somebody dumping."

"What?" Jake said. "Dumping what?"

"Maybe it was septic. You know, sludge. All the old-timers are still on wells and septics. But, my papa would've known septic. He would have smelled it. But this had no odor. This looked just like … water."

"Were there markings? On the truck? On anything?"

"I don't know, but the *ricos* don't drink from no tap. They get deliveries from *Agua Libre*, or one of those water-cooler companies. It sure ain't *libre* for us. Nothing's *libre* for us."

"Did he say where? Can I find the spot?"

"He weren't no cupcake. Papa let his pickers organize. He was one of the first, back when even pickers were suspicious of César. But that was before. That was before even me, or Manny. That was before they picked him up walking his own field."

"Who picked him up? Police? Who?"

"Just an old man in overalls, *Mija*. No wallet, and that northern New Mexico talk. You know? *La Migra* don't care if you speak English. If you're brown you're nobody. You don't belong."

Jake fidgeted, confused and conflicted by the coincidence of it. Maybe she was hearing only what she wanted to hear.

"They dumped him in TJ without a dime to make a call. He kept his mouth shut after that."

Jake's head began to throb just then. She stuffed her notebook back into her bag and pulled out the keys to the Corolla.

Another spell? Not another spell.

"I need to get back," Jake said and struggled to stand. "But, if I could talk to your dad, I might —"

"He don't want no trouble," Maggie said and giggled.

"I can quote him anonymously. Nobody would know."

"He doesn't think nobody listens anyway."

"Me. I'm nobody. I listen. But I really have to go and —"

Maggie giggled again, put one of her bakery business cards on the counter in front of Jake and touched the back of her hand. "Like I said," Maggie told her. "He's at the cinnamon bun place at The Memorial Promenade."

Jake dropped herself back down on the stool. "I'm so sorry," she said. "I get caught up. I forgot you said —"

"You just got passion," Maggie said. "Never apologize for passion, *Mija.*"

"It's this story," Jake replied. "It's got me running all over the place. I forget what it's about sometimes. I keep telling myself it's about water and —"

"Not water," Maggie said. "You know what César used to say? It's never about grapes or lettuce. It's people, *Mija.* It's never about the other stuff. People. Always people."

Jake stood and started for the door, then turned back to Maggie. "Problem is," she said, "people don't always want help."

"Never do," Maggie said. "Only way to save someone from drowning is to grab them from behind. Otherwise, you both go down."

Preserving Views Could Result In Strawberry Jam

By Keith Torrance
Pendulum Staff Writer

Waters End residents want strawberry fields forever. They just don't want anyone to cultivate, or pick the berries.

As a result, Save The Open Places will ask the Waters End City Council this week to purchase all remaining farmland within city limits.

The "Strawberry Preserve Initiative" would require the Waters End Deparment of Public Works to maintenance the farms as parkland. The initial cost to taxpayers would exceed $30 million, said Truthful Moonglow, vice president of STOP.

"We don't need to eat berries to enjoy our farms," Moonglow said. "I want to see fields of green, but not necessarily pickers in plaid."

Please turn to page A8

CHAPTER 7 – THE GIANT HEAD

Jake sputtered to a halt as she approached The Mayor's extra-large office door, awestruck at first, then chagrined at being so affected by something so trivial as a big piece of wood. It was twice as tall as her and broad as the span of her reach from fingertip to fingertip. The knob was enormous too, a cannonball in comparison to most, though proportionate to this particular portal. It was a textbook bully tactic, more deserving of disdain than deference. A big door like that was a modern-day drawbridge, a pitiful attempt to intimidate the hoi polloi, its breadth an implication that a mighty and mean force lay waiting to be reckoned with on the other side.

The Mayor wasn't a complete stranger. Jake had met him before, had experienced the discomfort of his hearty handshake. She'd even once been mistakenly seated at his table for a luncheon, at which he'd held court regurgitating ribald jokes about farmers' daughters and ministers' wives. Jake had also attended several meetings of the Waters End City Council, enough to ascertain The Mayor's opposition to being opposed. He was a guy's guy for the worst of reasons, for being unflappable, for being obstinate and for being seemingly impervious to political pressure of both the red and blue varieties. Money was what moved him. Campaign finance reports and roll-call votes confirmed that contributions opened The Mayor's door. For Jake, however, the barrier remained in place as she lingered and listened for signs of life.

There was no chance of a scheduling error. Jake had set up the interview by phone with The Mayor's secretary — another mysteriously absent individual. No pictures, pens, papers or baskets occupied the secretary's desk in the outer office, just a telephone and a lamp with a green plastic shade. Jake knocked on the door, but received no reply, the wood so thick and hard that her knuckle bones barely produced any approximation of a tap. Her appointment was justification enough to try the door knob too. If that was locked, she could decamp in good conscience and write *"unavailable for comment"* beside The Mayor's name in her story.

The knob was too big for one hand so she shoved her pen between her teeth, her reporter's notebook into her armpit and pressed the heels of both palms into the bulk of the sphere. With the strap of her handbag flat across her right shoulder, she tucked her elbows in at her sides and worked her back into the turn. The knob barely budged, but the strap on her shoulder started to slide. She made adjustments to catch the bag and to keep herself from falling. She thrust her shoulder up and cocked her opposing hip to counter the weight, but she went too far and dropped to the floor with a girly shriek. The door flew wide and she tumbled across the threshold. Her notebook fell open and her handbag emptied. She hissed and lay still with a mess of discount cards and grocery coupons around her head. Mayor Nimbus moved from his desk to her side, bent at the waist and extended his hand, though not quite far enough for Jake to reach without lunging for it.

"You allowed to accept help, young lady?" he said.

"I can handle it myself," Jake huffed and pushed herself off the floor with both her arms and legs.

Her face went instantly damp with perspiration. Her armpits felt wet too, same as the skin just beneath her breasts, though she didn't dare touch it to assess the severity, her blouse dark enough to go nearly black when soaked. Whatever a flop sweat felt like, she assumed this was it. She swiped her hand down her forehead and moved

TJ SULLIVAN

further into the room, her boot heels all clunky on the bloodwood flooring.

The room represented pure temptation with a Persian rug at the center of it. A couch and armchair sat atop the rug, each upholstered in chocolate velour. A cedar chest served as a coffee table with two catalogs on display atop it, one from Sotheby's and the other a "Review of the Season" book from Christie's Auction House. An antique-looking door at the far corner was open wide enough to reveal the white marble oasis of a private bathroom. In the opposite corner, next to a window overlooking the east lawn of City Hall, a grandfather clock stood sentry with gleaming gold gears and a matching moon-faced skeleton key in the lock. Opposite the windows sat The Mayor's desk, an ornate, carved mahogany altar, no comparison to anything in the newsroom, where every desk was made of pressed wood, plastic parts and glue. The walls on both sides were covered by half a dozen paintings, all depicting Mayor Nimbus in stately poses — in a chair, standing by a flag. Each portrait represented one four-year term, as noted on the little bronze plates at the bottom. Nimbus had been mayor since the city's incorporation.

"Six portraits?" she said.

"Thirty years," Nimbus replied. "That's long enough to piss off just about everybody except the gal who paints my portraits. Can't blame me for trying to keep at least one constituent happy."

Jake did the math. One was missing. "So where's the seventh?"

Nimbus pointed to his private bathroom door and snickered. "It's in my other office," he said. "And yes, there's a mirror in there too."

Behind Nimbus' desk was the biggest painting in the room, the only portrait not of him. It depicted the city's namesake, Calvin Waters, the man who bought the old military base, dug and drained the lake, and then built the town on top of it. His eyes in the painting were steel blue and he wore a plaid suit. The cane in his hand had a brass handle in the shape of a rabbit's foot and, at the base of the frame, a rectangular plate had been engraved with a quote:

*"The gentle man waits his turn.
The successful man finds a faster way."*

— *Calvin Oswald Waters*

Jake looked to the document on The Mayor's desk. It was a city declaration, a tribute to fruit farmers. It promised to honor the "salt of our community … the fathers of our strawberry fields forever." One large, gothic "F" highlighted the top, and a full-color seal of the city decorated the base along with a forked tongue of blue satin.

Nimbus stepped up and flipped the page upside down. "Miss Torrance," he said. "What can you do for me today?"

"Jake LaMotta," she said. "I'm Jake. I didn't take Keith's name."

The Mayor gripped her shoulders and steered her to the couch in the middle of the room. "Of course," he said.

Jake sat and sunk so deeply into the cushions that her arms flew out on reflex as her knees ended up higher than her hips.

"It'll suck the change right out of your pockets," The Mayor said. "That's how I buy lunch."

Jake cleared her throat and danced her buttocks to the edge.

"I'm not sure I understand what you want," he continued. "But I'm always happy to talk to a pretty woman."

Pretty.

Jake bit her teeth as The Mayor's eyes slithered to her cotton blouse, its collar open three buttons down. She hurried to close it at her neck.

"Do I get some small talk?" he said. "How's my buddy The Chief doing? I hope he's not letting that nonsense get to him."

"The Chief can take care of himself."

"A good, ole boy. He's been editor almost as long as I've been mayor. We have to watch out for each other, him and me. Who else will?"

Jake put her notebook on her knee and pinched her ballpoint at the tip, making the quick of her unpolished fingernails white with the pressure.

"About the plume —" she said.

The Mayor professed ignorance, said the terminology was as foreign to him as French. "*Plumé*," he seemed to say through a smile.

Jake ran down the rumors of water contamination with conviction and posed the possibility that nuclear waste — "tritium" — lay in wait above the city's aquifer, a Damoclean threat of cancer that was one big quake away from becoming the biggest environmental disaster since Chernobyl.

"The city's water has never been tested for that," she said. "We don't even know the picocurie count of what residents are currently drinking."

Nimbus reared back in his chair and laughed.

"Let's not get ahead of ourselves," he said. "Pico curry? That sounds more like lunch at Pancho Patel's Palace."

"Ms. Gonzales said her father might have witnessed contaminated waste being dumped from Copper-Sykes," Jake continued.

"I thought you were going to ask me something else," The Mayor said and sighed. "This water business? This is what your story is about? The cock-and-bull fairy tale no one even talks about anymore? It's years old. Ancient history. Even when it was an issue it wasn't an issue."

The Mayor cited his support of legislation that sought to ban the ground injection of fumigants by area farmers, and how he opposed the use of plastic sheeting to keep the chemicals in the soil. "An ineffective eyesore," he said and insisted that the comment be considered off-the-record.

"I just declared Saturday 'Berry Day,'" he said. "That's the story you should write; the end of an era in this town, and the end of fumigation. This talk of dumped waste is just … a waste of time."

"Maggie doesn't think so," Jake said. "Maggie says —"

"Is this the Gonzales woman?" Nimbus said. "Maggie Gonzales?"

Jake nodded, her pen at the ready.

"I can't talk about this," he said and thrust himself forward in his chair. "That woman has sued the city so many times we had her declared a 'vexatious litigant.'"

Jake continued scratching words into her notebook.

"The court decided she's a lunatic," The Mayor said. "And 'lunatic' is off-the-record, or we'll both be in for it. Listen here, pretty or not, you're not immune. She'll sue anyone, her and that mail-order attorney she uses. I ought to call The Chief and warn him. You're about to land him and his newspaper in the soup. He's got enough worries. Did you know his wife filed for divorce?"

Jake jerked her head up.

"The Chief's life is his life," she said. "This is about the lives of everyone in Waters End and Ms. Gonzales has a lot to say about it. A lot."

"Did you see her last night?"

Jake stopped writing.

Highlights of the previous evening's City Council meeting were replayed by The Mayor with dramatic hand gestures and head shakes so hard they shook loose half the strands of hair in his combover. As usual, he said, Maggie had arrived at the council chambers early, sat up front and was first in line to take the podium during the public-comment period. However, rather than read a speech, or a riot act, she'd spent her five-minute allotment of microphone time enacting a citizen's arrest, taking the city's Planning Director, Vic Vident, into custody for charges that included collusion and coercion. City police had been called into the chambers as Maggie held Vident by his shirt collar while also ticking off a list of ways city workers had harassed residents of The Knolls. She'd said the city wanted to squelch all opposition to annexation. The city had been trying for years to annex, supposedly because the lack of control over the rural community was a stumbling block to progress. The Mayor opined that the opposition went beyond paranoia. He told Jake he'd seen a few people like Maggie over the years, the sort who lived for the attention of the microphone on Tuesday nights. He suggested a restraining order may be the city's next step.

"Sometimes it's men, sometimes women," he said. "Always alone. They get it in their head that they missed out on having a family so they get pissed at the world and shoot accusations at everyone but themselves. Maggie's that kind. It's easier to make the city out the enemy than to admit the enemy is in her."

Jake crossed her wrists atop her notebook. "She's a businesswoman. She's a baker."

"She's a scofflaw. She's a fraud."

The Mayor characterized Maggie's bakery as an unlicensed panadería operating on a bacteria-ridden back porch. City code officers would close her down in an instant, if only city codes applied. Keeping half The Knolls in an unincorporated area of Covalop County, The Mayor suggested, was Maggie's way of keeping the city at bay for personal reasons.

"You want contamination?" he said. "Drop a few petri dishes on her kitchen counter and see what's what. Now that's a story."

"Ms. Gonzales is just one resident," Jake said. "I have others, informed sources who've seen … Has your staff ever mentioned tritium? Did you know Copper-Sykes had a meltdown in the '50s?"

"The '50s? If we haven't had any trouble by now, don't you think —"

The Mayor stopped, lowered his voice and began again. "This stuff is older than my secretary," he said.

Jake's mouth moved as her pen scratched.

Older than —

The Mayor waved his hands between her face and the notebook. "Now don't put that. You've got gadflies feeding you crazy tales. "

"You seem awfully upset," Jake said. "Doesn't the water issue and Maggie also threaten your business as a *ree-lit-tur*?"

Nimbus settled back into his chair.

"It's real-tore," he said. "Capitalize the 'R.'"

Jake grinned. "Why no test wells?" she said.

"Why haven't you been tested for small pox?"

"I've been vaccinated same as everyone."

"What about malaria?"

"Haven't been to the tropics," she said. "Same as I haven't been bitten by a dog, so I haven't been tested for rabies. But, the city's been —"

"A test for rabies?" The Mayor said and exhaled an exaggerated gasp. "There is no test for rabies. The only test for rabies is to wait. But, if you wait, you're a goner for sure if you got it."

Jake blushed, felt ignorant, as though she ought to know this. Rabies alerts were circulated every spring back home with warnings to stay away from prairie dogs and bats, both of which were more abundant in Española than pigeons and seagulls were in Waters End.

"Treatment's extreme," The Mayor said. "You can't wait for symptoms. You have to start right after being bitten. Maybe that's why there isn't a test. Either you act right away, die, or get lucky. I say we've been lucky with water the past 30 years or so. There's no threat, so why worry?"

Jake shimmied her shoulders and squared them. "Are you saying a test for tritium is pointless?" she said. "Is it the kind of result you'd rather not know? Are you willing to gamble with people's lives?"

Her pen scratched louder in the notebook.

"All I said was that if you haven't been bitten, why bother? But you're going to write what you want anyway, aren't you?"

Jake caught him looking to the office door and glancing to his wristwatch before he slapped a hand on the arm of his chair and shot to his feet.

"That's all the time I have today," he said.

He walked around to his desk and reached beneath the top of it. The big door flew wide open all by itself just then, revealing two men in suits seated side-by-side in the dim outer office. The taller of the two wore dark pinstripes, the other a powder blue suit that matched his hat, the brim of which hid his eyes. The tall one in pinstripes held a blueprint rolled and bound by a green rubber band. The smaller man had a small black dog in his lap. Neither of them reacted to the opening of the door.

Jake slipped her notebook into her bag and offered her hand to Nimbus. "I may call with a follow-up question or two," she said.

The Mayor's face crumpled, then popped into a smile as he gripped Jake's delicate fingers with a hearty squeeze.

"It's Chick," he said. "Chick's your buddy. Next time, come see me without the notebook."

Jake laughed and slapped a hand against her bag. "I memorize the quotes," she said. "The notes just remind me of what you didn't say."

Nimbus gave her a sideways hug that lifted her feet up off the floor.

"You do what you have to," he said. "I enjoy your professionalism."

Jake thought it odd that neither of the two men in the outer office stood as she made her exit. The Mayor made no motions or apologies either. It was as though the men weren't there at all. It prickled the back of her neck like an insult, as though she'd just been treated like a real-life Dorothy by the giant head of Oz, as though she were dreaming up the deceptions and the little man and the tiny dog. It felt like she was onto something, like they were afraid of her. Things like this couldn't merely exist in her head.

Another District Collects Taxes For No Purpose

By Keith Torrance
Pendulum Staff Writer

Waters End has no graveyard, but that hasn't stopped more than $1 million in tax payments from being funneled into a special cemetery-district fund each year for decades.

The Waters End Memorial Overseers Ward was established 25 years ago to maintain public cemeteries. But, when the town's only cemetery was razed to accommodate The Memorial Promenade shopping mall, the city failed to dissolve the special district. Property tax dollars continue to be collected.

"This is not a crime," said Mayor Chick Nimbus. "That money is for future use."

As mayor, Nimbus appoints the boards of directors for each special district, including the WEMOW.

Please turn to page A19

CHAPTER 8 – BAD JUMP

The thump of Keith's heartbeat made his head throb as he pressed his thumbs into Maxine Lugner's gullet. She thrashed beneath him, rocked her hips forward and pushed back against his chest, but Keith refused to relent. Her eyes popped open, but her pupils had fallen so far back that only a slight crescent of color remained visible. Her face was shiny wet, cheeks as red as rug burn. Her lips tasted of vanilla and cigarettes. Keith felt them go cold as he anticipated the pulsation of pleasure to come. He imagined it boiling in his uncertain center and blasting into Maxine with enough force to flush the last gasp of oxygen from her lungs. It would be his all-too-brief visit to blissful oblivion. Her legs went limp. She was almost there.

Maxine wrinkled her forehead, as though she wanted to speak, her lips open just enough to stutter a single staccato syllable.

"Kuh, Kuh, Kuh —"

Keith wanted it to be his name, wanted her to try to say it. *Just try it!* He figured it for a ploy, as if she wanted him to know her last thought was of him, to make him buck with greater force. She was like that, had such an insuperable desire to manipulate.

Such a cunning booner.

Keith responded in kind, pounded his hips harder against her, keeping time with the sound of the pile driver outside.

"Chud … Chud … Chud!"

Man and machine worked together.

"Boon!" Keith said. "Er … Fuh —"

A string of saliva trailed from his bottom lip to the hollow of Maxine's larynx, and the knuckles of his thumbs.

The bed began to spin after that as blood from everywhere else in his body flooded into his erect muscle.

"Kuh," Maxine coughed out.

He shook her by the neck, wanted to kill her, and yet, needed to be coddled. He kept hold of her throat.

"Muh," he said. "Muh."

He repeated it over and over, more quietly each time until it melted to a whimper. His hips jerked in tight thrusts and he spent himself inside her, spewed his warp and woof. His eyes fluttered. His face contorted and he finished with one final "muh!"

Beneath him, Maxine's head lay still, her nostrils flared, her mouth open wide, as though drowning on air. She appeared almost lifeless from the neck up, but her body remained defiant. She raised a hand and tapped Keith's elbow — their signal for release. She coughed her way back to consciousness from there. The red marks on her neck faded as Keith flexed the blood back into his joints. He collapsed beside her, his knees rubbed raw by the brown-and-purple motel bedspread. Maxine pet his bald spot.

"Baby made mommy feel good," she said.

He'd asked for it, had told her to use that word.

Mommy.

Before they got to the hotel he'd all but begged her to play the part, but now it made him twitch.

"Mommy likes her bad boy," she whispered.

He burrowed his hips into the mattress and fumbled to pull the flat sheet from underneath him. He tugged with all his strength, but the sheet slipped free and his fist flew and he punched himself in the eye. He saw sparks and cursed and wished he could knock himself out. He peeled the condom from his limp member and dropped it off the edge of the bed. Maxine snored as he flopped his fingers across the nightstand to get at the plate of lemon bars, which she hardly baked at all anymore. He pawed the plastic wrap on top and snagged one bar as the others fell to the floor with a thump. He jammed his mouth full and chewed his way into unconsciousness, flakes of delicate crust on his chin and a dusting of powdered sugar on his lips.

Keith awoke to Maxine pulling at the bedspread, which had become tangled between his knees. The belt buckle in his pants at the foot of the bed jingled. He looked to the clock. It was 10:45 a.m.

A knock on the door woke him a second time and shocked him upright.

"*Thwack ... Thwack ... Thwack.*"

"Maid —" said a voice.

"No!" Maxine shouted.

Keith jerked to see her sitting up too.

"*Que?*" the voice said.

"*Nada,*" Maxine yelled.

The knocking stopped and a shadow moved across the base of the closed curtains.

"Always pretending they don't understand English, just to fuck with us," Maxine said. "Yicka, yicka, yicka. No ab-lah the Ingrish."

Keith clapped his tongue off the roof of his mouth and brushed the crumbs from his chin. "Yeah, well, Jake's half Spanish, so —"

"Did the bad maid disturb Mommy's baby?"

"Don't you have to get back?" he hissed.

"In a minute. Is my boy all cranky now?"

The affair had started by accident over a lunch of two-inch-thick meat sandwiches and a hearty basket of greasy fries. They'd been thrown together by Buckwalter, who, for whatever reason, decided Keith and Maxine ought to be a team the day all the paper carriers got deported. It was Maxine's idea to dump the entire load and, instead, do a two-hour meal on the company credit card. She had a sense of adventure about her that Keith hadn't seen before. Throughout that first lunch, Maxine had gone on and on about what she deserved, and how she intended to take it. She packed Keith's brain so full of expectations and entitlements that he lost track of which ideas were his and which were hers. Pastrami and fried potatoes bloated his belly the way Maxine's talk did his head, and by the time the plates were pulled away, Keith felt euphoric. Maxine didn't lead and he didn't follow. They simply had similar interests, or at least she seemed equally self-interested. Maxine had sucked through 13 Dunhill cigarettes that afternoon. Keith kept count.

By the third lunch they were playing each other's games and picking each others brains for memories of hometowns and teen glory days, of skinny dips in gravel pits and sly moves in fast cars. Their talks about infatuations jumped to love; to marriage; to security; to happiness; to bad sex; to regrets; to wants; to needs; to depression; to boredom; to denial; to flirting; to Internet porn; to masturbation; to phone sex; to fetishes; to cheating; to being very, very good at being bad. Keith confessed a mommy fetish. Maxine copped to autoerotic asphyxia. How perfect it was, Keith thought, that the woman he both wanted to choke and fuck most in the world actually wanted him to do both at the same time.

The jackhammers at the construction site outside crescendoed as Maxine stretched to grab her cigarettes from the nightstand on Keith's side of the wobbly motel bed. "We better shower," she said. "I want to rinse off your juicy juice."

Keith winced, saved from further ponderation of that image by the ringing of his mobile phone, which was still in his pants at the foot of the bed.

A man's voice buzzed out the receiver as Maxine bounced into the bathroom with a lit cigarette between her fingers.

"I was hoping to get you," said the man on the phone. "Been trying to reach you all morning."

"Yeah … What's up?" Keith said, though he had no idea who it was.

"I'd like to talk with you and Jake," said the voice. "Can you make it at one? My office? I'll have coffee brought in, some sandwiches or whatever."

Keith turned away from the hiss of the showerhead that came through the bathroom door.

"Uh, let me see," Keith said, struggling to think his way back to real life.

Three loud raps sounded at the door again, just like before.

"Maid," a woman's voice said.

Maxine flew out of the bathroom with a froth of toothpaste running down her chin. "No!" she shouted.

Keith slapped his hand to the mouthpiece of the phone and shot Maxine a look.

"That Jake?" the voice on the phone asked.

Three quick raps sounded again.

"Just a sec," Keith said, both to the voice on the phone and to the knock.

Maxine's upper body was draped in a towel, her bare thighs strafed by ridges of cellulite so deep they put a vision of wind-whipped sand drifts in Keith's head. He squeezed his eyes shut and pulled the tatty bedspread around his chest.

"Key *aqui*," said the woman's voice.

"We *ah-kee*," Maxine shouted back. "Go away. *Vam-moze*."

Keith cocked his head at Maxine, then jerked his chin toward the bathroom, the phone still against his ear. "I hope she's not upset," the voice on the phone said. "I'd like a chance to make things right."

"The two of us?" Keith said. "Both at one?"

"Great," the voice replied. "It'll be good for you to see me."

Maxine's reflection filled the dark tube of the television as she wiggled into her clothes behind Keith, the distorted image a nightmarish bumblebee in black spandex tights, a black skirt, a black t-shirt and a canary-yellow blouse.

"Who was that?" she asked.

"Nimbus," Keith mumbled. "He says that same stupid goodbye of his all the time."

Maxine beamed and said something about how The Mayor was likely mad about Keith's property tax stories.

"Somebody's doing something with that money," she said. "Nobody in their right mind is going to let it all go to waste like —"

Keith stood with the bedspread still pressed against his chest. "Don't tell me what to —"

Maxine stubbed her cigarette in the sink and started for the door before he finished. "I told Fletch I had a gyno appointment until noon, so —"

Keith jerked his eyes around the room in a panic as Maxine pulled open the door.

"Where's the boonin' key?" he said.

A clicking sound came from beneath the doorknob, the source of which was the forest-green plastic bauble swinging from the keyhole on the outside of the motel room door. The key was still in the lock. A brown-skinned maid with blue eyes appeared just then and pointed excitedly. "*Mira, mira*," she said. "Key *aqui*."

Maxine jumped with surprise and shook a stiff finger at the woman. "You could have told us that, you stupid cow."

"Boonin' stupid," Keith spit, still wrapped in the bedspread.

Maxine shooed the maid, took the key to Keith and pet his head. "You're the man," she whispered. "That mayor's in for a surprise."

Keith turned the radio dial to "The Chad Habit Show" on the drive back to the office, a program Jake regularly refused to allow whenever she was in the car. She'd called it "The Bad Habit Show" a hundred times before, but Keith admired the performance regardless of whether he agreed with the content. Chad Habit was the go-to source for tension, tirades and testosterone, the best place on the AM dial from eleven to three each day. Besides that, Habit had written five books in five years, including "Disorder at the Mexican-American Border," "The Transgression of Political Correction," and "The Unmanning of American Men." Chad Habit was a shit stirrer. Armed with 50,000 watts of broadcast power and a caller kill switch, he consistently contradicted all Jake's beliefs and rules, which made listening to his program all the more enjoyable for Keith.

Habit was in the midst of another polemic on the housing market when Keith tuned in:

> "*... These reporters want you to believe this housing market is going to crash. They want to see people get hurt, lose their jobs, end up on food stamps. They want SARS, West Nile, Y2K. They want earthquake and tsunami predictions to come true. They want that little lunch truck at your office to have cockroaches, botulism and e coli because it'll keep you*

reading their papers and watching their TV
news. The Amazing Criswell Predicts. Long
live Criswell! —"

Habit reached into people's ears and grabbed them by the balls. Keith could do that too, if ever anyone would give him the chance. None of it would ever happen at *The Pendulum* though. Working for that newspaper smothered the best of him. No one could make it big while writing property tax stories and rehashing car accident reports. Jake magnified the injustice of it, the way she continued to squander a sure-fire scheme, allowing their future to flounder and defending the act as her dedication to fairness. Fairness was her excuse, her failure to pick a side ... her failure to pick Keith's side.

———————

The newsroom was awash in police-scanner squawk as Buckwalter stormed to his desk and cracked his keyboard with a folded copy of the morning edition.

"Goddamn copy desk!" he fumed. "A 16-page section and they jump the lead story to A19."

Jake shrugged, oddly comforted by his anger so long as it was trained on a target other than her. "Maybe readers will figure it out," she told him. "They might see it on their way to page 19."

Buckwalter didn't bother to look up.

"Readers don't know shit," he said. "We say A19, they go to A19. The trouble is they remember. Don't matter if you get it right every other day. Readers remember the fuck-ups forever."

"There he is," Jake whispered as she spied Keith dodging clerks and ducking coil-spring phone cords on his way back to the pod.

"There *who* is?" Buckwalter said, his eyes still buried in the paper.

Jake had tried calling four times, but Keith's cell was either off or out of range, which bounced her straight to voicemail each time. She left messages, but they'd gone unreturned. The Mayor had said Keith knew about their meeting at one o'clock, but she didn't trust The Mayor. It was 12:30 already. They'd have to leave soon.

Jake twisted her chair around, stretched her legs into the aisle and smiled at Keith. She had her turquoise-colored boots on again, the length of her black skirt just enough to reveal the cool coffee-and-cream tone of her bare knees before her legs disappeared inside the sleeves of her Luccheses. For some unexplainable reason she needed Keith to notice her, even if all he did was look. She'd worn her lacey white blouse special, the one he once said made her look like Penélope Cruz. She'd brushed her hair straight. She wanted to feel a little like she felt in the beginning, back when they had firsts to spare — their first lunch, their first dinner, their first kiss.

Buckwalter cut Keith off before Jake did. "You see your story yet?"

Keith's chin was wagging before the question was complete. "No time," he said. "Had an interview after I dropped Jake this morning and I'm just now —"

"All morning? I better see a daily."

"Source stood me up."

"So where the hell you been?"

"Got stuck in traffic, stopped for lunch. We supposed to punch a clock?"

"Bullshit," Buckwalter said. "You're full of bullshit. The director of that cemetery district says you never tried to reach him, that you didn't even call."

"Oh, give me a break; I called twice," Keith said. "I put it in the fifth paragraph '... *couldn't be reached for comment.*'"

Buckwalter stripped the cellophane from a fresh pack of cigarettes and crumpled it into a ball. "Twice?" he said. "You called twice? One, two? Are you shittin' me?"

Maxine cleared her throat and pulled two Dunhills from her desk drawer, along with what looked like a pink Bic lighter.

"There was no answer," Keith said. "How many chances am I supposed to give somebody to ignore me?"

Buckwalter put up his thumb and pointed it at Keith, then Jake, then back to Keith again. "This is exactly what I'm talking about. Doesn't matter how much you do right. I remember fuck-ups."

"But I didn't," Keith said.

"Vacation time," Buckwalter told him. "Mark it. Your morning comes out of your vacation time."

"You don't have the —" Keith started.

"No," Buckwalter said. "You don't know the difference between a last chance and a last paycheck."

Keith sat down hard.

Jake scooted her chair around to Keith's as soon as Buckwalter and Maxine made for the dock. She licked her fingers and pet down several shoots of hair on his head. "You had the car windows open, didn't you?" she said. "You look like you rolled out of bed."

Keith shoved Jake's hands away and raked his hair back to how it had been before. "I don't care," he said.

"Did Nimbus get you?" she whispered. "He called about meeting with us. I left messages."

Keith gave a queer look.

"He left me voicemail," she said. "He said you agreed we'd meet him at one o'clock? Both of us. Why both of us?"

"All he wants is to bitch about your story," Keith said. "That makes him the only person who believes you're actually going to publish it."

Jake scuttled closer, half listening and half hoping Keith would look to her legs, or at least detect the perfume she'd rubbed off a sample ripped from a copy of Cosmopolitan in the women's restroom.

"So, you talked to him?" she said. "What did he say? Does he think my story's true?"

"True?" Keith replied.

"Yeah, true. Did he say that?"

"What do you mean 'true?'"

"I just … it might be true. But I need more. I don't trust him. He's after something."

Keith pushed Jake's chair away, mumbled something about "self-sabotage" and pulled a pocket comb out of his top desk drawer.

"Fine then. I'm out," Jake whispered. "I can't prove anything. I don't have a story."

"Just like that?"

"I'm telling Buckwalter. I'm telling him the truth."

Keith's eyes went cold. "Buckwalter doesn't want the truth," he hissed. "He'll get someone else to do it if you back out now. He'll get Maxine. He'll use the versions you've already written."

"I hid those on the hard drive and … I can just as easily erase them before he tries any —"

"At least see what Nimbus wants first," Keith said.

"Why you then? This isn't your story. Why'd he insist on inviting you to meet with him too?"

"He's a man. I'm a man. Maybe he thinks I'm on his side."

Jake allowed Keith to take the lead once inside City Hall, content to follow behind like a minion, all the way to The Mayor's office, only to be disappointed when he stopped at that big door without so much as trying to knock or turn the knob. Keith simply crossed his arms and looked at it, as though he might suddenly blink, or mutter some secret word to make the whole thing whip right open for him.

It happened a silent second later.

Suddenly something clicked and the door flew inward with a whoosh to reveal Mayor Nimbus seated in his high-back chair with his right hand underneath the desktop, that same spot Jake had seen him reach toward at the end of their last meeting.

The Mayor waved the two of them in the direction of the couch in the center of the room. "So good for you to see me," he said.

Jake whispered: "How?"

"What do you mean 'how?'" Keith replied, his voice loud. "He's got the button. The Mayor's always had the button."

The room looked different than before. The bathroom door was closed all the way and the top of The Mayor's desk hadn't a single document on it. The cedar chest coffee table was clear too, no more "Review of the Season" books or Sotheby's catalogs. In their place lay a service of cups and saucers, an elegant silver coffee pot, and a porcelain plate of slim cucumber sandwiches.

Keith snagged a sandwich as he lowered his butt to the couch, his hips sucked so deeply into the cushions that the hand with the sandwich went high above his head, as though he'd fallen into water and wished to keep the food dry. Jake eased herself onto the sureness of the couch's edge, her knees and boot heels held tight together.

"Did you forget the couch?" she said as Keith wiggled forward to right himself. "The Mayor's always had the couch. It'll suck the change out of your pockets. That's how he buys lunch."

Nimbus grinned, already at work on a cup of coffee, dropping his third cube of sugar. "This is for all of us, for Chrissakes," he said. "So, spare me the ethics lecture and have at it."

Jake flashed a polite smile and poured for herself — black with no sugar — then snapped as Keith's mouth opened to take his first bite of the finger sandwich. "I thought you ate," she said.

Keith replaced it on the platter. "Habit," he said. "And, anyway, it's free, and who are you to tell me what I should and shouldn't —"

Nimbus got right to it and encouraged them both to share their best guesses about what he wanted. Jake took it as an opportunity to reiterate her refusal to be swayed and promised to publish any threats — direct or veiled — in the pages of *The Pendulum*. Implicit bullying would be put into context and printed verbatim. Readers deserved the truth, regardless of whether it was obtained on the record, or not. She advised The Mayor that off-the-record provisions were never absolute in the company of politicians. Elected officials were held to a higher standard, which became a double standard when they attempted to conceal bad behavior with off-the-record caveats. She declared that nothing would hinder publication of her water story, nothing other than hard facts. Blackmail would hasten her deadline. If pushed, she'd risk her own reputation in the interest of doing the right thing.

"Boundaries," she said and poked the armrest of the couch with her index finger. "If this conversation crosses the line, we go on the record. Fair is fair."

"Fair?" Keith hissed. "Since when is anything you do fair?"

The Mayor's face went clownishly tight, his chin low, his eyebrows high. "Should I be flattered, or miffed?" he said. "Did you practice that? Tell me you didn't just think that whole speech up. Tell me you got that from a handbook or something academic."

"Most journalists wouldn't be here right now," she said. "And it doesn't make any difference that Keith's here either."

Nimbus raised both his hands, as though signaling surrender. "You keep proving me right," he said. "You're validating my genius."

"No," Keith said. "She's just being 'fair.'"

The two men laughed as Jake shot Keith a look. He balked as their eyes locked, gave her a defiant glare, then launched himself forward and shoved two whole finger sandwiches into his mouth.

"I know more than you think," Nimbus said. "And you know too much not to listen. This is a good opportunity for the three of us. That's why you're both here."

He put his hands out in front of him, as though wading into an imaginary lake, his arms level with his shoulders, just above the surface of water that wasn't there.

"All this," he said, "everything around us, everything you see … erase it."

Jake shook her head. "You lost me."

The Mayor laughed, then proceeded to talk in more riddles. One minute he was on about the time wasted knocking on doors, and the next he was talking about scaling walls and climbing into hearts and minds. Persistence, patience, passion — The Mayor eyed Jake especially long and said it again.

"Persistence, patience, passion."

Jake could tell he was headed where she'd told him not to go — right over the line. She rubbed her tongue to the roof of her mouth, just to keep it busy, just to keep from speaking up. If he wanted to hang himself, she had to let him finish. Keith, meanwhile, looked oblivious, those shoots of hair still sticking up despite several swipes with that comb of his.

The Mayor droned on and digressed with bits of background information. Fumigants had been outlawed. The farms had been closed. The STOP restrictions were scheduled for a vote and sure to be repealed within days. No doubt. Big changes were certain, and not solely in the open spaces of land within view of the freeway. The seeds of tens of thousands of dwellings were prepared for planting. Agreements and orders had been arranged with contractors, subcontractors and all the ancillary enterprises that supported such efforts. Backhoes, bulldozers, cement mixers and steamrollers would soon start to wail and whirl. The marathon would last until every vacant lot was serving the residential purpose for which it was zoned. Buildout was assured, and current city occupants were guaranteed to resist. The trick was to take them by surprise and turn them around before they hired attorneys and tied the whole plan in a knot.

"We need to tell them what to think before someone else does," The Mayor said. "That's where you come in."

He tried to put it in terms of milk. "Cream rises," he said. "But you've got to stir things up once and awhile to keep the bottom of the barrel from festering into something that'll spoil the bucket for everyone. We've got to stir this pot to spread the fat around. And I want the two of you to help us."

Jake let out a laugh, unable to contain it for the images that accompanied the clichés. Cream floated, sure enough, but the concept proposed by Nimbus was an oversimplification. One thing rose higher, a detail easily detected by anyone who'd ever actually lived a rural life. Milk left to sit was always topped by a skin, a nearly undetectable layer of scum, invisible only so long as the surface remained undisturbed. *Scum.* All she had to do was poke it. It was her job to poke, not stir.

"So, what you're saying is that you want to tell me where and when to get people riled up," Jake said. "You're telling me to lay off the water investigation and do this *for you.*"

"No, no, no," The Mayor said. "I'm telling you that I know what young couples like you are going through. It's hard to work up here and live down there."

He raised and lowered his hands as he said it. *Up here — down there.* Jake squirmed in the slickness of his presumptions. As if The Mayor knew what it was like. As if a man whose office door opened at the push of a button had ever departed and returned to his residence in the dark, day after week after month after year. Did he shop for groceries at 11 o'clock at night? Did he know his neighbors only by the shouts that came through thin apartment walls after one o'clock in the morning? Was The Mayor's life on hold because he didn't have a house? Chick Nimbus was greeted on sight as "Mr. Mayor" throughout Waters End. Jake still had to show ID to prove she was who she said.

"We rent *down there*," she told him. "We sleep *down there*. We eat *down there*. But we don't *live* down there. We don't *live* anywhere."

"Exactly," Nimbus said. "So work with me. Live and work up here with us."

Affordability. Living wage. The man knew what words to use and what buttons to push. He said he had a plan to make Waters End more than a bedroom community, more than just a maze of upscale office parks and million-dollar McMansions.

Jake pulled her purse strap up over her shoulder. "Mr. Mayor, I don't think we can help you," she said.

"Let him finish," Keith told her.

She jumped, having forgotten Keith was even there.

"We've got cops and firefighters who drive in here from Glencaster," Nimbus said. "We want 'em here. We want 'em with us. What if there's a wildfire? What if there's an earthquake?"

Jake tried to cut in, to stop The Mayor long enough to plant her declaration of "no" and leave, but Nimbus kept up at such a pace that he perturbed her to a stutter. His destination was "now." The STOP laws were "nonsense." Its supporters were "elitists." Sky-high housing prices served "no one's interests."

"That's why I want you," he said. "I want our city to get what it deserves."

Jake snorted with laughter and slapped her hand across her mouth, embarrassed by her loss of control.

"Let me finish," The Mayor said, his eyes twinkling with glee.

The Mayor's main goal, he said, was getting national news programs to scramble north from Los Angeles to relate the tale of Waters End — the genesis of the next great American trend. Suburbs had run their course. Now was the dawn of the "sub-exburb," a model of self-containment, a community that protected and served the same workers who served and protected it.

"Now don't start picking a fight with me," he said. "This is a vision, not a final draft. Future visions are always blurry, even in the movies. Details will come later. The first step is to get you to jump over to our side."

Keith grabbed another sandwich. "You want us to make you look good," he said all matter-of-factly. "We could do that."

"No," Jake said and stood. "I won't write stories that aren't true."

"Sit," The Mayor said. "Sit, please. I wouldn't ask you to do *that*. I'd want you to leave the paper, of course. It's us, or them. I guarantee you'll be paid a lot more than you're being paid now, enough to buy a house here; enough to *live* here."

"Of course," Jake said as she sat back down. "And I guarantee the Council would shred us into little pieces. No way they'd approve this. We quit. You hire us. They fire us. Then what?"

Nimbus slapped his knees. "That's why we have friends."

The way The Mayor explained, the employer would not be the city, but rather a private interest with common interests. Anyone could say nice things about Waters End. There was no law against that. Businesses, organizations or individuals could even pay someone to say nice things about the place. The Mayor pitched it as a promotion of positive thoughts, which, according to him, meant the endeavor could hardly be considered lobbying. It involved no candidate and no ballot measure either. Campaign finance laws and antitrust provisions would not apply. No public money would be involved, so public disclosures were not necessary. The only paperwork the government would see was whatever Jake and Keith filed with the IRS, the state Board of Equalization, and any other agency that played a part in the documentation of personal income for the purposes of taxation and regulation. The Mayor rattled off a list of benefits. Health insurance, life insurance, long-term disability, dental and vision coverage — all would be figured into fat and frequent paychecks.

"You will submit invoices as private contractors to a private business owned by a friend of ours," The Mayor said. "We know how to contain embarrassments. No questions will be asked, and none will be answered. We'll get you into a house. We'll make sure you're taken care of. You won't even know we're doing it."

Jake was caught in mid sip, the coffee cup still at her lips when Nimbus leaned forward to inquire about their current wage. Keith answered before she could swallow. He said she made "about $25" and that he was "not too far behind." Jake glared at him. In truth, Keith made $18 an hour and she made $22.

Nimbus offered $35 — to start.

Jake did the math quickly. "Seventy three thousand a year?" she said.

"Each," Nimbus replied. "Absolute minimum. Guaranteed. Of course, you'll work more than 40 a week. Fifty. Eighty. Who knows? Put in for it. You'll get it. We'll talk bonuses later, but now I need you to commit. I need to know you're serious."

"Serious?" Jake said. "Serious about what? I don't mean any disrespect, but we're not going to throw our lives away for a promise that sounds … unreal."

The creases at the corners of The Mayor's eyes grew deep and dark. "Your future employer is a friend. He knows I'm protective. He wants the same for the city as me — school teachers in the same neighborhood as the kids they teach; police who patrol their own streets. We want a hometown with a mix of young and old. We want the best, and that's why we want you. Don't you think you're the best? Is that so unbelievable?"

"No," Keith said and swatted at Jake's hand.

"Yes," Jake said. "It's unbelievable because it's —"

Her brain choked on the concept, the enormity of it too much to comprehend so quickly. "It's just shiny," she said. "All it is is shiny. We need a couple days to think and get back to you."

"Can't do it," The Mayor snapped. "The Chief won't be happy and I don't want a battle. You tell him you're leaving today, or you don't tell him about this conversation. Never ever. My first offer is my last, and he won't match it anyway. I know what you know. Remember?"

"This is what I was talking about," Jake said. "You can't do this. It's blackmail. I told you."

Nimbus pet the air in front of Jake's face. "Here's what's what," he said. "You'll take this job because it's good for you. But, if you don't … if you betray me to The Chief … I'll tell him you're a liar. I'll say I never made any offer. I'll also suggest that it's your little ploy to get a pay raise. You're mad about the raise he didn't give you. He knows it. He told me. He says you're behaving like a prima donna."

"He told you … " she said. "A prima … A what?"

"Layoffs are coming," The Mayor said. "The Chief and I have been friends longer than you've been alive, and we've both been businessmen longer than that. It's OK to be professional about this. Do what's right for you, for all of us."

Keith wrestled to take hold of Jake's hand, pulling it from her lap to the middle of the couch. "Let's talk," he said.

Jake bit her lip and yanked herself free. "But it's black —"

"It's business," The Mayor said and sat back. "You'll learn to see the difference."

"I see it now," Keith said.

Nimbus slipped a business card to Keith and moved to press a button on the armrest of his chair that made the office door shoot open like before. "You need husband-and-wife time," he said. "Been there. How's five? Call me on my cell."

Jake looked from the armchair button — which she hadn't noticed before — to the outer office, where the same little man was seated. He was alone this time, dressed in a white panama hat and a slightly different shade of powder-blue suit. There was no little dog.

The Mayor patted Jake between her shoulders as they both stood. "This is good," he said. "People are already lined up to live here and we're moving you to the front of the line."

Jake shrunk from The Mayor's touch, and inhaled to speak, though only one word came to mind. "No," she said. "No."

"You call me later," The Mayor said.

The little man in the outer office stared forward as Jake and Keith passed. Keith hooked his arm into Jake's and steered her all the way out of the building, across the street, and into the parking lot of *The Pendulum*.

"He wants to kill the story," she said. "That's it. There's nothing else to make him do this. I just need a document, a record to hang it on. A couple hard facts will fix this. I can find it. I just need a couple days, a week tops, and the story will be solid."

Keith snuggled her closer and she inhaled his faint scent of Dial soap, perspiration, and some indeterminable funk. *Bacon? Campfire smoke? Whatever.* She felt drunk on the sensation of his embrace, along with the renewed hope her story might actually turn out to be true. It was all happening. It was all coming together. She'd endured it for all the right reasons. Her story had become something so big The Mayor had tried to bribe her with what everyone was supposed to want — a house, financial security, the comfort of a community. She was *that good*. Properly intuitive. Practically clairvoyant. She breathed deep, hugged Keith tighter and shut her eyes.

"No way," Keith said and pulled away. "There's nothing to flush out. We take this offer."

"It's a bribe," Jake said.

"It's fair. It's only fair," Keith told her. "You decided to get us into this mess on your own without talking to me first, so I get to make this decision for the both of us. OK? You want fair? That's fair."

"But ..." Her throat was swelling and her eyes were welling up. "He gave us less than a day to decide. That's what swindlers do."

"You didn't even let *me* decide. You went off and hatched this whole water-story scheme on your own. If that was fair then ... so is this."

She couldn't argue. He was right.

"We'll get it all on paper," Keith said. "We'll do it now. We'll tell him to get us a contract by five."

"Even then ..." Jake said. "We don't know —"

"It doesn't matter who's paying the tab. The Mayor's the one calling the shots. This is what you wanted. This is your way out. We're *that good*. Or is this about me? You doubt it because he included me in the offer, don't you? You don't think I'm *that good*."

"No," she said. "No, no, no. You're —"

Keith slipped his arm around her hip and caressed the small of her back with his fingertips. "Then do this," he whispered.

"You've already decided," she said.

"It's my turn to decide. That's what's fair."

Maxine perked up as Jake and Keith arrived back at their desks. "How'd everything go with The Mayor, you guys?" she said.

An urgent need to cough caught Jake off guard, the gears of her brain suddenly so bunged up that her body couldn't even breathe right. "Wha…" She tried to speak between hacks. "How did …"

"It was nothing," Keith said.

Buckwalter thumped an index finger in the cradle of Jake's phone before she could finish dialing Keith's number.

"I want the story today," he said. "Whatever condition it's in, I don't care. Get it to me by five."

Jake dug both her boot heels into the carpet beneath her desk. She could sell this. Buckwalter would wait if she offered a hint about how rattled The Mayor had become. "They're nervous," she said. "They're about to break. I can link some big names to this. I can prove what's really going on if you give me —"

"We print what we've got now," Buckwalter said. "Whatever else we get, we print later."

"But —"

"This story is horseshit," he said. "Every story we print is horseshit. We drop them one lump at a time all over the goddamn place and the readers follow like flies. All we got to do is keep regular. Otherwise, people start to realize you're just plain full of shit."

Jake's mobile phone saved her from a response as it began to ring. She twisted around in her chair and put Buckwalter at her back to answer the call. It was her "Undetermined" friend again, nothing but static on the line.

"Where are we going with this?" she said into the phone. "We're wasting time. Why did you keep it secret for so long? Why did it happen this way? Why all those lies?"

The familiar sound of nothing hung on her every word.

She clapped the phone closed and declared to Buckwalter her immediate need to leave, said she'd only be an hour, maybe two, but that she'd come back with *the answer.*

"This is my source. I need to go meet my source."

Buckwalter splayed the fingers on his right hand and held them up. "Five," he said. "Five PM." Then he turned and walked away.

Jake nodded and typed an instant message to her husband, requested the keys to the Corolla and promised to meet him on the dock at four o'clock.

Once outside, however, Jake got only as far as her car. She locked the doors, kept the windows closed and the keys in her lap. She shut her eyes, opened her mind and breathed deep that dry, hot, ever-fading scent of comfort — the smell of eight-year-old French fries and spilled coffee, the last remnants of her college years, the scent of composted hope.

Keith kicked at the concrete pad of the dock and hissed with laughter as Jake offered her surrender on one condition: No more lies.

"Is that all it's gonna take?" he said.

"We do this honestly," she told him, her head still hot and shiny wet from sitting in the closed-up car. "Straight up. No padding. A fresh start."

Even if the worst was true, and maybe it was, she hadn't proved it. Part of her wanted to take the risk, but her reasons were indefensible. She wanted to be vindicated, to acquit herself of a capacity for deception and greed. She wished the whole mistake could play out as a happy accident, an act of clairvoyance, or luck. But Buckwalter was right. The story was horseshit. Every story was horseshit, and so was she. Her story had no ending. Without an ending, a story was just a long sentence. As wrong as it felt to take The Mayor's offer, as much as she doubted his promise of a new start, at the very least it was an end, and, at the moment, that was her best option.

"I'm tired," she said, her heart pounding, head swimming and knees about to give way. "It's only fair."

Keith scooped her into his arms as she drifted forward, as though he'd mistaken her lack of balance for an expression of affection. She was only half-conscious at the first touch of his kiss, but bit down to block his tongue. She groaned and pulled her head back, her teeth still tight together.

"I just want a house," Keith whispered and took hold of her neck with both hands. "I want to get it for you."

She slipped free of his grip, licked her lips and puckered. His kiss tasted bittersweet, like lemons and a vanilla something.

"Are we good?" he asked.

She said nothing as she watched his grin grow.

Buyers Troll Obits, Funeral Notices For Vacant Homes

By Maxine Lugner
Pendulum Staff Writer

Competition for homes in Waters End has pushed some buyers to dig up divorce records, bankruptcy filings and death certificates in search of an edge.

"I'd be surprised if every funeral director isn't in some agent's pocket," said Peter Kenlford, a local real estate broker.

One of his clients, Jackie Carbonara, found her house in an obituary that detailed the departed's love of birds. Carbonara, an attorney, attended the funeral, found the family and offered to maintain a birdbath if they would sell the house without listing it.

Please turn to page A10

CHAPTER 9 – THERE IS A BUNNY

Jake panicked the second the Corolla reached the top of Watercress Drive.

Keith was swaying and mumbling behind the wheel, half singing every other word of whatever was on the radio, the volume up and the windows down. Jake was belted into the passenger seat, her thoughts far away when it — whatever "it" was — sent a salvo of pricks and shivers from her head to her heart and back. It shocked her into consciousness, back into the car and back into her body. It made her hold her breath, as though it — the thought — was a sneeze about to come, almost ready, but not quite. It was right up front, as near as her forehead, so close she could almost feel it tingling beneath her skin and skull, teetering, on the verge of complete comprehension. Then Keith began to sing and it knocked her concentration off kilter. The thought went tumbling the other way, all because of one lyric from some song about living an easy, underwater life in a submarine.

Suddenly all Jake saw was red. All four corners of the windshield and the windows on either side of the Corolla were consumed by it — red rooftops, a multiplicity of terra cotta tiles pieced together on street after street, down the hills and across the valley floor. They didn't reflect the sun so much as they absorbed it and glowed like embers. Jake's belly seemed to float as the Corolla continued down the incline, the sight of row after row of rooftops almost like descending stairs, at once wonderful and wicked. She wanted to turn around, to get out of the car and run away. *But why?* Intuition told her she'd missed something important, though whenever, wherever and whatever that might have been was lost in her head.

She pulled the Thomas Guide from beneath her seat, to see if she could figure which of the rooftops out her window might be their destination, but there was no way. The map in her lap was a mess, its pages puckered by too much yellow Highlighter ink. She used to keep track of their house-hunting excursions by tracing each drive in the atlas, but finally stopped once their Sunday drives began to bleed together. Now they all looked like one big stain.

Jake sucked her cheeks and looked to Keith. Not since they were newcomers to California had he seemed so eager to start a Sunday, his fingers laced atop the steering wheel, the tip of his tongue pinched out the corner of his mouth. He'd already decided and he hadn't even seen the house. She could read it in his face. But, whatever his idea of home might have been, it wasn't likely she'd agree. Jake wanted to make Keith understand, to see that a house required more than four walls and a roof to qualify as a home. *But how?* Translating the feeling of a home was as difficult as explaining why her favorite color was teal, or what made strawberry ice cream better than both vanilla and chocolate. *It just was.* She could have at least told him the practical stuff, that to be a home it must never leak during rainstorms, and never whistle in the wind, not even in the most sinister of Southern California's Santa Anas. She might have said a home had to feel the opposite of lonely on Sunday mornings. She thought to say home was a matter of choice, but this time the choice was up to Keith. She no longer had a say. It was all about him now. It was fair.

Keith slowed at the neighborhood's entrance, both sides flanked by open iron gates and more than a dozen open-house signs. An engraved marble stone sat just outside Jake's window, its letters caked with weed-whacker splatter, barely legible but for the part that said "Bernin Ridge." She squinted at the bottom line, could only make out the words "community conceived …" and what looked like a name that ended in "… COW." It didn't matter. No one cared who built a house, so long as the walls were solid and the roof didn't come down. The same was true for whoever sold it, all those middlemen who thought themselves so important, staking their satin flags with sharp sales pitches like capitalistic conquistadors, gentrifying entire zip codes one escrow at a time. Fact was, homes were made by homeowners, not the guy who got the permits, or the one who passed along the keys after all the papers were signed.

Jake decided to try to talk Keith out of it all, but her cell phone rang and pushed that thought out of her head too.

"Jake, Jake, Jake —"

It was a woman's voice.

"*Eee*, you've got to do something —"

It was Maggie.

"*Mija*, you gotta. Gotta."

Jake's body jerked forward as the Corolla rocked to a halt at the end of a cul-de-sac. Keith cursed, threw the gearshift into reverse and whined back down the block. Jake bent over her knees and plugged her finger into the ear opposite the phone.

"The Wells," Maggie said. "They sucked us dry. They want our land. They took my brother's farm and now they're gonna take me too. I told you they're no good."

Jake dug into her purse in search of one of her blank notebooks, all of which she'd turned over to Human Resources several weeks before. They'd even made her return the ballpoints — Sanford Uni-Balls — her favorite. They'd cut up her press pass and her key card for the building. They'd have taken her cell phone too, if she hadn't happened to have her most recent invoice in her purse as proof that she was the owner.

She slapped her purse shut and tried to slow the pace of the conversation. "Maggie," she said. "I don't know anyone named Wells. Who do you mean?"

"Not 'The Wells,' *Mija*, my well. Everybody's well. *Agua, Mija. Agua.* Every place out here is on well water and every place is dry. The old timers got no water. You gotta do it. You gotta."

"Maggie, I'm not there anymore. *No trabaje allí mâs.* We quit four weeks ago. We don't do that anymore."

Keith hit the brakes hard again and jerked his head around. "Help me find this boonin' place," he said.

"Maggie," Jake said and cupped the phone closer. "How do you know The Mayor did anything?"

"We're not gonna take this sitting down," Maggie said. "We're gonna march. We're gonna give Nimbus what's what. That silver spooner is a crook."

"I … I'm not a reporter anymore. You know that, right Maggie?"

"Did they fire you, *Mija*? Did they do it to shut you up? Don't worry. I've got people. We'll picket. We'll get that John Streusel on TV to set up a hidden-camera sting."

Jake inhaled to speak, sighed and began again. "Don't understand me so fast," she said. "It was me. Nobody. Me."

Maggie promised to get to the bottom of it — the water, the paper, Jake. There was a man in Frazier Park, a geologist. Maggie had asked him to help.

"You gotta stand for some things," Maggie said, "otherwise, you'll sit through everything."

The lack of privacy in the car made the conversation complicated. Jake begged to talk later, offered to call Maggie back. Maggie said a face-to-face visit would be best. They left it open and promised to reconnect.

"Water, *Mija*," Maggie said. "People are made of water."

Keith opened his mouth as soon as Jake's phone was folded shut. "Who wants what done to Chick?" he asked.

"It was a friend," Jake said. "A source."

"The Mayor's our only source. We don't have any other sources. He's our boss. What he says, goes. Give it up, Jake. We're not reporters anymore."

"I didn't ask her to call me," Jake said. "I didn't ask Maxine to call either, but you didn't complain when I got stuck with her this morning. You left me alone for *that* phone call. You left the room."

"You should have told her," Keith said and eased the Corolla to the curb outside the single-story house they'd come to see. The post-and-beam sign out front had the usual for-sale language, plus a second slot card on top that declared "FAMILY STARTER" in big, red letters.

"I don't have to tell *that woman* anything," Jake said.

"You could have given her names."

"My sources? Give her my sources?"

"Yeah. Why not?"

"I quit so I wouldn't have to be a part of that anymore. And, you want me to help *that woman*?"

Jake put her hands to her face.

"Don't even start," Keith said. "You quit because you screwed up and I saved us."

"Who do you think you are?" Jake said. "Where's the guy I met in … I gave up my career for … Was it all for —"

She thrust her hands out her open car window and toward the house.

"This is what you wanted," Keith said and pointed to the house too. "This is what we wasted all those Sundays looking for. When was any of that going to change? You're always so right, always 'no' this and 'no' that. You say 'no' to everything, including 'fucking,' and I don't just mean the word. You don't fuck anything, including me. I'm your fucking husband and I'm fucking tired of it. That's what's fucking wrong. You're the one who fucked us up, Jake. You —"

Jake opened and closed the glove compartment, unlocked and locked her door, tensed with the need to storm away and relaxed to wait it out. "What else haven't you told me?" she said. "What else do you blame me for?"

"You see what you want to," he said. "Everybody lies. The world isn't fair. It's always been like this. But you want to pretend it's not."

"That's not what I asked."

"You're the worst liar of all because you lie to yourself. I can't even ask you about your parents without you getting all —"

"I'm not going to argue like this. Not now. Not here."

"See! You're the never-ending cliffhanger, always next week, always 'on the way back,' always 'wait and see.' You're always waiting for nothing to fucking change."

"That woman will be here," Jake said.

"What? Who?"

"You know who."

"Why would Maxine come here?"

"Maxine?" Jake said. "I meant the real estate agent that The Mayor referred us to. Why would you even think I meant Maxine?"

"Just give her your goddamn sources."

"They were 'anonymous,' Keith."

"So?"

"I won't reveal anonymous sources."

"There are no sources! You made them up. They're imaginary — munchkins, scarecrows, tin men. Wake up! There's nobody to betray. So give Maxine some names and make her think you tried. We might need a favor from —"

"I can't violate a sacred trust, imaginary or not. Maxine will think it's real. She'll think I betrayed someone. That's my reputation. Mine. What else have I got?"

A dark-skinned man in white overalls began to unload a Toro push mower from the back of a pickup truck across the street. Keith turned toward him and mumbled what sounded like "yicka, yicka, yicka."

"What?" Jake snapped.

"Just give her one of the stories then."

"Can't. Don't have them."

The lawnmower started up and Keith shouted over the roar. "You threw all those stories away?"

Jake gasped. "It" came back — that thought she'd been thinking when Keith cracked into her head with his singing, right before the Corolla crested the hill with that vision of red. Suddenly she remembered what she'd left undone. "It" was the stories! She hadn't deleted a word of them, had left them where anyone could get at them, in what had been her computer on what used to be her desk. Escape had been too much of a focus. She let go of everything that day. She gave up and gave in. Keith had taken control. Keith had called The Mayor. The Mayor had called The Chief. The Chief had called Buckwalter. And Buckwalter had called Jake out. Everyone in the building knew she was leaving before she'd come to terms with what it meant.

The Chief's goodbye e-mail had even followed a burst of laughter that sounded from behind his office door.

The missive was more list than letter, a tick-tock that ran down all but whether Keith and Jake should depart through the side door or the front:

TO:	HR
FROM:	Chief
CC:	JLamotta, KTorrance, FBuckwalter
SUBJ:	rush process 2 resignations

effective immediately
voluntary resignations
2 editorial staff

emp id JL-5768
emp id KT-3689

collect all company property
terminate electronic access
publish 2 FT staff vacancies

Jake remembered reading it for what wasn't there — her name — neither in the "TO" line, nor in the text. Besides that, her position was set to be advertised, *not* downsized. She hadn't even rated a complete sentence. No punctuation. It was less than no "goodbye."

She'd never before considered what sort of send off she'd rate, but, in retrospect, she at least expected an attempt to persuade her to stay. Even people she'd seen forced out had been given handshakes. Some got cake. She'd have been grateful for a simple nod, or a halfway grin. She deserved to be addressed directly. A voicemail. A personal e-mail. A finger gesture flung from an office window. The Chief was the reason she'd stayed in Waters End. He was why she'd said "no" to offers from other papers in LA. She'd been sustained by his praise, inspired by his encouragement. She'd defended him against the criticisms of coworkers. She hadn't been a "prima donna." She'd believed.

It took Maxine to make Jake remember. Maxine had been assigned Jake's story and wanted Jake's help to write it. She wanted sources and direction, but Jake had said "no" and little else. *That woman* would get nothing. Maxine was the worst of the profession. She represented the problem that had driven Jake to make her fictional pitch in the first place.

All four versions — four individual tales of poison and deceit — were still in the possession of *The Pendulum*, each one password-protected and disguised as mortgage statistics. Jake had to get them back. Even a slight risk of discovery was unacceptable. She had to go.

The lawnmower across the street choked on a lump of lawn as Jake mumbled. "How could I forget?"

"Give them to Maxine," Keith said. "Let her rewrite the whole thing her way. If she crashes the market, it'll be her fault. She'll make it even easier for us to buy a house."

Jake tossed her arms up and let them drop limp in her lap. "I've got to get them back."

"The hell you do."

A dark-blue BMW eased into the driveway of the house and broke up the conversation. It was the real estate agent, Rusty *Something*. Jake had put it on the Post-it, but forgot it on the kitchen counter in Reseda.

"I drove up here to do this," Keith said as he got out.

Jake watched him walk to her side of the car, playing the part of the loyal husband, making a fuss over his wife with curb-side service.

"Not to worry," he said as he reached in the open window to unlock Jake's door. "Not to worry."

The agent looked like a Nancy Reagan wannabe — tight hairdo, red blazer, matching skirt. She introduced herself to Keith first. "Rusty Tirzah," she said and took his hand. "You must be Jake. The Mayor has told me so much —"

The small circle of bulls-eye glass in the center of the front door swirled with the appearance of two pale people on the other side.

"Normally I use the lock box," Rusty explained. "But the owners wanted to meet all prospective buyers. He's Charlie. She's Clara. Charlie was in the industry — Disney. He actually knew Walt. She's a homemaker. Salt of the earth. You're gonna love them."

The door opened and Keith stepped ahead first, catching the toe of his right shoe on the corner of the mat. It flipped vertical and wedged between his knees, threw him across the threshold and made him clap his feet down hard on the white linoleum of the entryway. The old couple stepped back fast as he landed upright with his shoulders against the wall. The doormat flopped face up at his feet. "Welcome To Our *Loverly* Home" was printed across it in big, black letters.

Clara reached to Keith, as if to pet his aura.

"Did you hurt anything, dear?" she said, a white kitchen apron across her chest, gray hair in a ponytail, her feet flat in sensible old-lady shoes with double-knotted laces.

Charlie followed. "First day with the new legs?" he joked, so tall he towered over both Clara and Keith, six-foot-five with a waist like an oak tree, and hands big enough to palm a pumpkin.

Keith stuffed his hands deep into his pants pockets and shrugged. "I'm fine," he said.

Jake drifted immediately, wandered into the kitchen and was overwhelmed by the aroma of fresh-baked bread — an old real-estate ploy to make a place seem more homey. No surprise there, but, other than that, this place looked and felt different from all the others she'd seen in five years of Sunday open-house visits — the modest appliances, the framed family photographs on two walls in the adjoining den, bric-a-brac on nearly every inch of shelf and mantel space. There were porcelain figurines, hand-painted teacups, and dozens of tiny silver spoons. More of it sat in the window box above the kitchen sink, on top of the Kitchen Chef microwave oven, and all across the end tables on either side of a couch that slouched in the center like an old horse. People actually *lived* in this house.

Jake could feel Clara behind her, same as she sensed the warmth of the oven.

"All these precious things, so delicate," Clara said. "I should trust the movers, but I just don't."

"They must mean a lot," Jake said and reached for a porcelain kangaroo.

The figurine depicted the marsupial on its haunches, eyes downcast and stern with wrinkles down the top of its nose. It gave Jake a twinge of guilt, as though she were being judged by those painted eyes.

Suddenly Charlie was at her side, his big feet surprisingly quiet in thick, white cotton socks, no shoes. "We got that one up in Soledad," he said. "We call the little feller 'Lunch,' don't we Clara?"

Clara swatted his arm and smiled. "Pay him no mind," she said. "He thinks he's a comedian, but he's just a silly old fud."

"Old?" Charlie said and laughed again. "I may be silly, but I'm sure as shoot not old."

Jake bent to inspect another of the figurines — a mother hen and baby chick.

"Solvang," Clara said, her voice softer as she got closer. "Every one of these came from someplace else and that one's from Solvang. That's our rule. One thing. We pick one thing from every place, and it has to be small enough to fit in a pocket. It seems silly now, all these dust magnets, but, oh, I just love them. These memories have been good to us. I don't know what we're going to do at the new place. I don't know if that cottage has room."

Jake traced a few trips around the world in the makeshift diorama of the couple's life. There was a windmill and an Eiffel Tower, a Big Ben, a Samurai warrior, a Statue of Liberty and a tiny kachina doll.

Jake pointed to the kachina. "Acoma Pueblo?" she asked.

"No one's ever guessed that," Clara said. "We got that the year of my first. Nearly had him in the car between Flagstaff and LA. Mr. Funny here was joking the whole way."

"You laughed," Charlie said. "You encouraged me."

Jake looked to the photographs next, a tribute to the lives of three children. There were black-and-white pictures of baby-carriage bundles, color pictures of black-and-white graduation robes, toothless smiles and baseball uniforms with stirrup socks. A little girl was wearing pink ballet shoes in one photo. A little boy wore a big, blue football helmet in another. Most every inch of every wall was covered, the frames tiled together like an unplanned puzzle with gaps too oddly shaped to fill. The oldest of the photos looked to be the sepia-toned print in a stand-up frame on the bookshelf. It was Charlie and Clara on their wedding day. He was in a traditional tuxedo. She wore a lacey gown. Jake turned to find Keith, but he wasn't in the room. She and Keith didn't even have a photo of their wedding day, hadn't thought to borrow or buy a camera before or after going to the courthouse. Jake took hold of her ring-bare wedding finger and squeezed it.

Clara started to speak, but stopped as another couple appeared in the archway that connected the kitchen to the living room and the front door. They were about the same ages as Keith and Jake, the man that much older than the woman. The man and woman said nothing at first, stood side by side with their arms akimbo, fingers splayed over taut abdomens. His left foot was slightly left of her right, their combined silhouette a kind of caduceus, a double helix of rawboned bodies held tight by the elastic fibers of identical, black FCUK turtlenecks and straight-legged GAP slacks. The woman's raven hair was shiny and short. The man's hair was peppered with strands of gray. They each wore the same dark, thick, rectangular eyeglass frames, with lenses that made their eyes seem to protrude from the sockets. They were almost each other.

The woman in black spoke up first, asked something about contingencies, which made Clara's face turn to Charlie, who looked at Rusty and wiggled his nose.

"Well —" Rusty said, as though unsure of the answer. "The house is paid off, and Charlie and Clara are moving into a rental home in Newport Beach, so —"

She paused and swung her arms from front to back. "There was something about the cat," she said and stuck out her chin at Charlie. "The cat ... the cat ... the —"

"Yes, yes," Clara said. "The cat. We have the loveliest little cat. Bunny. We call her Bunny. She's been here her whole life, since the kids were in middle school. It would be terrible to make her relocate to the harbor with all that water all around. All she knows is the inside of this house. Never been outside. Never touched the grass with her little paws. Not once. But she's happy, goes the whole day laying in the sun on that dresser in the front bedroom, watching people go up and down the street. Oh, I wish she was around so you could see. She's shy with new people."

The skin on Clara's wrists went red as she twisted each in her hands.

Charlie took over. "Rusty told us it would be ok to ask whoever buys this old house to keep old Bunny," he said. "It's important. This may just be a house, but it's the end-all, be-all for Bunny. It's the only home she's ever known."

Keith cleared his throat, but the woman in black started back up before he could speak.

"We love cats," the woman said.

The man in black perked from a blank stare. "Adore them," he said. "May I ask … short, or long-hair?"

"A *loverly* angora," Clara said and rocked herself in her arms. "She sheds, but she's so good, keeps to herself. Like I said, you'll never notice her, unless you wear a lot … of … black … things."

Clara bit her upper lip.

"Hardly ever," the woman in black said and snickered.

"What are lint rollers for?" the man in black said.

The room bubbled with polite laughter.

"I've always wanted another cat," Keith said. "Love 'em."

Jake cleared her throat loudly and turned away.

Both house-hunting couples divided to wander the place solo. Jake spotted Keith and the man in black out the window box in the kitchen, each of them at an opposite end of the kidney-shaped pool in the backyard. The woman in black was stretching a tiny tape measure across the front door as Jake passed on the way to the bedrooms. The smallest one looked like a well-kept college dorm room, its tiny bookshelves lined with Signet Classics. Jake spied the cat in the master bedroom up front, resting atop a six-drawer dresser beside the window, its eyes trained on the front walk, its face and Jake's reflected one inside the other in the double-paned glass.

Clara joined Jake and touched her shoulders from behind.

"It *does* feel like home … like a home is supposed to feel," Jake whispered. "I'm afraid it's just —"

"The money?" Clara said, her hands still there on both Jake's shoulders.

Jake shook her head. "Not really."

Clara persisted. "Just afraid?" she asked. "Everyone is afraid at first, dear. It's such a big, big decision."

"I adore the cat."

"But —"

"Everything," Jake said. "Big, big decisions."

Jake used to laugh when Keith told a story about how, as a boy, he'd cut a calico's whiskers for no reason other than to watch it trap itself between two uneven fence slats. Back then she'd laughed to make Keith feel good. But now the memory of it made her long to confess. She felt dirty, like she needed forgiveness. She wanted to tell Clara. She wanted to tell Maggie. She wanted someone to be as close to her as her mother and father used to be, but no one could be all that at once anymore.

Who can you trust if you can't trust your parents?

"Big, big decisions," Jake said.

Jake found Keith outside, in the driveway, his hip propped against the back of the agent's BMW, holding court with the couple dressed in black.

The man nodded to Jake as she stood behind Keith. "You believe all that crap in there?" the man said. "That bit about the cat? Fuckin' priceless."

"That cat's gone soon as I get the keys," Keith said.

"Promise breaker," the man in black joked as he and his wife turned toward a black Ford Excursion at the curb.

Keith bounced himself off the Beemer and went along after them.

"You gotta keep your promises," the man said as he climbed up and into the SUV. "My Rottweiler would want me to keep *this* promise. He'd love that cat to pieces."

The woman in black sat on the passenger side and opened the window. Keith positioned himself just outside it, his left foot on the running board, his forearms crossed on his knee. "When I was a kid," he said, "we took this cat and —"

Jake slapped a flip-flop hard on the pavement behind him.

"Seriously," the man in black said across his wife's lap, "You two aren't actually going to bid on this, are you? We're out. It's too much to gut. Paneling. Linoleum. That's *real* linoleum."

The woman in black chuckled as she adjusted her seatbelt.

Jake turned her hand up in front of Keith. It was her silent request for the keys.

Keith slapped the ring into her hand as the man in black continued talking. "Ophelia and I have a place in Woodland Hills that's perfect for you two. We're listing next week. Want to see? You can follow us. Where's your car?"

Jake turned away and moved toward the Corolla, which was concealed by the big backside of the SUV. The agent stood waiting there, her hip propped against the weather-beaten front fender, ready with a handshake and a business card.

"You ought to make an offer right away," Rusty said. "Another couple is set to do a walk-through this afternoon and —"

"It's all too much," Jake told her. "It's a wonderful place, and they're such a nice couple, but —"

"Are you working with anyone?" Rusty asked. "I assumed you —"

Jake shook her head and Rusty's eyes shot open wide.

"Oh, darling, you've got to have an agent," Rusty said. "You go alone and you end up like those people who disappear in the woods. Everyone who ever got lost knew exactly where they wanted to go. They just didn't know the way. You end up going in circles. You end up right where you don't want to be, sometimes right back where you started. I've seen it."

Jake squeezed the ring of keys. "You know, we can't do this," she said. "We're self-employed and the financing's never going to —"

"It's an industry town," Rusty said. "My specialty is people who don't have 'job-jobs.' Normally, I'd tell you to never let the seller's rep be your rep, but this one's different. Clara likes you. Charlie too. And, well, you come *highly* recommended by The Mayor. This is what we call 'Special Circumstances.' So, how about I buy you lunch and we can talk about an —"

Lunch!

Jake already had an appointment for lunch, another in a series of networking attempts with former sources and spokespersons, her new life so dependent on how many people she knew and how much they liked her. And then there were those stories. *The stories.* Her heart pumped faster and the world began to spin. The house, the agent, the Corolla — everything went from noon to nine and back. That submarine song replayed in Jake's head with its promise of ease and the fulfillment of every need. The ring of keys slipped from her hand.

Jake woke up on the couch in Charlie's and Clara's den. She sniffled and licked the taste of salty snot from her upper lip as Clara dabbed a wet washcloth to her forehead.

"Somebody got too much sun," Clara said and winked. "It'll zap you sometimes."

Jake sat up and put her feet to the floor, the strands of the deep shag carpet cool between her bare toes. *The boots.* Someone had removed them. She looked quickly around the room as Clara curled Jake's fingers around a tall glass of water, the base of it wrapped neatly in a paper towel.

"This will help," Clara whispered.

Jake heaved a sigh upon spying her turquoise-colored Luccheses beside the fireplace. "I drink so much coffee," she said by way of an apology. "It's the caffeine, I think."

The men were staring at her. Keith stood behind Charlie, whose knees were bent, butt on his heels, weight on the balls of his feet.

"She does this," Keith said. "She gets these spells sometimes lately."

Clara's forehead wrinkled as she turned back to Jake. "I used to get spells too," Clara whispered, "right before I found out about my first. You should see your doctor, just in case. Young people aren't supposed to faint, even if they are in a 'family way.'"

As impolite as it seemed, Jake couldn't keep from laughing. The one problem she didn't have was pregnancy.

"You got to drink that water up," Charlie said. "Eight glasses a day. It ain't easy, but you've got to make yourself do what's right."

Pendulum Names New Editor-In-Chief

By Maxine Lugner
Pendulum Staff Writer

Fletcher Buckwalter, 42, was named editor of *The Pendulum* Tuesday, succeeding Eli Woundwort, who's served as the paper's chief since the publication's formation.

Woundwort, known to staff and friends as "The Chief," announced his retirement at the same time as Buckwalter's appointment.

Buckwalter was "an obvious choice," said Todd Slayer, vice president with Denny Dukat Newspapers, owner of *The Pendulum*.

"He's pro-churchgoer, pro-reader, pro-business and pro-homeowner," Slayer said. "He doesn't mess around. He gets results. And he'll be there when people need him."

Buckwalter was out of town and unable to be reached for comment Tuesday.

Please turn to page A11

CHAPTER 10 – FOXES AND BUCKS

The sport coat caught Jake's attention before she realized The Chief was trapped inside it.

It bespoke genuine ugliness, a plaid blend of torpid blue and vile green with shoulders that bunched and a breast pocket that drooped like the bottom lip of a big fish. The brown buttons didn't match each other and the yellow lining spilled out the sleeves. Jake made a conscious effort not to grin too broadly, suddenly hypersensitive to the fine line between joy and sass. She owed her old boss a smile, at least. He'd broken the ice, contacted her himself by phone and extended a gracious invitation to lunch. Whatever his reason, she felt grateful to matter as much as a meal, particularly after her somewhat dubious departure. Nonetheless, the sight of him in that coat made the corners of her mouth turn up. She heard the threads snap from two tables away as he pulled at his collar and flinched, seemingly stuck by a pin. He sucked his right index finger and waved his left hand wildly, clearly in pain, notorious for his short supply of patience.

"What the Sam Hill took you so long?" he said as Jake arrived at her chair.

He whined immediately about having sat alone "forever," forced by the maitre d' to wear a club jacket despite his stature as a community leader, not to mention that, given the earliness of the hour, no one else was around to witness the "goddamned unsuitability" of his attire. From the moment The Chief had stepped into the dining room of the Waters End Country Club he'd had the place to himself, though that was certain to change the nearer it got to noon. He called Jake's attention to several marks on the nearby bay window, each of which he claimed to have witnessed as sliced shots from the driving range had smacked into the glass. The green-and-yellow paint marks left behind by the projectiles matched The Chief's jacket perfectly. Their similarity, however, was not the point he was trying to make.

"Every five minutes, 'BAM,' another son-of-a-bitchin' golf ball hits the window. Pain in the … I'd have got up and goddamn gone, but what else am I supposed to do with my day? Where the hell you been?"

Jake wasn't late. She'd race-walked through the parking lot and down the grand hallway in her boots, all to meet him at 11:30 as agreed. She'd have been early if the maitre d' hadn't hassled her, his disapproval so intense she sensed it a hallway's length from his podium. Whatever the club's definers of fashion considered "dress casual," her outfit had to qualify — a caramel-colored, knee-length skirt; a brown v-neck pullover; and that pair of turquoise boots. She'd sought to pre-empt any objection the maitre d' might have had, volunteered the fact that her skirt was linen — not denim — and remarked about boots being "the new flip-flops." He'd made an issue anyway, called her "Annie Oakley" and inquired of "Wild Bill." She offered her correction kindly with a wink, whispered that Annie worked with *Buffalo* Bill, but that *her* name was "Jake LaMotta."

"Of courth you are dear," the maitre d' had said with a lisp. "And I'm Betty Page."

The Chief grunted, squirmed and snapped more threads in the seams of the sport coat as he snatched his menu from the server's hand. "Damn attorney. Says I got to demonstrate my use of this membership or lose it," he told Jake. "The paper paid it off. My name's on it. But Hazel and that damn lawyer —"

Despite the lack of any official pronouncement, The Chief's divorce was common knowledge at the paper and around City Hall. Still, Jake hesitated to join in any discussion of it. So many weeks had passed between her and the newsroom that she scarcely recalled who'd said what regarding The Chief, let alone which parts of his personal life she wasn't supposed to know about, and which she was. Rather than chance it, she tried to turn the talk back toward a resolution, assuming there was still something worth fixing left between them.

"I'm very … you know … leaving the paper and all," she said. "There was probably a better way, but it just happened so fast and —"

The Chief hissed and squirmed, his torso still sparing against that sport coat. "Those bastards got what they wanted," he said.

Jake opened her menu and restrained the reflex to rectify his statement. Technically, The Chief had been one of *those bastards*.

"You gotta look out for yourself," he said. "You gotta insist on what you're worth."

Jake let him ramble as she combed through the menu, puzzling over its lack of prices. "How are we supposed to know how much?" she said, sotto voce.

"If you don't know, I can't tell you," The Chief replied.

"No," Jake said, looking up from the bill of fare. "They don't tell you."

"They don't tell any of us, goddammit. It doesn't work like that."

She gave a slight snicker, figuring his crack for sarcasm. "But, how do you know?" she said. "What's to keep them from taking you for everything you've got?"

The Chief's fist struck the table with such force it bounced the place settings out of alignment. "They took my goddamn job," he shouted. "Is that what you mean?"

Jake blinked and jerked her head back, her grin laid flat by the blast.

"I had a business to run," he said. "I did what was expected. I delivered and got screwed. That's the price I paid. We all gotta eat shit sometimes."

Jake pet the shoulder of The Chief's coat, then pulled her hand away quickly. "I didn't mean *that*," she said, suddenly overcome with the urge to comfort him. "I meant the menu and … It doesn't matter. So, what now? Got anything else?"

The Chief grunted as he straightened his fork, knife and spoon.

Jake continued to press. "Other newspapers must be chasing after you to work for them."

"Newspapers," he sputtered. "Don't matter whether they print it on high-grade toilet paper, or this damn new Internet. It's all the same shit. I'm done. The house is sold. The divorce is almost final. I'm headed to your old stomping ground to do some fishing."

He looked away and stared off into space, his eyes so shiny it made Jake feel as though hers might start to water too. They didn't.

"You mean Ketchum?" she said.

"Did you know Hemingway fished that same Stanley River?" The Chief said. "He wrote '*The Sun Also Rises*' at the Sun Valley Lodge. There's a Jake in there, too. A reporter."

"Really?"

"Poor bastard got castrated in the war. What good's a writer with no balls?"

"Hemingway?" she said and cocked her head.

"Hell no," The Chief said, halfway through a belch with his fist to his lips. "Papa died with his testicles intact. I'm talking about Jake … Jake Barnes."

————————

Although Keith had never before dined in a sushi restaurant, he was absolutely certain the Japanese did not eat ChapStick.

Maxine, however, expressed a willingness to entertain the possibility.

"Orientals are such little trendsetters," she said, turning heads at the nearest tables and up at the hostess stand. "They're wearing skirts over pants now. So crazy. So no wonder they eat lip gloss."

Keith set her straight, the volume of his voice deliberately louder than hers had been. "The hostess," he explained, "said 'chopstick,' not 'ChapStick.' Chopsticks, as in two sticks used to eat quickly? Chop, chop."

He didn't want to be there, had agreed to come despite his better judgment. He'd insisted they meet in a secluded spot, someplace they wouldn't be seen by anyone who knew them. Sushi, Maxine had reasoned, provided the perfect cover. "*No take-out,*" she'd explained. "*Nobody at the paper eats nothing but take-out.*" Keith had no other ideas, and no choice in the matter. Ten calls a day was too much. He had to do something to make her stop.

"You never call back," Maxine said as she reached across the table for Keith's hand. "It's so hard since you've been gone from the paper."

"Listen," he said. "You've got to —"

The server, a slight woman in a silk kimono with her hair done up in a French twist, interrupted to offer Maxine a cup of "hot tea." Maxine gave a blush and a breathless whisper of thanks, then dipped her chin down close to the tabletop and sputtered with glee.

"No waitress nowhere ever called me a 'hottie,'" she whispered.

Keith rolled his eyes up, then dropped them to his lap and shook his head. "She was pouring you 'hot tea,'" he said. "That's what she was talking about. 'Tea.' As in *tea* that's hot; not *you*."

Maxine did not react, but fussed with her napkin and cup. She said her world had been turned upside down because Buckwalter had hired two new reporters to replace Keith and Jake.

"So he goes and puts me on Jake's story, right? Great. So, guess what? No one knows anything about nothing in the water. I've talked to everyone. The Mayor says it's all some old gadfly telling lies. And maybe it is, but I can't tell Buckwalter *that*. I mean, like he'd ever believe Jake got it wrong. He wants that story no matter what."

The arrival of the food provided Keith a diversion — two oblong "bento" boxes, or so the menu had called them. They looked more like lacquered utensil drawers, each rectangular compartment filled with a different shade and form of fleshiness. Besides that, steamed white rice had been portioned into separate, small bowls that resembled skullcaps turned upside down. Next to that was a dollhouse-sized dish of Play-Doh-green paste.

"Wassa-by," Maxine said and pointed to the green blob. "I read somewhere that it was spicy hot."

She left the box lay and pulled a Chinet paper plate from her big purse. The plate contained half a dozen lemon bars all bound up in plastic. Keith wrested one from the layers of wrapping and shoved it into his mouth, grateful for anything other than the tissue cultures in his bento box.

"What's the matter with Jake?" Maxine asked. "What does she care? Why won't she help?"

Keith scrunched his face, chewed and mumbled through yellow mush. "I couldn't say. Can't help you there."

"You could say her source. I know you know, Kiki. Tell *Mommy* what you know."

Her toes ran across his right ankle, which made his leg jerk. His knee slammed up into the table and splashed tea out the cups.

"What are you doing?" he spit.

"What is *Mommy* doing?" she corrected. "Don't you want your *hot tea?*"

Keith fished another lemon bar from the folds of wrap. "What if I give it to you?" he said. "Would you keep it secret? Secret no matter what?"

Half of the lemon bar vanished in one bite, leaving behind traces of sugar and pieces of crust on Keith's chin and across the untouched contents of his bento box.

"Tell me the name," Maxine begged. "Tell me, tell me, tell me."

"Not even Buckwalter," Keith said. "You can't even tell Buckwalter."

Maxine did a double take. "Why would I do that?" she said, her tone suddenly serious. "If I get the story, it's my story. I get it. I earn it. I don't see anybody else baking for you. I'm doing this. Me!"

She wiggled and bounced, the smile already back in her cheeks, the booth such a tight fit that her breasts spilled over the tabletop and caught a portion of the yellowtail in her bento box. Keith watched as the fleshy strip of fish stuck to a button on her blouse and slithered after her as she sat back. It rolled down her chest and flopped to her lap. She snatched a napkin and followed after it, slapped and smushed it to her spandex-clad thigh. The force of her motions suggested to Keith that she not only intended to catch it, but to scour it to death.

"Do you want my water?" he said and offered his glass.

"I want you to get me that source!" she demanded. "I'm through screwing around."

"OK. OK. I will. I will."

Maxine stopped rubbing and put both hands flat on the table. "OK?" she said. "You will?"

The waitress interrupted, pointed to the untouched lunches and asked if everything tasted good. Maxine waved the woman away and kept her eyes locked on Keith.

"OK?" she repeated. "You got it? You have it now?"

Keith snagged a third lemon bar. "Did you look in her computer?" he asked and sat back.

"Hello?" Maxine spit. "I'm not stupid. There's nothing in the system."

Her lips stayed flat.

"Don't you get it?" Keith said. "That's the key to everything. It's not in the system. It's on the hard drive. Look harder. The file is called 'mortgage statistics,' or whatever. The password is 'Pop.' That's it. You've got to do something for yourself. I can't fix Jake's screwups and do your work too. And don't ask anyone else for help getting it. This isn't everything else."

Maxine's spittle hit Keith's cheek before he even heard the words.

"Don't go all Mister Mister on me!" she shot back. "I do everything myself. Everything! No one claims credit for where I am, or where I go. Not you or Stan, or anybody. 'Lucky?' He's so full of shit. I'm not 'lucky.' I deserve what I get. I've gone through hell to get this far. I've earned all this and I got more coming."

She banged the table so hard with her hand that the cups spilled more tea. The whole restaurant went quiet after the outburst, making it possible for Keith to hear the faint music sprinkling out the ceiling speaker above his head, a symphonic rendition of a familiar song about a she-devil. He lowered his voice and leaned forward.

"Who said you were lucky? Not me."

"Never mind," Maxine replied. "But you're just like him. You're all alike."

"I just told you where to find the story, but I figure you would have found it anyway —"

"Story? What do you mean 'story?'"

"That's gotta be better than a source, right? All the work has been done. It's all there on the hard drive."

"The *hard* what?"

"Get IS to help you. Tell them it's for a report on computers, or whatever," he said. "They'll show you the hard drive. They'll explain what to do. Just don't let Fletch … er … Buckwalter find out what you're doing. He'll give credit to Jake. She can't do what you do. She doesn't even care."

Maxine's shoulders drooped and her forehead went smooth. "I know, Kiki," she said. "Don't worry. I've got Fletch covered. I got control."

"Pop," he repeated. "The password. Pop."

He refilled his cup with tea and watched shredded bits of leaves gravitate to the sides. Maxine fished a pill bottle from her purse and swallowed the two white capsules that came out of it.

"I'll take the credit," she said. "But, I need the source. I have to actually talk to him, or her, or whoever."

"I can't tell you that," Keith said, the mush of a third lemon bar stuck to the backs of his front teeth. "I told you where to go for the story. That's enough."

She reached across to his hand and dug in. He winced and focused on the seams of her fake fingernails, each of them lined with tiny, hardened bubbles of glue.

"Tell *Mommy* what she wants to know," she said. "Chop, chop."

Keith yanked his hand away. "Fuck," he said. "You drew goddamn blood."

"You're such a boy. You don't even know what it is to bleed."

Jake assumed the blonde was her replacement.

The woman was three tables away, next to one of the big bay windows with a view of the first fairway. Beside her sat *The Pendulum's* new Editor-in-Chief — Fletcher Buckwalter — along with City Editor Neil Thrumming and another man she didn't know, more of a boy really, likely the new Keith.

The blonde had longer legs and shapelier hips than Jake. She looked to be younger too, a fresh college graduate, about 23, maybe 25, optimistically clad in a dry-clean-only outfit. That wouldn't last, not on *The Pendulum's* wages. The woman's eyeglasses were particularly offensive, the same kind of catty frames Jake had been wearing for years.

In contrast, the old Keith was nothing like the new one — a short-haired boy about the same age as the blonde. His shirt was a wrinkled white Oxford tucked into a pair of rumpled khakis. A reporter's notebook was sticking out his back pocket, its ringed binding hooked into the tail of his plaid club coat, identical to the coat the maitre d' had forced The Chief to wear. Jake imagined the two of them together in their plaid costumes and grinned until The Chief slapped his butter knife flat on the table.

"Your problem is you think this is all about you," he said. "You got this goddamn sense of entitlement."

Jake pulled her feet back beneath her chair and sipped her Perrier straight from the little green bottle. She didn't mention the new Jake or the new Keith or the new Chief just a few tables away. She just nodded in passive agreement and poked at the brown rice on her plate.

"I know what you think you were doing," The Chief said. "I was onto you from the start."

Jake tensed and froze. "Doing what?" she replied.

The Chief leaned his elbows on the table, clasped his hands and rested his chin on his knuckles.

"Everyone thinks what they do is so God-almighty important," he said. "You thought you'd change the world with a few phone calls and a couple open-records requests. You told yourself: 'Once this gets out, the people won't stand for it!' But you should've known better. You might've caused a few ripples and rocked a couple boats with a big story or two, but, girly, you're way too little to make waves."

Jake sat back, her head already starting to spin. She fought to control her breathing, to conceal her panic as she gripped the seat of her chair with both hands, still lucid enough to fear fainting forward into her brown rice. The worst of her worries was coming true. The Chief was about to call her out, to tell her he'd found the stories in her computer at work. Fuzzy as her head was in that moment, she could see the end and it was almost a relief. The Chief was turning her over. This was how he planned to redeem his career, by getting even. He'd pull Buckwalter into it too, no doubt. The Chief was not on Jake's side.

Keith was right. Keith was right.

"You've been away from the stink long enough to smell what you were shoveling," The Chief said. "You know. I know you know. I know what you know."

Jake had once read about a cancer victim who'd chronicled her chemo treatments for a newspaper, only to be outed more than a year later as a terminal wannabe. The woman had made it all up. She was never dying, had never had cancer. But there was no way out. Much as she had tried — quitting her job, moving away — her story had no ending. Readers demanded an ending. She'd betrayed them. She didn't keep her promise. She didn't die. Well-wishers became witch-hunters. Friends became enemies. Friends. Jake had none of those to lose, only Keith, and lately she'd begun to doubt he was ever her friend to begin with.

The Chief glanced toward Buckwalter's table across the dining room and stopped. His eyes narrowed and the wrinkles at the corners grew deeper.

"I read every e-mail," The Chief said, his attention still half diverted by the other table. "I read everyone's e-mail."

Jake objected. "I never put anything in e-mail," she said.

The Chief continued talking, seemed not to hear a word Jake said. "Judas, Brutus, Benedict Arnold … Different reasons, all personal," he said. "They all made it personal."

Jake stuttered. "But … I didn't. I never put anything in e-mail."

The Chief turned to her. "You weren't the first."

"I didn't want it for myself."

"That's exactly why you didn't get that pay raise," he said. "Reporters like you don't want money, or a house. If you wanted that you'd have picked another profession. You're smart enough. No, you wanted me to keep you hungry, but you didn't want to admit it. Giving you more money would've killed your motivation. It would've made you do some other stupid thing, like go and have a baby. A baby! You don't want a goddamn baby."

More threads snapped and the seams at the shoulders of The Chief's coat opened up, releasing blooms of yellow lining, like frilly epaulets.

"Then why do this now?" Jake said. "I did everything you asked. I made a mistake. It was stupid. I know. But, I was only trying to prove a point and I was trying to fix it and —"

"Goddammit!" The Chief said. "It doesn't matter that you quit. It wasn't a mistake to leave. Your mistake was thinking you could make a difference. You should've known better. Reporters got no say. All you had was a job."

Jake let go the seat of her chair. "You're not upset about the water and the —"

The Chief flipped his fingers toward her green water bottle and jiggled with laughter. "I don't give a good goddamn if you drink Perrier or pink champagne. It's on *The Pendulum's* tab, not mine."

"But the story —"

"Story?" The Chief said. "What fucking story?"

———————

Maxine's hand brushed the front of Keith's beige khakis as she pressed her body into his outside the service entrance to Yo Mahmah Sushi. She'd trapped him against the fender of her Land Rover, a doggie bag in his right hand, his other hand groping for leverage, to keep from falling. She smushed her icy cheek to his, huffed her hot breath across his lips and contaminated his senses with a scent of sick and cigarettes.

"Tell me the name," she said and squeezed the front of his pants harder in her fist, sending a spasm from his balls out to all four limbs and up the back of his neck.

"You've got to stop," Keith said and squirmed. "Now! Get your hand off my —"

Maxine gave a quick goodbye squeeze, then let up and stomped her foot so hard a hairspray-stiffened limb of hair dropped across her forehead.

"Is that it?" she shouted into his lips. "Is this 'good-fucking bye?'"

Keith whipped a finger to his mouth, to wipe away the spittle, but forgot the bag of sushi still in his hand. The bottom busted out. Broken Styrofoam and fish parts fell across his shoes and onto the pavement. Maxine bent over and reached for it.

Keith looked to the back of her head, half an inch of dark roots revealed at the part in her hair. "It's not goodbye," he said. "I don't want to upset you. Things are tense and —"

Sweat beads formed on Keith's forehead. For the first time he perceived Maxine as a threat, unstable, so opposite the predictable manipulator he'd believed she was. He tried to inch himself along the Land Rover's fender to move away from her, but she shot straight up and threw her purse on the hood, her arm blocking his escape.

"I know a fucking kiss-off when I see one," she said.

She shook a handful of white rice and gravel-encrusted tuna an inch from his chin. The raw red flesh hung limp between her fingers, the rice was mashed to a glutinous pulp that oozed across her thumb knuckle.

"You think you can end it like that?" she said. "You think I'm going to let you walk?"

Her pelvis bumped his hips and shoved him back against the Land Rover. Her hand returned to the front of his pants, the lumps of smelly fish and rice still between her fingers as she ground it into the fabric and his flaccidity underneath. She heaved and coughed and dropped her head to his shoulder. She convulsed with sobs and sniffled and rubbed her runny nose into his shirt.

"I don't know … what I'm gonna … do to … you … make me —"

Keith stood stiff, arms at his sides as she blubbered against him. "It's ok," he said. "It's me. It's the change, the new job and … and —"

He hesitated.

"— It's the baby," he said.

Maxine slurped and dragged her bottom lip across his collar. Keith felt the wetness soak through.

"I forgot the baby," she said. "But that's not the end of us. We can help each other. I got changes too. We've got new reporters who think they're God's gift. I've got to get that source. I need it. I deserve it for all the dookie I've been through Kiki."

Keith spied a man walking in their direction so he yanked Maxine by the elbow and pulled her into an alcove concealed by a curtain of bougainvillea.

"Be cool," he whispered as she pulled free.

Mashed remnants of raw tuna dripped from the front off his pants to the pavement as the two of them watched the man pass and continue down the alley.

"We're friends," he said and brushed at the remaining blobs of pink flesh, the rice now a hazy shadow on the fabric.

"So be my friend," Maxine told him. "Tell me."

He slipped his hands around her throat and pet it with his thumbs. "I'll tell you," he said.

"Who?" she rasped, her eyes bright.

"It's —"

He gave up Burton Brand, the director of the Mosquito Abatement District. The one who'd been in the car accident and ended up in a coma. The guy whose wife hit his car with hers and died at the scene.

"He doesn't know I'm Jake's husband," Keith said. "And I'm not supposed to know that he's her source. Jake doesn't even know that I know."

"Well ..." Maxine said and blinked both eyes over and over. "It's not like she and I talk or —"

"You have to promise to keep it to yourself."

"I promise. I promise. I even promise not to tell him I'm your lover. How's that?"

She pushed past Keith and out of the bougainvillea-draped alcove, back to the Land Rover and to her purse on the hood.

"Mommy's gotta go," she said.

Keith again scrubbed his fingers against the fishiness on his pants. When he looked up she was already behind the wheel.

"Love ya, mean it," she said, wiggling her fingers out the window. The tires spit gravel as she skittered away.

Keith kept his hands across the front of his pants as he walked quickly to the nearest Starbucks a block and a half away. He marched directly to the back, past the register and the espresso bar and into the bathroom. He switched on the light, locked the door and pulled a ballpoint from his pocket. He pressed the tip hard into the wall at eye level above the toilet and tried to write Maxine's home phone number, but his pen was out of ink.

———————

Fletcher Buckwalter approached Jake's table as The Chief was signing for the check.

"Life after newspapers," Buckwalter said. "I thought you'd be drinking beers in green bottles, not water."

The two young reporters stood quiet behind him. The young woman's grin had a nervousness about it, and the young man's hands were in and out of his pockets every few seconds. Jake caught his eyes licking the light cocoa skin of her knees, just above her turquoise-colored boots and beneath the hem of her light-brown skirt. She tilted her toes up slightly, wagging them at him until his cheeks went red.

"Fletcher Buckwalter," The Chief said. "You're starting out same as a puppy, I hear, already pissing all over the place. You think you're the first to change the comics page? It's all the same shit. You just wait. You're going to find out just how many people were reading that 'Darcy Mallnuts' strip you cut. You're going to get letters like you wouldn't believe. It's all been tried. You're gonna figure that out."

Buckwalter smirked, then jacked a thumb over his shoulder toward the young woman and the boy. "Got the new recruits on board," he said.

"Did you name them yet?" The Chief said.

The one with the eyes piped up first. "Michael," he said.

"Bobby," said the woman. "Bobby Fuchs."

The Chief picked a pinky nail into his teeth. Buckwalter turned, as if about to leave.

"Ever do any hunting?" The Chief asked.

Buckwalter spun back around. "Not a lot of hunters manage to stay married to vegans," he said. "Same with journalists, right Jacqueline? Not a lot of reporters stay married to flacks, unless they both convert."

Jake stretched her legs and let her skirt ride almost to mid thigh. The young man noticed and bounced his eyebrows.

"Ever hear of St. Matthew Island?" The Chief said. "Up in the Bering Sea?"

Buckwalter straightened his yellow-tinted eyeglasses on the bridge of his nose.

"My father was stationed there with the Coast Guard in WWII," The Chief said. "They put a couple dozen reindeer there as an emergency food source. Then the war ends and they abandon the reindeer. This island the size of Malibu's got no predators. It's Eden. All these deer got to do is eat and fuck. So, in 20 years, they overtake the place. We went back, my old man and me, in 1960. Must have been 50 deer on every square mile of that bump of dirt."

"I really have to —" Buckwalter said, but The Chief cut him off.

"This one guy says 'that's nature,'" The Chief said. "But, my old man says 'it's a fucking natural disaster.'"

Buckwalter raised his hands to the shoulders of each of his reporters and started to steer them out, only to stop again.

"You know what?" The Chief said. "You don't know shit. That's the whole point. Just like you, those deer didn't belong there, but they weren't smart enough to realize it. Someone else put them there. So, the deer just did what came natural — they fucked and ate the place down to the nubs. Then, whoosh — one hard winter comes and all the deer were wiped out. You know what their legacy was, Fletch? Not one deer survived. The whole fucking island is back to what it was, filled with artic foxes. The foxes were there before the deer, and the foxes lasted through all the snow and shit. The foxes waited. They waited for the deer to die and then they ate the goddamn deer. Now, you tell me — What do you know, Fletch?"

Buckwalter tapped the bulge of the cigarette box in the breast pocket of his suit coat. "Well," he said. "I know I've got a newspaper to put out."

The Chief launched to his feet as Buckwalter made his way toward the entrance with the two reporters on each side. "You're too stupid to see why they put you here," The Chief shouted across the dining room. "You don't belong. Go ahead, graze the place down to nubs.

Fuck yourself into oblivion. I'll wait. I'll wait and pick your hollow vegan bones. I was here before you, goddammit. I was here before you and I'll be here after you!"

Jake pulled her skirt back over her knees and stayed seated as The Chief knocked over his chair, tore off the shredded, plaid club coat and threw it at the floor. He offered Jake no handshake, no "goodbye," not even a look as he stormed out the emergency exit and set off the alarm.

The maitre d' rushed to Jake's side and shouted over the door buzzer: "Who doth that man think he ith?"

"I guess I don't really know," Jake said. "But I don't think he does either."

Secret Offers Not So Secret As Thought

By Maxine Lugner
Pendulum Staff Writer

Real estate agents in Waters End say buyers shouldn't assume that their secret bids stay secret for long.

"Spit handshakes and spoken promises are for playgrounds," said one agent, who spoke on condition of anonymity. "I work on a commission. I'm here to make money, not friends. You want bargains? Go shop eBay."

Randy Lamont, who lives in the commmunity of Walden, learned from experience when he bid $1.2 million on a three-bedroom house, only to lose it when his agent betrayed his confidence to another client, who was willing to pay more.

"I wish I'd thought of it first," Lamont said.

Please turn to page A12

CHAPTER 11 – STORE-BOUGHT CAKE

The spark in The Unabomber's eyes made Maxine go wobbly in her chair.

He stood silent beside her desk, an oversized hoodie shading his face, the sleeves so long they hung past his knuckles. He kept his right arm stiff as he raised it, one skinny pale digit pointing out his cuff at the oblong box on Maxine's mouse pad. Afterten's coffee cake. She'd purchased it on special at the Raleigh's grocery store down the street.

"Second breakfasts?" he said.

Maxine looked to his fingernails, all painted black. The white iPod ear buds dangling out of his hoodie looked almost like earrings.

All of a sudden, after weeks of nothing, there he was, blurting out question after question. "Elevenses? Luncheon? Afternoon tea? Dinner? Supper?"

Maxine felt so excited to finally make contact that she could barely breathe. "Yes," she whispered. "You can … Cake for you."

He lowered his arm and turned his mouth down. "Not into Tolkien?" he said.

"Are you kidding?" Maxine replied, her voice restored. "I *tolk* in my sleep. I'll *tolk* you silly. You're the one who never does any *tolk*ing. All you ever say is 'reboot,' and you haven't even said *that* to me."

The Unabomber laughed a laugh that sounded sweetly similar to a whinny, then pulled up a chair and pried at the lid of the box. He offered to share the crumb-covered, cheese-filled strip of cake, but Maxine shook her head, her lips pursed as she watched him stuff the first bite between his teeth.

"It's after midnight," she said. "I never eat this late."

Crumbles and puffs of powdered sugar fell to the desktop and she brushed them away, less concerned about neatness than the way the sugar stood out against the granulated contents of the two Ritalin capsules she'd emptied on the cake out in the Land Rover. The dome light had tricked her, concealed a contrast as subtle as the difference between arrowroot and table salt. Not that it mattered. The Unabomber appeared oblivious, the whole of his mouth ringed in white.

"Reboot," he said and laughed again.

Maxine pushed the box of cake closer to him and scanned the length of the newsroom, to be sure they were alone. Two copy editors loitered a dozen desks away, proofing the first few papers to come off the presses, the last step before putting the whole thing to bed. So long as they detected no major misspellings, or bad story jumps, both men would be gone in time to make last call at the first bar across the county line. Maxine had memorized the drill. Fifteen minutes to go. She tapped the space bar of her keyboard and heaved a sigh.

"I wish I could *tolk* to my computer," she said.

"Reboot," The Unabomber mumbled and snorted through the mush of half-chewed cake.

Maxine giggled then tried to speak the language she'd heard the copy desk speak whenever something went wrong. "It's not a 'meltdown,'" she said. "No 'blue screen of death.' No 'bad command' either. I just can't find … the *hard* thingie."

"I can teach you," The Unabomber said and shoved another hunk in his mouth. "Piece of cake."

Maxine had worked 14 days straight to get this close, far longer than she expected it to take. Methods of persuasion that had previously worked without fail on men in management had proved useless in her effort to

168   TJ SULLIVAN

sway the 20-something boys who controlled *The Pendulum's* computer universe. The entire lot kept to themselves, a clique so tight that no one outside their ranks seemed to know their real names. Other than trips to the soda machine and the men's room, they stayed sequestered in that windowless den of theirs, staring at super-sized monitors beneath the twinkling of a hundred tiny lights on giant, electronic wall panels. When called upon by writers and editors in distress, the boys in the IS Department responded first by phone, and always with that most special word — reboot — the meaning of which Maxine deduced to be *"turn off and try again."* When that failed, one boy would emerge to commandeer the corrupted workstation and proceed to make it right without explanation. Maxine needed more than that. She had to find a way into one of their heads.

She'd targeted The Unabomber because he worked the worst hours. As the lone late-night occupant of IS, he'd seemed easier to coax in secret than any of his daytime counterparts. Maxine had stalked him from afar at first, pretending to work overtime at her desk as he bopped from computer to computer. Night after night, the look of entrancement on The Unabomber's face had slowly burned itself into Maxine's brain. She'd watched as he pecked keyboards and inserted disks that made the monitors display bizarre geometric patterns. He'd demonstrated the necessary proficiency, but his aversion to eye contact had confounded her efforts to exploit his talents.

Maxine had resorted to basics at first, broke out her baking pans and whipped up an assortment of sweets intended to attract a growing boy's attention. But all she managed to catch was extra-special treatment from the janitorial service worker, who'd never before cleaned her phone so thoroughly or frequently. Her next step had been to dye her hair a brighter shade of blonde, but that went horribly wrong, the result of some drug-store prankster switching the contents of the box, and yet, the store refused to exchange it. If only every problem could be solved by a bottle of Oops.

She'd discovered the coffee-cake solution during her final act of desperation. Lost for options, Maxine had armed herself with one of Stan's flashlights and rifled through the trash baskets in the IS office. The Unabomber had been called out at the time, to attend to a newsroom meltdown so serious it threatened to push the press operators into overtime. The empty Aftertén's box buried in the trash had winked at her, despite being partially covered by several crushed Mountain Dew cans, five Magna comics, and a broken *Marion Ravenwood* figurine from the *Raiders of the Lost Ark* collection. It was no wonder he'd refused her homemade treats. The poor pale kid was the product of a processed environment.

The Unabomber lingered beyond the last bite of coffee cake, contentedly digesting as Maxine praised and probed him with questions about computer navigation. The distance between them shrank with his every response until, eventually, her beleaguered hair brushed his cheek. She placed his hand over hers and urged him to help guide the mouse in tandem. He dropped his hood after that, revealing a face of fair skin contrasted by bushy eyebrows and a shaggy head of hair, both black as boot polish.

His name was Norman Palm. He could spell in binary code and was one semester away from his degree at UCLA. His parents had promised to buy him a red Porsche for graduation, not exactly like the one Bill Gates drove, but as close as his uncle the car broker could get. The most harrowing moment of his life was the time he was nearly arrested at a California DMV office for insisting his home address *really* was "127.0.0.1." His heroes, in order of preference, were Tolkien, Gates, Peter Jackson, Kevin Smith and Emo Phillips. His favorite book was *The Cuckoo's Egg* by Cliff Stoll, and his favorite movie was *The Matrix*. For all the actors he could have picked, he liked Doris Day. He told Maxine she sounded just like her when she whispered, so she whispered just for him as she asked him to share his turn-ons.

"Kissing and cuddling," he said and blushed.

"*Kay Sarah Sarah*," Maxine said and gave her chair an awkward scoot, bumping her cool cheek to his warm one.

Sweet nothings and tender touches filled the three nights of tutorials that followed as The Unabomber helped Maxine locate not one, but four stories on the hard drive of Jake's computer, each of which opened as promised with the password "pop." Why Jake broke the whole thing up into four parts made little sense, unless she'd been vying for her own special section, or a series spread out over four days.

Such an ego, that one.

Buckwalter wanted a single story with everything, which was exactly what Maxine would give him — one cataclysmic collection of cover-ups that included a nuclear meltdown, perchlorate contamination, a petroleum spill and the intentional negligent use of fungicides by area farmers.

Maxine cut and pasted all the important bits into one document, then permanently purged the files from Jake's computer with The Unabomber's help. He promised her a "35 pass overwrite" to clear it from the memory banks.

"It means I'll erase it a lot," he explained.

"The future's not theirs to see," Maxine whispered and planted a kiss on his forehead.

"Ours," he corrected. "Not *ours* to see."

Maxine winked. "It's not us I'm concerned about, baby boy. It's a newsroom. You can't trust anybody in here."

The night on which Maxine planned to cut The Unabomber loose she found the IS office lit by electric candles with a blanket on the floor beside a box of coffee cake and a six-pack of a syrupy, red energy drink.

"Four nights," he said. "Our first non-prime anniversary."

Maxine agreed to stay, but opted for the fancy Aeron chair instead of the blanket on the floor. It took her almost 20 minutes to get The Unabomber to sit still, and another 20 minutes after that to complete a cold-fingered handjob through the zippered fly of his camo pants. But this too was absolutely necessary.

"Pull it, sir," she wheezed. "Pull it, sir. I am going to win the Pull-It-Sir Prize, aren't I Normy?"

The Unabomber responded with what resembled a gurgle, then a sigh, then a gasp.

"Reboot," he whispered. "Reboot."

Maxine smirked, smeared her hands clean with a blue handkerchief, then slipped it into a sandwich bag.

"That's all now," she said as she pinched the seal shut. "Not a word to anyone about you helping me, or me helping you. We don't want anyone in HR to find out about your little meltdown just now. I'd hate for the mess you made in my hands to mess up your plans for that red car, or your graduation."

The Unabomber sunk back into his hood and handed Maxine the unopened box of Afterten's cake.

Maxine pushed it back at him. "Now, now," she said. "You've got your whole future to be with all kinds of people, unless you screw it up with me."

———————

The double doors of Crestcare Medical Center parted as Maxine flicked the butt of a half-smoked Dunhill into the stony flowerbed outside. She marched into the lobby, a frosted sheet cake balanced on one hand, and breezed past the candy striper at the information desk. One of the three elevators sat open and waiting. She stepped into it, pushed the button for the fourth floor and blew a kiss to some guy working a floor buffer down the hall. If she was going to play the part of a rich relative she'd have to be especially nice to the help.

Maxine had taken extra care to dress the part. She wore makeup so thick it altered her complexion from white to peach, and donned dark sunglasses big enough to cover the tops of her cheeks. The long, black cashmere shawl that draped her spandex pants was intended to complete a look somewhere between heiress and Dame. The trick, Maxine decided, was not to sneak, but to ramble, to behave like a woman comfortable with her station in life. If she believed she belonged, everyone else would too. Burton Brand would have to appreciate her going to all that trouble. He'd have to talk to her then.

She found his room without incident, then sat beside the mechanical bed and looked him over. She knew him better than anyone she'd ever interviewed, had accessed every news and feature story written about him since he took charge of the Waters End Mosquito Abatement District. But for all Maxine knew about *who* Burton was, she had no idea *how* he was. Keith's report of the auto accident said Burton's wife had died and that Burton was admitted to intensive care. That's it. No follow-up, no condition. Maxine didn't dare risk rejection by asking for more. A call to the medical center's spokesperson, or a nursing supervisor, would only have given Burton a chance to say "no." Better to simply show up. She had a way with men like that. She had a way of getting her way.

"You poor thing," Maxine cooed as she scooted her chair closer to Burton's bed. "They got you drugged, don't they?"

She fished in her purse for her supply of Ritalin LA, which she'd replenished over the weekend, popped two capsules into her mouth and considered briefly what might happen if she shared one with Burton. It always made her feel so much more conversational, so focused on even the most boring things. Both Burton's eyes and mouth were open, as though he expected her to share. His skin looked healthy enough. His hair was combed and his face had been shaven. No lumps, bumps or bandages. Although a couple of tubes and wires snaked out of his bed shirt, it was nowhere near as bad as what they showed on TV doctor dramas. The way he mumbled and gurgled sounded like a song. Maxine wondered if her costume reminded him of his wife.

"She's looking down on you," Maxine whispered. "She's happy that you're doing the right thing, that you're talking to the newspaper like this. I'll help you do good. I promise."

Maxine moved to the door, cracked it open and peered up the hall to the nurse's station. Staffers had already found the sheet cake she'd purchased from the bakery at First Harvest Grocery. She'd personalized the top, pushed in 329 Red Hots candy dots, one dot short of the number necessary to spell "THANKS A BUNCH," which she hadn't realized until the last letter. She'd improvised and nudged a couple dots to turn the "H" into an "O." It spelled: THANKS A BUNCO. *Close enough.*

Returning to the chair beside Burton's bed, Maxine slid forward and bumped the guardrail on accident with her shoulder, moving the bed several inches. Tubes and wires clanked against metal hooks and rods, a flash of fuzz appeared on the readout of the green machine that beeped, and Burton's head rolled to the side, pointing his open eyes right at Maxine's chest. She pulled her shawl across her front and giggled.

Old men always stare. Always.

"I was a friend of Jake at *The Pendulum*," Maxine said. "Jake's not with us anymore, so … I've taken over. I'm your reporter."

Burton's chest rose and fell in that same steady rhythm. Drool dripped out his mouth and his gassy song stopped.

"You haven't asked me to leave, so you must want me to stay," Maxine said. "Is that right? You want me to stay?"

She drew the shawl back off her chest, exposing again the shiny valley of puffy flesh between her breasts.

Burton did not react, just continued to stare dead straight.

"I saw this once in a movie," Maxine said. "I'm going to go over everything, all the facts about how the water got poisoned. I'll tell you how the whole thing was covered up, and, if you don't stop me, that means the story is right. If there's anything wrong, then you start singing, or humming. OK? If it's wrong, you sing like before. That way you won't be telling me anything. You'll just be singing, or not singing. I know how this stuff works. You can trust me. OK? I'm just going to start."

The green machine above Burton continued to beep as Maxine pulled out a copy of her story and began to read aloud. All 70 column inches of text were shared, as promised, from the part about the secret dumps, to the unreported nuclear accidents, to the unheeded hazards. Bullet by bullet Maxine looked to Burton's face. He was rapt.

Just as Maxine finished, a gnat flew between Burton's lips. She jumped to the edge of her seat and looked inside after it, then tucked his chin to close his mouth.

"That's that," she said and stood. "I brought a cake. I left it down the hall."

Burton's head rolled back the other way, his eyes closed and his mouth opened.

"Ahhhhhhhhh," he said.

"Now, now," Maxine said. "I'll be back. I promise."

Off-Shore Quake Saps Water Wells In The Knolls

By Bobby Fuchs
Pendulum Staff Writer

State geologists say an off-shore earthquake caused the catastrophic loss of all well water in The Knolls, threatening the health and welfare of residents in that portion of Waters End.

Although about half the homes in The Knolls are located within city limits, efforts to extend city water and sewer lines to those dwellings have been hampered for years by activists who claim such a move would make the area more attractive to developers, and, as a result, force out working families and older residents.

The loss of well water last month, however, has dramatically changed the situation and reinvigorated the city's efforts at annexation.

Mayor Chick Nimbus says the move is "critical."

"These *wack*-tivists made a mess of this," he said. "But, the city will make it right."

Please turn to page A13

CHAPTER 12 – DIRT RULES

Jake drove the Corolla north in a trance, surfing the long shadows of early morning up Highway 101 from Reseda to the far side of Waters End. Her face was slack, half hypnotized by reflector-flecked signs and painted lines, the route so familiar her hands and feet could have done the drive solo so long as her eyes remained open. Without thinking to do it, she soared up the same exit ramp she'd ascended every morning for five years and bombed through the same streets of the same downtown, hesitating only at the corner of Apple and Main, her arms so conditioned to turn into *The Pendulum's* lot that her muscles tensed even when she wasn't at the wheel. She corrected the mistake before she made it and continued past the newspaper building and City Hall.

The city was the same as always, though the further she got from her old routine, the more foreign it appeared. She cruised beyond the first of the phase-one subdivisions to the latest fully-wired residences — high-tech domiciles strung together with fiber optics and tricked out with 24-hour surveillance cameras at every right angle. Within minutes she was flying through the forlorn beige blur of neighborhoods so new that all the trees were leafless saplings and the stuccoed sound walls were bare of bougainvillea. The houses dwindled soon after that, but the painted lines went on and so did Jake, the road bisecting a fresh crop of surveyor stakes, their Day-Glo orange plastic blossoms flapping in the breeze.

Then her calm journey exploded into a calamity.

The steering wheel shook and the metal Starbucks' mug in the cup holder spat bursts of day-old coffee. The ribbed rubber collar around the gear shift was soaked, same as the knobs for the heat and the air. The pile of new mail Jake had placed on the passenger seat flew in every direction, fliers and envelopes suddenly all over the front and back of the car. Her ring of keys remained in the ignition, all those jagged pieces of metal flogging the steering column so hard that silvery scratches began to wink through the flat black paint. The brown hills in the distance seemed to slide counterclockwise at first, then disappeared altogether in an amber cloud of dust. Jake jerked her head around, unsure where to look, her mind jammed by too many possibilities. The car was fishtailing, but what was it? *A blowout? An earthquake? An eruption?*

Her arms and legs moved without prior calculation. Her foot pumped the brake and her fingers gripped the wheel, directing the tires into the skid. When the Corolla finally crunched to a stop it was face to face with a tractor in a field across a culvert. She was on the edge, but not quite over it.

The person inside the machine slid open a window and looked out. It was a brown-skinned man in a baseball cap. He cupped both hands to his mouth and shouted. "*¿Que paso?* You OK?"

Jake rolled down her window, lifted herself halfway out to answer and shouted back. "OK. Thank you. Where is this? *¿Dónde?*"

The man pulled his ball cap off and laughed hard, his white teeth bright in the sunlight. "*Aguas Final, Gringa,*" he said and slipped back into the tractor's cab.

Jake waved, spit the bitter taste of dust out her window and rolled it closed. The tractor was answer enough. It told her she was where she meant to be — alongside the last farm on the old road out of Waters End. Maggie had told her what to look for: "*Keep on past the pavement, all the way across the washboard, and don't expect no signs.*" From Jake's side of the hill it was the only way into The Knolls.

Jake cursed at herself. Had she paid attention, the spinout never would have happened. She grew up on dirt. She knew the rules were different. Logical as it seemed to hit the brakes and decelerate when confronted by bumps, what felt right was wrong when it came to dirt. The education cost her $100 the summer she turned 16 — the cost of a new drive shaft for her father's pickup.

Jake restarted the Corolla and backed away from the culvert. She applied steady pressure to the accelerator and let the shock-absorbers work. The tires jumped from bump to bump, the speedometer hit 45 mph, and the tremors of the choppy road were transformed to a soothing vibration.

Over the first hill and through a grove of mature eucalyptus trees, the first signs of life in The Knolls emerged. Warped longboards stood propped against clapboard houses and metal mailboxes gawked with open mouths, their sides tattooed with names and decorations — peace-symbols, yellow smiley faces, and faded "Brown For President" bumper stickers. Jake had met him when he ran for president. She'd shaken his hand once in Santa Fe and always remembered what he'd said: *"We have to deal with where we are."*

Satellite dishes commanded most front yards in The Knolls, their circumference as substantial as tractor tires. Stubbly fields separated houses and vegetable gardens ringed by wooden stakes tied round with ragged lengths of twine. The whole place appeared as a colorized reproduction of Jake's northern New Mexico home — all the brown swapped for green, the squat piñons stretched into leggy eucalyptuses. The Knolls was an oasis.

Politicians and editors did not count The Knolls as part of "Waters End *proper*," despite the fact that almost half of it lay within the city limits. Shared control was no control, a characteristic that cemented sub-suburban status for The Knolls — an unofficial no man's land. In legal terms, nearly half the residents of the community were bound to abide by city laws and codes, like the rules that dictated the height of hedges, or where inoperable vehicles were permitted to be parked. In practice, however, legality morphed into abstract reality. The unincorporated, non-city section ruled the whole place, which meant no rules applied. No newcomers dared to enter. Although legions of suburban trailblazers skilled in the artful use of attorneys and razor wire existed throughout Southern California, Waters End officials considered the potential for confrontation reason enough to put a halt on permits. A moratorium on new construction had been in effect for almost 15 years.

Mayor Nimbus degraded the place as "The Gnomes," a nook where bumpy people lived shaky lives. The local cops pilloried their partial jurisdiction as untenable, called The Knolls a haven for halfwits and ne'er-do-wells. The newsroom engendered the worst of it. Events that rated as front-page news elsewhere were mostly considered a nuisance when they occurred in The Knolls. Reporters and photographers were conditioned to perk at every prolonged squawk of the police scanner, but rookies were ceremoniously ridiculed if they paid any attention to a disturbance on Lookout Road. *Nothing but tweekers and bangers up there*, or so the copy desk said. The attitude was as infectious as it was toxic, and Jake proved to be as susceptible as the rest. She didn't choose to believe it, she just did. No investigative urges were suppressed or denied on her part. The inspiration just never came. Jake followed the journalistic mantra "follow the money," but no money trails ever led in or out of The Knolls. As far as Waters End was concerned, the city terminated where the road turned to dirt. Clichés kept the curious away. No one wanted to be the guy who *stuck his nose where it didn't belong ... had no business being there in the first place ... got what he deserved.*

Eucalyptus trees shrouded Lookout Road in a cave-like darkness as Jake rolled past Maggie's mailbox, a red one with no name, just the silhouette of an Aztec eagle painted within a circle of white. It was half past seven, too early to knock, so Jake pulled the Corolla over, across from a rickety roadside sign that had just enough letters missing to make its barbershop advertisement read: "BAR----HOP O--N WEEKENDS." She left the engine running for the heat and jumped at the sudden slap of fat raindrops on the windshield as they fell from the branches above. She laughed and looked to the mess of mail on the floor. She had more than enough time to sort it out.

The bulk of the mail was trash — circulars from hardware superstores and postcards from real estate agents. Two pre-approved credit card applications from the same bank promised her two different interest rates, each of which was touted as "the lowest rate guaranteed." A full-bleed flier from Pinston-Schilling Realty depicted a house engulfed in flames beneath the caption: "Don't get burned, sell while it's hot." And a rack card from an air-and-heating service boasted of odor-free employees, as though the handyman industry was rife with smelly ones. Most shocking, however, was how easily accessible Jake's new address appeared to be. Her Waters End post office box was less than three weeks old, and already it had attracted more direct-mail than she'd ever received in LA. Keith had insisted the box in Waters End was worth the trouble, said an address in town would establish the appearance of success — temporarily, of course, until they grounded their new life with the purchase of a house. All the box provided so far, however, was a heap of refuse.

Jake tore through the stack like an automaton until she reached the envelope with a curious pink cow in the upper left corner. She recognized it only after she'd torn it in two. *The first paycheck. Destroyed.* Her initial reaction was relief. At least Keith was not around to witness it.

The pink cow was the COW Co. logo, and COW Co. was Jake's and Keith's new employer, which was as much as Jake knew about it. For all the investigative energy she used to expend in her journalistic pursuits, she'd done nothing but bite her tongue before leaping into her new career. Avoidance was both her goal and all the new job required. Each day consisted of making phone calls, writing letters, retrieving mail, and returning to bed. Except for her networking luncheons, contact with others was minimal. Some days all she said was "yes," and sometimes "paper" or "plastic." Her most complex, routine challenge became the choice between standard or commemorative postage stamps. Even the conflict in her marriage had disappeared in the weeks since departing *The Pendulum*. Had The Mayor e-mailed a request for Jake to dig a hole she'd have dug it without concern for what he intended to bury, or uncover. The sole purpose of her new life — as Keith repeated daily — was to get paid. But, now she'd screwed that up too.

Jake puzzled the torn pieces together in her lap to discover more than she requested, not one check, but two — a total of $16,000 — two weeks compensation plus a $10,000 "signing bonus," as designated on the stub. Her hands quivered as she lifted the pieces up to look closer. It was more money than the Corolla had cost, more than she and Keith had saved in five years. Much as she'd demonized it, money felt good.

The tree branches above the car swished and swayed. More fat drops fell and hit the windshield like face slaps. *Stupid. Stupid. Stupid.* She was in The Knolls. Suddenly all those newsroom tales of methamphetamine addicts and rapists came to life in her head. *The Knolls.* Torn or not, voided or otherwise, a paycheck was reason enough to get killed in The Knolls.

Nothing but tweekers and bangers up there.

Jake bucked up and laughed as she reached absently for her Starbucks mug. "Tweekers," she muttered and sucked a shock of cold, bitter coffee across her tongue. Three sharp cracks against the passenger window made her jerk. She dropped the mug in her lap, dribbled coffee down her chin, and let loose the pieces of the paychecks.

A man was standing outside the window.

"Open up," he said and mimicked the cranking of the handle against the glass.

Jake stared at his hands, the fingernails caked with what looked to be grease, or blood. A black smudge darkened his cheek and his eyes were ringed in pink, obviously irritated and blearily trained on Jake's lap. Her hands flew to the upturned mug, the last of the coffee now a dark stain the size of a big hand on her white skirt. The man huffed and stomped around to the driver's side. Again he made a cranking motion with one hand while the other tapped the glass. The ring on his middle finger made the knocks more drastic.

"What?" Jake said and rubbed desperately at the stain in her lap.

"Roll it down," he said.

"What do you want?"

"Listen lady, I'm not going to hurt you."

Jake's catty eyeglasses slid down her nose. "Why are you doing this to me?"

The man pet the stubble on his cheeks then held his jaw between forefinger and thumb. "I'm Maggie's brother," he said. "She saw you out the window; asked me to get you; said you're that newspaper woman friend of hers."

Friend.

Jake fumbled to unlock the door, her face hot and her fingers numb. The moment the door was open the torn pieces of the checks took flight on the breeze. She let them go, stepped out and put herself between the car and the door.

"I'm so, so sorry," she said. "I didn't know Maggie had a brother. Or, I didn't know that he was you, or that you were him. I'm Jake. I mean, hi, I'm Jake."

She offered her hand to shake, but the man pointed to the paychecks dancing across the dashboard. Jake jumped in after them and, following several fitful grabs, managed to snag every piece. She stuffed her catch into her purse, turned off the engine, then shut the door without locking it.

The man pointed again.

"It'll be OK," she told him. "There's nothing in there."

"Nothing, huh?" he replied and pulled the door back open. "I caught a crankster in my truck last week and he said 'nothing' was exactly what he was looking for."

He gave her a wink and a grin as he locked the door and slammed it closed.

Jake looked to his left hand and the ring that had cracked against the window — a turquoise stone with silver inlay. There was no wedding band.

"I'm Jake," she said again. "Jake LaMotta."

He did a double take, then appeared to think better of it as he swiped his hand down the front of his shirt and took hold of her fingers. "Yeah, Jake," he said. "I guessed that. I'm Maggie. I mean, I'm Manny, Maggie's my sister."

"*Mija!*"

Maggie's embrace was soft and warm, so soothing it filled Jake with sorrow for how long she'd gone without a hug. "Holden's late," Maggie said, "but we got coffee."

Jake took a seat at the round kitchen table, careful to keep her hands in her lap to cover the coffee stain, the heels of her turquoise-colored boots together on the floor.

"Holden?"

Maggie giggled. "My friend, Holden Woodcock. *Eee*, you think with a name like that he worries about splinters?"

Maggie's brother grabbed her shoulders from behind and gave her a playful shake. "She's only doing that because I'm here," he said. "Maggie thinks her mouth is too small for bar soap."

BOON   **183**

Maggie grabbed hold of Manny's right wrist, held his grimy hand up and winked at Jake. "Does this look like the hand of a man who knows how to handle soap? Eee, my bro is *loco*."

Jake watched as Manny slipped out the screen door and disappeared beneath the open hood of a yellow pickup out back.

"He's widowed," Maggie said quietly.

Jake scooted her chair to the table. "What?" she said. "I mean no. No. I'm not looking."

"Of course. He says the same thing."

Maggie's kitchen was a virtual peninsula, surrounded on three sides by five-gallon bottles of water stacked one atop the other, all sideways in square plastic crates, red caps pointed out. Jake counted 45 bottles, not including those in the bed of the yellow pickup. Besides that, the kitchen was equipped like no other Jake had seen in anyone's home. Mixing bowls and bags of flour littered the counter between cooling racks loaded with cookies, churros, and muffins. There were cartons of eggs and milk, and a frying pan on the stove, right next to a plate of fresh tortillas. The adjoining living room, which consumed the remainder of the first floor, was equally cluttered. Post-it notes hung like droopy yellow ears from the fireplace mantle and an overloaded bookshelf. A desk equipped with a computer monitor and a stack of photocopied documents sat alongside an entertainment unit of unfinished pine. The television was tuned to the "Today Show," its volume up just enough to be audible in the kitchen. The weatherman was judging a pie contest in Pennsylvania.

Jake pointed to the bottles. "That your earthquake stash?" she asked.

"No, *Mija*. That's why you're here," Maggie replied. "You're gonna tell the world what Nimbus did to us, and those bottles are part of it."

Jake combed her fingers through her hair and pulled her ponytail apart. "Maggie, I'm —"

The oven-door hinges creaked as Maggie pulled it open to retrieve a tray of muffins. "If you're hungry, I've got potatoes cooked up," she said. "Eggs are easy. And I've got warm tortillas. Every day is a delivery day, so —"

Jake wrung one hand in the other above her stained skirt. "I really only want to borrow a towel," she said.

Maggie looked to the stain and immediately pulled a soup bowl from the cupboard. She filled it with water from a cooler beside the sink, then grabbed a towel from the oven door handle. "We'll make it OK, *Mija*," she said and mixed salt into the bowl.

Jake dampened the towel and pet it gently to her skirt.

"Manny's got a box of Borax," Maggie said. "And Bernie's got a bleach stick upstairs. The washer don't work without water, but I'm going to a laundromat in Woodland Hills later on today."

Jake turned up quickly, her forehead wrinkled.

Maggie grinned. "Bernie's his daughter. She and Manny been here with me since he sold the farm."

Jake returned to working the stain, her gentle strokes getting more firm.

"Holden's gonna cheer us up," Maggie said. "He's gotta say Nimbus did it. Water don't run dry for no reason. I've never seen it. It's not logical. Plain unnatural."

The stain looked worse to Jake. She grabbed the salt shaker and shook it directly over the fabric.

"*Pinche* speculators," Maggie said. "The day this whole place gets annexed we'll have building inspectors, police dogs, cops with shotguns ... *Cucarachas*. They'll put us out for every little thing, for Chevys up on blocks, for old trucks with flat tires. One of them tried to red tag my house for an orange extension cord I had strung out to the shed. Said I wasn't 'up to code.' Code. You know what 'code' is code for? It means you ain't rich."

Jake let up on the stain, took a deep breath and glanced out the screen door to the clicking sounds of socket wrenches coming from under the open hood of Manny's yellow truck. Much as Maggie might have had a point about code enforcement, she stood little chance of discrediting the city's claim of being on the side of public good. The law was the law. Jake hadn't the heart to tell her what she already knew.

"Nimbus wants to turn the whole place into one of those arty farty paintings they sell in shopping malls," Maggie said. "They'll slap up some stucco, a couple fake lantern streetlights, and a few vigas and give us some *loco* name like 'Amber Blossom Estates,' or 'Stepping Stone Acres.' No more Knolls. That's for sure."

Jake scrubbed harder, exposing her kneecaps as the skirt rode up.

"Developers," Maggie said. "They threw their rings in the hat a long time ago."

Jake wrung the towel and applied more salt to the stain. Maggie offered to soak it, said she'd get Bernie to lend Jake something to wear, then shuffled through the living room toward a stairway nook that Jake hadn't noticed before. "Bernie!" Maggie yelled. "That hotel man's gonna fire you if you keep going late."

After a long pause she yelled again: "Bernie!"

Somewhere far above came the muffled reply: "It's a motel, *Tia*," the voice said. "I wish that assclown *would* fire me!"

Several minutes later, Bernie bounced down into the living room.

"*Tia!* Stop yelling," Bernie said.

"This is our source of thunder," Maggie said to Jake. "Hard on the house, and a head as hard as her papa's."

"Oh, wow," Bernie said as she leaned to shake Jake's hand. "That stain is hella ugly."

Jake scrunched her mouth, covered the spot with the towel and looked into Bernie's eyes. They were the bluest Jake had ever seen.

Maggie jingled a set of keys and told Bernie to take the car out front. "Your papa's working on the truck and I'm gonna need it to haul more water. But get Jake something to wear before you go, so I can soak that skirt."

Jake preferred not to stay, but had no place else to go and didn't want to lie. "All I need is maybe another towel," she said.

"*Es* housekeeping," Bernie joked in a mock Spanish accent. "You want *toallas*?"

Maggie bubbled into a giggle and covered her mouth, as if embarrassed by her own laughter. "Take your wallet," she told Bernie. "I'm serious and you know it. I don't want to get no collect call from Tijuana."

"*Tia*. You're old school," Bernie said and flipped back her hair. "*La Migra* never messes with motel maids. Besides, all I'd have to do is explain. Like I even *sound* Mexican."

Bernie bounded back up and through the house, thumped the length of the upstairs and returned with a pair of baby-blue sweat pants. Jake draped them across the back of her chair as Bernie flashed a two-fingered peace sign and left through the back door.

Maggie wiggled a finger at the sweats. "Upstairs, first door on the left," she said. "Put that skirt on the sink and I'll get the water and Borax. I'm good at getting things out."

A fuzzy old man was in Jake's seat when she returned from changing into the sweats. He looked at least 80, maybe 90. So thin and bald on top. Harmless. What little hair he had was curly and gray. His skin bunched in the wrinkles that ran across his forehead and up the middle of his chin. He burst into a big, brown smile as soon as he managed to draw focus on Jake through the smudgy lenses of his wire-rimmed spectacles.

"This little Bernie?" he said and lacquered her with moony eyes. "You grew like a weed, Thumper. You remember me? You probably don't like people calling you 'Thumper' no more, do you?"

Jake drummed her fingers on her bottom lip to keep from laughing.

Maggie set a mug of coffee on a saucer in front of the old man. "Oh, Holden! Stop," she said. "You know good and well this is my reporter friend. I just got done telling you Bernie was off to work. I know what you're up to, and you're not about to make me feel guilty. She was late. It ain't my fault. You'll see her some other time. You know how that girl gets. She wasn't even born on time."

Holden snickered and raised his right arm to offer Jake a handshake. "Holden Woodcock," he said, suddenly all sober and serious. "You spell that 'E-N,' like the actor, not 'I-N-G,' like the asset."

"Holden …" Maggie said.

Jake gave the drawstring waistband of the sweats a tug and took the seat beside Holden. He had a stack of papers in his lap and flipped through them between sips, his bulbous nose inches from each page as he squinted at scribbled numbers and notes in the margins.

"I don't share data," he said. "Not with reporters especially."

"That's just it," Jake said. "I'm not a reporter anymore, so —"

"But," Holden said in a raised voice, "because the state saw fit to release its findings to the papers yesterday, I might give you mine. Only because you know Maggie, and because my data is more complete."

Jake turned to face him, then couldn't seem to look away. Coarse gray hair shot out his ear canal like clumps of ponytail grass. The back of his neck was a downy blur. Both ends of his jawbone sprouted crops of slate-black hair. His eyebrows were yet another color, reddish blond, same as his nose hairs, which fluttered when he spoke. Jake wished she had a camera, not to show his picture to other people, but because it was rude to stare and she wanted to look closer.

She gripped her knees through the blue sweats and rocked forward, her bare toes spread like fingers on the floor. "I'm not a reporter," she said. "I'm a —"

"She's a friend," Maggie said.

Holden wiggled his left pinky finger into his ear. "We're not at the end," he said. "You have to listen, not just hear. It's the same as the state said. It's uncertain how long it's going to be until anyone knows when the end will come."

Jake and Maggie raised eyebrows at each other as Holden erupted with a severe cough. Maggie rushed him a glass of water, but he shooed her away and spat into a hankie.

"I'm not dying," he said.

"You better not," Maggie told him. "Not until we bury Nimbus."

He spat again. "It's not political. It's hydrogeological. Blame the fault, not 'The Man.' It's that 5.1 we had off the coast on —"

Maggie knocked a knuckle gently to the side of Holden's head. "English, professor, English."

"An earthquake made the water go *hasta la vista,* baby," he said.

"I didn't feel no earthquake," Maggie said.

"You didn't hear me hit your mailbox either, but that doesn't mean it's not laying on its side right now. You also didn't feel the 7.9 quake in Alaska that pushed up water levels in Wisconsin by two feet. And that temblor in Pennsylvania that dried up 120 wells also escaped your finely tuned levels of perception."

Holden continued rattling off his list of natural tragedies, even as Jake's attention drifted to the screen door.

"These things happen all the time, whether you believe they do, or not," he said.

Maggie paced from the kitchen to the living room and back. "Holden, I flush my toilet with a bucket," she said. "I boil bathwater on my stove. You gotta tell me how we fix this. You gotta give me someone to blame."

Holden stared at Maggie for so long a silence that Jake reached for him, to be sure he was alright. She jumped as he resumed his lecture.

"The earth doesn't work that way, not like a house," he said. "It's rocks and sediment, not pipes and basins. By human standards, it's inefficient and unpredictable. You move a tectonic plate around in one place and sometimes you can make water appear or disappear in another place. Sometimes nothing happens."

"*Tectono*-what?" Maggie said. "Holden! Nimbus did this! You say it was an earthquake. OK. How do we prove that Nimbus made the earthquake? People can make earthquakes."

Holden dug his thumb into his nose, pinched and squinted and tugged. "That's highly unlikely," he said. "They've done it in Egypt, but it's not something you can create with wires and circuits from Radio Shack. You need heavy equipment. You have to inject massive quantities of water back into the —"

Maggie stomped her foot so hard it made the metal pots on the countertop ring like bells. "That's it!" she said. "They've been injecting water up in Oxnard. They shoot water into the ground to push the salty seawater back. Saltwater is no good for crops. *Hijole!* That's it."

Holden sucked his teeth. "Then blame the farmers," he said.

"Not the farmers," Jake interrupted.

Maggie sat and raked her chair across the floor to scoot closer to Holden. "No, not the farmers," she said. "Nimbus. Nimbus is cheating them. He's using them somehow."

Another long pause followed. "Don't just hear me, listen to what I'm saying," Holden said. "Yes, we can make earthquakes; on purpose, and on accident. But that doesn't mean we can control them. It's like that Whac-A-Mole game. You hit the Earth here and something pops up there … or there … or there. But, unlike Whac-A-Mole, the Earth has billions of holes. It's too random. We don't know which hole to hit to make it do what we want. We might pull a fast one now and then, but Mother Nature always gets even."

"So what," Maggie said. "That's just what *you* say."

"Water levels could rise back a month from now, or never," Holden said. "The Earth doesn't make promises. Either you respect it, or you don't. It doesn't care."

"We aren't selling out," Maggie said. "If we lay down, the vultures will swoop and gobble us up."

"I'm a geologist. I can only tell you the facts and guess at what they mean."

Jake's heart began to beat faster as Maggie pointed at her. "If you write something, people will see," Maggie said. "You were gonna write that before you got pushed out. Write it now. Write it for someone else … for the big paper … for some other one. For the Internets."

Jake gripped her chair, her eyes all glassy. "Maggie, I —"

"*Mija*, there's nothing you can't do."

A warm rush was in Jake's chest as she panted out an explanation. "Maggie … I'm not … who you … think. I'm … working for —"

Holden stood and shuffled to the screen door. "You're done with me," he said. "I don't need to attend another meeting of *La Raza*."

Maggie touched a hand to Jake's shoulder on her way to help Holden out the door.

"You did your best," Maggie told him.

"That mailbox was too close to the street," he said.

Jake was up and searching for her boots when Maggie returned. "I should go too," she said.

"At least let the skirt soak awhile yet. I'll throw it in the dryer before you go."

Jake clapped her palms to her hips, the sweats a perfect fit. "I can wear these. I'll bring them back."

"You don't want to wear those outside with *that* on your backside."

Jake looked around to see white letters across the seat of the sweatpants. They spelled "JUICY."

Maggie laughed and caressed Jake sweetly between her shoulders, her fingers splayed and firm as the rub became a gentle back scratch.

"I quit," Jake said. "I don't write for the newspaper anymore."

"You didn't quit your gift. You can always write."

"No. No I can't. Not anymore."

"Come. Sit. Please."

Jake's long hair bounced and fell across both her shoulders as she flumped into the nearest chair.

"You got *fuego*," Maggie said. "You're a younger, skinny me. You love justice, *Mija*. You were born to put wrongs right. I can tell. You know it. You know it sure as —"

Jake's chin was at her knees. She was hugging her thighs and humming.

"That Nimbus got everybody in his pocket," Maggie said as she pet Jake's hair. "You don't have to say it. I just know he got you fired."

Jake began to rock. "I left because I couldn't —"

"*Mija.* You quit cause you couldn't let them do you like that. You stood up. You refused to lay down. You're a fighter."

"No, no, no," Jake said and shot upright. "Stop. Please stop. You don't … I quit because I didn't *want* to do the story. I quit because I'm a liar. It's my fault. Don't you see? I'm the fake. I did lay down, and … No, I didn't. Instead of laying down, I just stood there. I stood there and took it. I didn't even try to defend what was right."

Maggie's lips were flat.

"I left because The Mayor offered me a job," Jake said. "There. I said it. I sold out. Maybe Nimbus didn't want me to write that story, but I didn't either. I made it up, Maggie. I made up a lie about poisoned water. I let my pride … I snapped. I was only trying to show them how wrong they were and … Before I knew it, I was the horrible one. I was the bad guy. At first I didn't confess because I didn't want to kill my career. I thought I could fix it. Then, I didn't say anything because I thought my lie was true. But that's just because I *wanted* it to be true. By then it was too late. I couldn't lie in the paper. I couldn't hurt people. All I could do was escape, and there was The Mayor offering me a job and money … I took it. And I can't even say I sold out to be happy. I'm not. I don't even want a house or a family anymore. Not like this. Tell me you hate me. You should hate me. I hate me."

Maggie cupped Jake's tear-soaked cheek.

"I can't help you," Jake sobbed. "I can't help me. I can't even help —"

"*Mija*," Maggie whispered. "You didn't hurt nobody."

"All I did was work. All I did was work and we still couldn't buy a tiny house. All I wanted was a house, but … I wanted out and there was Nimbus with this COW Co. friend of his. They threw money at me and I don't even want it. I don't … My life doesn't feel like a life. My husband doesn't feel like a husband. All I want is to lie down and sleep and sleep and sleep."

Jake reached for her purse, pulled out the remnants of the two paychecks and threw them to the floor.

"There," she said. "I don't want it. That's more money than I ever had at once and I don't want it. This isn't me. This isn't how I'm supposed to be. I don't cry. I don't lie. I'm not … And, you … You're so good. You're like my only … All I do is work. I don't even have a mom anymore. I didn't even call my mom to tell her I got married. I just want to run somewhere where nobody knows me and —"

"*Mija*," Maggie said. "Why not call your mom?"

"I can't," she said. "It just happened. First I didn't call cause I was upset. Then I was upset that she didn't call. Neither of them called. Him, or her. When I got over being angry I was embarrassed. I was the reason. I'm what broke them up. My name. Me. Jake LaMotta. My fault. Maggie, it's my fault."

The screen door shut with a thwack as Manny entered the kitchen. Maggie picked up the pieces of the paychecks and Jake grabbed the towel to wipe her face. She tasted the salt on it and stopped before it reached her eyes.

Maggie pished and waved a hand. "You bent some rules, *Mija*," she said. "I make up stories all the time. How do you think I keep them *güeros* from poking around? *Hijole!* You should see those *ree-lit-turs* when I tell the story about the *rico* speculator who got mauled by a pack of pit bulls before he could get to his Bentley. I swear, they believe it. Let 'em think it. Helps keep 'em out. You think the politicos never bend no rules? You think they never tell no lies? All of them, *Mija*. Ain't that right Manny?"

Manny's butt was resting against the kitchen counter. "Your name really Jake LaMotta?" he said. "Like the fighter?"

Jake convulsed with sobs.

"He was talking about fighters like César, weren't you Manny?" Maggie said.

Manny nodded rapidly, his lips pressed together, tight and straight across.

"Fighters like César, they all got through it," Maggie said. "*Ricos* swindled César's papa out of his house. They smeared Martin Luther King Jr. and Malcolm X and John Lennon. It's a war, no place for *conejitos*, *Mija*. You gotta be as big as you are. Non-violent protest don't mean toeing no line. They keep moving the line. They keep telling us to stand in line. Wait. They always expect us to wait!"

Jake wrapped herself in her arms. "This isn't supposed to be me," she said and stood to retrieve her cowboy boots. "I should go."

Maggie puzzled the pieces of the checks together on the tabletop and gasped. "This is a fortune. Wait. Manny. Where was that outfit that bought your farm?"

"FARM Co.?" Manny said. "How could you forget a name like FARM Co.?"

"No, no, no. Where, bro? Where was it?" Maggie asked.

"Studio City? It's in those papers on the desk."

"Moorpark Street?"

"*Si!*" he said and laughed. "Kraproom."

Jake pulled on her boots and tucked the sweatpants inside the sleeves, but before she could leave, Maggie rumbled into the living room and returned with a two-inch stack of papers.

"Look," Maggie said and stabbed a finger into the document on top. "The same address."

Maggie held the torn corner of Jake's envelope to the stack.

"Yours says 12801 Moorpark Street and this says the same," Maggie said. "COW Co. and FARM Co. They're at the same address."

Jake leaned in. "It's a coincidence," she said.

"No, no," Maggie said. "Look here. If The Mayor is your boss and your paychecks come from this place, then this proves that The Mayor is the one who bought up all the farms. See? They're in the same office, the same building."

"But it's …" Jake said and stopped and pointed to the computer. "Can that get the Web?"

Jake surfed for an hour online, clicking through news archives, state Corporation Commission records, federal Bankruptcy Court documents and fictitious business declarations. She took apart assumptions and reassembled the facts where they fit, rather than where she expected — or wanted — them to go. The skeleton that resulted looked like something The Mayor would want buried. She continued to dig.

Maggie gave her a start as she crept up from behind. "What is it *Mija*?" Maggie asked and leaned over Jake's notes.

Jake snatched up the legal pad, the torn pieces of her paychecks and her purse. "You have to trust me," she said and moved toward the back door.

Manny slapped his denim-clad thigh so hard it resembled the crisp crack of a whip. "Looks like she knows what she's doing," he said.

"I can't promise I'll be able to do anything about anything," Jake said. "I don't know exactly what I'm doing. But, I'm going to try to do what's right."

Maggie threw a finger into the air and shouted: "*Viva la raza!*"

Jake nodded and grinned, preoccupied by the ideas in her head. "You better hold onto that skirt," she told Maggie.

"It'll be here, *Mija*."

"All because you remembered Moorpark Street," Jake said and tapped the legal pad against her thigh.

Maggie elbowed Manny in the belly. "It's the backwards game," she said. "'Moorpark' backwards is 'kraproom.'"

Jake laughed and nearly collided with a gray-haired woman who came hobbling up the back steps with a stock pot in her hands. Jake apologized, but the woman ignored her and continued to trudge unfazed to the nearest wall of water bottles.

"Mrs. Roybal," Maggie said, "*como estas*? *Es tiempo*? Time for your *agua* already? I'm making another run this afternoon."

Jake waved and went out the way she'd come in, back around the house and up the weed-lined path to the dirt road in front, now so brightly lit by the sunlight streaming through the trees. More old women were on their way to Maggie's, each with an empty pot clutched in both hands. Jake swung her legal pad around to cover the white letters that spelled "JUICY" as she passed. She bounced on the soles of her boots and skipped from rut to rut to the Corolla. For the first time in weeks she felt alive and wide awake. It had been so long since she last knew exactly where she was going.

Agents, Brokers Get Licensed In Record Numbers

By Michael Spunkmeisel
Pendulum Staff Writer

The California Department of Real Estate says the number of real estate agents in the state is now higher than the number of teachers, nurses, and firefighters combined.

"If I became a nurse, I'd have to work all year to make $60,000," said Jan Kinkinos, an 18-year-old senior at Waters End Country Day School. "But if I sell a house for a million bucks, my share of the commission is $30,000. Who wants to be a nurse?"

Kinkinos, who got her license last month, plans to use her first commission to pay for breast augmentation surgery.

Please turn to page A14

CHAPTER 13 – KRAPROOM

It was the toe again.

Keith recognized the sound of the snap and the immediate sensation of numbness in the joint. He'd broken it. Again. He was up on the ball of his one good foot before the agony began, bouncing from the living room to the hall, the cell phone still pressed to his ear, the call still connected. He counted through the rings same as he had during each redialed call since six o'clock. This was call 39, the very reason he'd kicked the futon couch to start with. He slowed to a hobble near the bedroom door, stopped cursing and leaned into the wall. He needed to keep Jake in the dark, and asleep. He bit his bottom lip and listened as the voicemail greeting picked up again:

> *"You've reached Maxine Lugner, senior growth writer for The Pendulum. I'm off on a major project, so if you're returning a call, or passing on a story tip, please press the pound-cake key and leave a message. Otherwise, please call the City Desk. Oh, and have a nice day."*

"Fuck you," Keith whispered.

He hung up at the beep, then shuffled back to the living room, dropped himself into the couch and pulled up his foot for inspection. For Keith, broken toes were more common than paper cuts. No hospital visit required. He'd squandered that co-pay before, five hundred dollars to hear nothing but *"tape it."* Doctor upon doctor. Always the same. *Tape it. Tape it. Tape it.*

He tried Maxine's mobile again and hung up halfway through the recording. Leaving a message was like leaving a fingerprint. Either she was avoiding him, or already at home with Stan, the two of them tucked beneath those 600-thread-count sheets she'd gone on and on about. Motel sheets made her itch. Crazy. Pure crazy. Keith knew it for sure. He sighed and pressed redial again, certain that her cell phone had to be switched on. If not, there'd have been no rings to count. It'd have simply jumped right to voicemail.

Jake was snoring on the other side of the living room wall as Keith looked into the empty whiteness of it. He imagined he could see through to the bedroom and into her open mouth. It was as if she were mocking his situation — their situation. If she knew … she'd be awake too. She'd be fighting for the cell phone and pounding the "redial" button. Keith intended to see that Jake never found out. The ache in his foot pulsed to a puffy warmth as he raised the phone to dial again.

He watched his own silhouette reflected in the darkness of the television screen as he alternated between "redial" and "end call." His mind tripped back from there to a revived vision.

Redial … End call.

Life at the age of 10.

Redial … End call.

An Easter Sunday long gone.

Redial … End call.

There was a chocolate bunny and the neighbor's Pekingese.

Redial … End call.

He'd tried in his 10-year-old mind to make a point, to disprove his father's insistence that chocolate was dog poison. It had taken 15 hours.

Redial …

The animal had dug its own hole before it died.

… End call.

A twinge in Keith's foot pricked him back to the business of Maxine. The next call would be number 57.

————

Jake awoke at three o'clock to find Keith still absent from the bed. She rolled to the middle, felt the coolness of the sheet against her back, and stared up through the dimness at the bumps on the ceiling. A hard stretch and a yawn pushed a smile into her cheeks, her head still spinning with the tribulations and revelations of her day. Not a knot remained in her neck, shoulders or stomach. When she breathed deep she could swear the pores of her skin inhaled too. To call it giddiness seemed flippant. To describe it as satisfaction downplayed its effect. It was whatever word described what made her dance down church steps after each and every Saturday confession as a child. *Redemption*. She hadn't felt as right with the world since then.

The sunrise drive to Maggie's house had only been the beginning. It had broken Jake down, built her up and sent her Corolla roaring out of The Knolls with a purpose. After that, the drive back to LA was almost spiritual, her easiest ever at midday, all five lanes filled yet humming at 70 mph, every vehicle in every lane seemingly in sync and soaring beneath a blue sky. No congestion. No confusion. No angry fingers or flashy guns. No spit-soaked curses and no car horns. It had made Jake feel a part of something, as though she were a bona fide member of an efficient army, machine-bound and aligned to achieve an unstated, yet noble goal. It had been harmonic, as though everyone in every car, truck and SUV was absolutely certain of their destination and on track to meet their estimated times of arrival.

The morning, with all its stains and sobs and snot, had cleared Jake's head of a lingering clog. The trap was clear. Her future was in flux once again. She replayed what happened that afternoon in her head, too enthusiastic to sleep anymore.

————

Jake parked kitty-corner from 12801 Moorpark Street, outside Feabul's Market, a mom-and-pop convenience store with an entryway facing away from the street. It had double automatic step-to-open doors and big windows painted over with sales advertisements in orange and blue acrylics — *40-ounce bottles of malt liquor $2.99; pre-paid* *phone cards $20, California Lottery scratchers $1*. Jake chose it as neutral ground, as well as for the way it concealed her Corolla from the office building windows across the intersection of Moorpark Street and Coldwater Canyon Boulevard. Sometimes the lack of a cool set of wheels could result in a chilly reception.

She smiled at three men standing in the entryway of Feabul's, a vantage point that offered both cover from the sun and the occasional blast of AC whenever someone came or went. The wide grins they paid Jake did little to mask their impishness. They threw whistles once she passed by. She figured the "JUICY" sweatpants were to blame, and maybe the turquoise-colored cowboy boots. The attention pushed her smile higher and put a spark in the sway of her skinny hips as she crossed the cracked concrete blocks of sidewalk pavement. She strutted both lengths of the intersection to the opposite corner, her concentration increasingly focused on the dark entrance of the seven-story brick building with the four majestic spires.

No name appeared on the building's face, or on its black, steel-plated door. Jake picked up the phone receiver that hung inside the entryway, punched the numbered keypad and batted at the silver switchhook. No tone. No buzz. No static. The door had no handle, though the silver eye of its mortise lock suggested it would open inward from the right. Jake put both her palms against it, planted her boots in a wide stance and pushed with every muscle from her toes to her back to her fingers. To her surprise, the only resistance was the weight of the door. Her hands slipped from the steel to wool cloth. A body. Someone's chest. A man. A shirt button jammed into her cheekbone. Someone's fingers were in her hair, gripping fistfuls and pulling, making her wish she still had it tied up in a ponytail. A familiar voice huffed into her head, so close that each word blasted like steam into her ear canal.

"Watch out," it said. "Watch out. Whoa!"

Jake did not let up. She wrapped her arms around the body and dug her heels into the carpet. The front door slammed shut behind her and still she bulled forward, clinching the way a fighter might, blinded and nearly breathless, determined not to go down. She shoved harder and deeper into the shadows of the hallway. Forward was power.

"Whoa now!" the man said as he let go of her hair and went reeling back.

Slow as her eyes were to adjust to darkness, she could make out the shape of a second man behind the one she'd hit. She let go as their backs struck the wall with an "oomph." She bent slightly, hands on her knees, catching her breath and looking to see who else was there.

The bigger of the two men was correcting the tilt of the smaller one's hat.

"I got you covered," the bigger one said with a laugh. "I got your back ... and I got your front too."

It was Mayor Chick Nimbus. No doubt.

The little one didn't answer, though the more Jake looked, the more he resembled the odd man she'd seen outside The Mayor's office. He was dressed in the same sort of powder blue suit, and had a similar hat. She scanned the floor, just in case the little dog was somewhere too. Instead, she found her eyeglasses, her purse and her legal pad, all of which lay around her.

She bent down to collect her things, the "JUICY" backside of her sweatpants turned toward The Mayor. She picked up her pad, put her eyeglasses into her purse, and retrieved several pieces of paper — including the paychecks she'd torn apart at Maggie's house.

The Mayor flashed a slight smile. "Jake?" he said. "Why are *you* here?"

She tossed her hair off her shoulders, blinked fast and tightened her voice to affect a perky personality. "I work here, remember? Well, not *here* here, but … yeah. Here, I guess, even though there's no *here* here, but you know. 'Here, here,' Mr. Mayor."

She gave a giggle and thrust her hand forward to shake, forgetting she still held the paycheck pieces. The Mayor focused on them, the COW Co. logo showing face up.

Jake fumbled for what to say. "Uh, I tore up my paychecks this morning. They got mixed in with the junk mail by accident. Junk, junk, junk. Probably too damaged for the bank to take, so … I hopped down here to get new ones. Wouldn't want to bother you with that, Chick, so … It's good for you to see me, huh? I mean, even if I'm not working *here*, or for *you*. You know?"

She winked.

The little man in the powder blue suit sputtered with a throat-clearing hack, the smooth skin on his chin puckering. Jake couldn't see his eyes, the brim of that Panama hat too low.

The Mayor slicked his combover back into place and brushed his necktie flat. "Of course," he said. "What you can do is, uh —"

Jake heaved a breathy, starlet-like sigh and shot her right arm ramrod stiff to shake the little man's hand. "I'm Jake LaMotta," she said.

The little man's head turned up, his steel-blue eyes looking to The Mayor. "She's who?"

"Jake," The Mayor said. "That newspaper guy I told you about? This is his wife."

"The flack!" the little man said.

"Yes sir," The Mayor said with a go-get-em swing of his fist. "Public relations."

"This is the flack?" the little man said.

"She's the one, er, one of the two of them. The wife."

The little man did not respond, his arms limp at his sides, suit sleeves hiding his wrists. His ears were so big they bumped the bottom of his hat.

The Mayor cocked his chin toward the end of the hallway. "Accounting is up on four," he said. "Catch the elevator at the end. I'll ring security from the car and tell them you're OK."

Jake giggled and gave her shoulders a girlish shake. "Okie dokie. I'll figure it out."

She rolled her fingers in a wave as The Mayor helped the little man outside and down the steps.

For the first five floors, the elevator opened to dank hallway after dank hallway, a series of urban caves complete with sprinkler heads and security cameras. The hum of photocopier gears filled level three, and the distinctive whine of vending machine motors was the sole sign of humankind on four. No phones rang. No conversations buzzed. No laughter broke out. The first person Jake encountered was up on seven, a woman with a corrugated face who sat beneath recessed ceiling lights at a crescent-shaped counter. Behind the woman hung a large, wall-mounted version of the company logo, the same silhouette featured on the front of Jake's paychecks. The name COW Co. appeared in black letters across the middle of a pink cow, the whole thing backlit by bright pink and blue light.

"How did you get in here?" the woman said.

"Chick," Jake chirped. "I'm a consultant. I'm Jake. Jake LaMotta."

The woman picked up her phone and dropped her eyes to her desktop. "You mean Mayor Nimbus?" she said.

"That who you're calling?"

"Colleen, this is Dani," the woman said into the phone.

Framed family pictures sat in a row on an oblong table behind the woman's desk. Most were snapshots, pictures of children and adults. The oldest grownup looked less than half the age of the receptionist. Two crayon drawings taped to the counter's interior flanked what looked to be a company phone directory. Only first names were listed, and in no apparent order — Madison, Prescott, Austin, Cleveland, Dallas, Remington, Burlington, Bryant, Billings, Constance. Jake feigned interest in the artwork as she committed to memory as many names and numbers as possible.

She felt the woman staring. "Why is it you're here?" the woman asked, the phone still in her hand.

"I needed to get the lay of the place," Jake said. "I'm on contract. It's so nice here. Oh, and … I'll need to see someone in accounting about these."

She flashed the paychecks, the torn pieces all fanned out like playing cards.

The woman sniffed. "Did you submit an invoice?"

Jake nodded. "Kids," she said. "They don't know the difference between scrap paper and mommy's mail. But, of course, you know about that. You have *such* a beautiful family."

"Invoice number?" the woman said.

Jake neatened up the stack of paycheck pieces and handed them over. "The number's in there somewhere, I think."

The woman looked to the scraps and tapped a fingernail to the mouthpiece. "LaMotta," she said into the phone. "Initial 'J' … Well, how many can there be?"

"Accounting is on four, right?" Jake whispered. "I'll just look around until —"

The woman's lips contracted as she set the receiver back into the cradle. "No you won't," she said. "There's nothing to see. This is an office. People work."

Jake nodded to a crayon drawing of purple trees. "Did one of yours draw this?"

The woman heaved a sigh and sat back. "My granddaughter."

"You?" Jake said and popped her eyes open wide. "You can't be a grandmother."

The woman waved her hand as though shooing bugs, a move that sent the ticklish scent of French-milled soap into the air. Jake pinched her nose to keep from sneezing.

"All visitors to the property must be escorted by an authorized representative," the woman said. "The CEO's assistant is unavailable. I don't know how you got into the building, but you will have to call back to make an appointment."

The woman produced a business card for *Lauren Hudkins, Office Manager*. Jake took it and did a double take at the name beneath the name — *Calvin Waters*, CEO.

"Waters," Jake said. "Calvin Waters. Waters End. The *Waters End* Calvin Waters."

"Ms. Hudkins is the one you call, not Mr. Waters."

"Right, because she's ... But this ... Waters —"

"You call Ms. Hudkins."

"Calvin Waters," Jake said again. "*The* Calvin Waters. The *Waters End* guy.

His image was more mythical than physical. A painting. A name on a plaque. Not a person. He was one of those larger-than-life figures who transcended flesh and blood. Assigning him a heartbeat gave birth to a host of alive-or-dead uncertainties. *Harper Lee ... Henry Kissinger ... Margaret Thatcher ... Jake LaMotta*. Dead to the world did not equal departed.

"So Calvin Waters isn't ... gone yet," Jake said.

"You do not see Mr. Waters and Mr. Waters does not see you," the woman said. "Whether he's here or not, he's gone indefinitely, as far as you're concerned."

"But, he's here," Jake said. "Not *here* here, I mean, but ... here. He's here among ... his office people. This office. It's his office."

"Ms. Hudkins' number is on the card," the woman said.

Jake was spewing sentences just to buy time to think. "I live in Waters End," she said. "I mean, I'm going to live there. *We're* going to. My husband and me. And our kids, of course. Kids and their crayons, cutting up Mommy's mail and —"

The woman handed Jake back the pieces of the paychecks.

"Accounting is on Four," she said. "An escort will be waiting. Provide her valid proof of identification and your bank drafts will be reissued."

On the elevator ride to the fourth floor, Jake jotted down the list of names and numbers in her head — phone extensions for "Burton" and "Chick" and "FARM Co." and "BARN Co." A red line had been run through Burton's name on the company list, the sort of mark that implied termination. It had to be him. *How many Burtons could there be?*

Another rumpled face met Jake outside the elevator on Four. The woman stood with her arms at her side, shoulders stiff and back straight.

"Jacqueline LaMotta?" the woman asked.

Jake held up her California driver's license and the torn pieces of the paychecks. "It's Jake," she said. "Just Jake."

The woman snatched the ID, but pushed away the paper scraps. "Never mind those," she said. "Follow."

Jake stayed close, batted her eyelashes and smiled as she was deposited in a vacant office furnished with oil-shined antique furniture and freshly polished pewter fixtures. She peeked inside the empty drawers of the desk and thumbed through a "Review of the Season" book from Christie's Auction House until a third woman came to get her.

"Next time, we'd prefer to courier," the woman said and presented a sealed envelope addressed to "Mr. J. LaMotta."

Jake pointed to the name on the envelope, but was interrupted by the chimes of a grandfather clock sounding out the top of the hour. Three o'clock.

"They tow vehicles parked on the street after four," the woman said. "You should move your car."

Jake tried again to explain about the name, but the woman went silent. Jake kicked the elevator doors as soon as they were closed. She had none of what she'd come to get, no proof of a scandal or scam, just numbers and names and restored paychecks.

"Calvin Waters?" she said and kicked the doors again. "I'm working for *Calvin Waters*?"

Jake slumped in the afternoon heat. Her Reseda apartment was a mere eleven miles away, but the drive would surely take almost an hour with traffic. The thought of doing as she'd been told made her feel dirty, so she turned and roamed the length of the office building's exterior, stomping weeds in the sidewalk cracks with the heels of her boots. She spied a row of garbage bins down the alley, behind the building, and, for a moment, considered dumpster diving for documentation. At the very least, the likely confrontation with security that would result might wash away her funk. *But to what end?* She didn't even know what to look for.

"Calvin Waters," she mumbled as she drifted down Coldwater Canyon Boulevard. "What the —"

She ducked, almost hitting her head on a post-and-beam sign. It said "Little Brown Church" and the building to which it belonged was exactly that — little and brown and churchy. It completely escaped her attention until she was right up on it, an entire structure concealed in plain sight, blanketed by the long shadow of Calvin Waters' big, brick fortress.

The church entrance looked nice enough with a lush garden of red roses and impatiens across the front, all hemmed in by a hip-high picket fence. Jake pushed through the gate and bent to smell a rose. She shut her eyes halfway and breathed deep until she caught sight of a slim body on a bench two feet away. She squeaked and jerked and knocked the little old man's hat crooked as her hand bumped the brim. He left it askew and patted the space beside him, inviting Jake to sit. She crouched on the grass at his feet, in no mood to be lectured, but not wanting to be rude either. The Mayor was nowhere in sight.

"You waiting for something?" she said. "Where's Chick?"

A smile crept slowly into the man's cheeks and she worried he might be having a stroke. She scooted closer and watched his blue eyes as he began to recite a verse of something like poetry: "This tree above me is free / As free as I long to be / If I be as free a tree as thee / I hope you'd sit beneath me with me."

Jake choked back a chuckle. She judged him healthy and harmless, and pushed herself up to join him on the bench.

"I wrote that," the little man said.

"Really?" Jake replied and flipped her hair off the shoulder closest to him.

He looked away and began again: "I think of her before I start / In slumber's arms I lay / I tinkered with my lover's heart / Each heavy beat I must now —"

He stopped and turned back to Jake. "You with that new family?" he asked.

"No, we … We met just now. You and me. Back in the hall? I'm Jake, Jake LaMotta."

He took Jake's hand from her lap and shook it. "I'm Calvin," he said. "But everyone calls me Cal."

"Calvin Waters? *You're* Calvin Waters?"

"Calvin Oswald Waters," he said and perked up his chin.

"COW," she whispered.

The old man threw a playful fist up in front of his chin and shook it, a crinkle of devilishness in the corner of his eye. "Anybody calls me that I'm supposed to punch 'em in the nose," he said.

He still had hold of Jake's hand, his fingers so delicate they felt to her as though they'd crumble with the slightest squeeze.

"Where's Chick?" she asked.

"Went to the other side," the old man said and laughed. "You met my Ma yet? What's your name?"

"LaMotta. Jake LaMotta," she said, unsure of whether she was being played for a fool, or if the little man was genuinely confused. "I work for you."

"No … Pa don't hire no people who … no girls. He don't hire no girls."

His statements were lucid, but his tone was childlike. No doubt, he was delusional.

"Chick Nimbus," Jake said. "The Mayor? Remember? I was writing for *The Pendulum* when he hired me away to —"

Something about the comment seemed to affect the little man. Excitement faded from his eyes, his smile went slack and his forehead went wrinkly. He threw Jake's hand away. His knees came together, his back straightened and his shoulders broadened. It was as though a whole other soul slipped into his body in an instant.

"That was pure clumsy foolishness," he said.

Jake looked around her, to see if she'd sat or stepped on something. He still had his hat, though he'd since straightened it. Her hands were nowhere near him, and the nearest she'd come to damage was the dandelion blossom bent beneath her left boot.

"Do what?" she said.

"That fool story," he barked. "I made things, built communities, fulfilled dreams. But you … you journalists … You make nothing. You make trouble."

Spittle flew from his lips as Jake scooted down the bench.

"They ought to do a story on you, don't you think?" he said.

Jake wanted to retort, to hit back with words, but then she thought better of it, heard Maggie's voice running through her head, talking about how "*you can't quit your gift.*" Jake could wait. She could listen a little longer. She could do this. Silence was a weapon, especially when used against people who felt compelled to fill it.

Mr. Waters opened his eyes so wide that a lunatic fringe of white encircled the whole of his irises. "Every time I give a dime to a campaign, you people deem me a 'special interest,'" he said. "By your definition, a 'special interest' is anyone who sells or produces anything that anyone needs or wants. That's pretty much the entire populace except, of course, newspapers. All you make is trouble, and nobody needs or wants it."

Jake wiggled her back straight.

"Used to be a daily paper on every porch up the block," he said. "Now they're scarce as lawn jockeys, not that I ever had a thing against those. You people are no different. You're a business like any business, except you paint yourselves in that public-service nonsense. Hypocrites."

He clapped his hands together and pointed all his fingertips at Jake's face.

"You wouldn't have slowed me down one bit," he said. "You people don't understand. Nothing would ever get done if we all stood in line and filled out every form."

Hot as it was even there in the shade, a shiver rippled through Jake's shoulders, down her arms and into her fingers.

"You stuck your nose where it didn't belong," he told her. "Nobody elected you, but there you were, set to foul this up and sic the federal dicks on us, all for no damn good reason."

Jake nodded to herself, his accusations as good as a confession, confirmation that what she'd suspected was all starting to fit into place. His grin caught her by surprise. Did he think she was agreeing with him? She felt compelled to clarify.

"No, I know what you did," she said. "Bullying farmers and buying them out. FARM … COW … Burton Brand. They're your shills. You've got Mayor Nimbus fixing the zoning so you can build houses on the farmland. You've got me making everybody think it's all about helping working families. You have no right. You know what's in the water —"

"I know more than you," he barked. "I know what you wanted to write, and why you wanted to write it. You were not out to *help* people."

Jake repositioned herself on the bench, her spirit struck dumb.

"No one was forced to sell," he said. "With or without me, those farms were doomed. I'm the one taking the risk. Me. All me. All you wanted to do was make trouble, to make a name for yourself."

Jake inhaled to interrupt, but he cut her off.

"Those districts will get back every penny, provided no other fool gets curious enough to poke around and foul it up before we're finished."

"Districts?" Jake said.

"Yes, districts," he snapped. "Districts. Those districts. Don't think for one damn minute they were my idea."

"Which districts?"

"All of them," he said. "What do you think? You think I'm a thief? They'll all get it back. They'll all get reimbursed."

The notion staggered Jake.

"You see," Mr. Waters said. "It's a different story now, isn't it? Not as juicy as you thought."

"Juicy," she said in a daze. "Not what I thought."

"That money was doing nobody no good sitting in a bank. There's no land to build parks on up there, no cemetery to tend. And mosquitoes? Bah. A boondoggle. I'm doing what's right. I'm putting wasted earmarks to good use. I'm turning lost causes into capital investments. Once we turn a profit, all the money will go back. No one needs to know. And you get to be part of the solution, instead of the problem."

"But why take it?" she asked.

"No interest," he snorted. "You can't take money from banks, or investors, without telling them what it's for. People talk and profits walk. My business is *my* business. I keep things quiet. That's how I get things done."

"But the water. There's no … It's in the water and —"

"Water, bugs, cemeteries … I told Nimbus 30 years ago those districts were a pitiful waste of money. What good was it all doing in there? What good?"

"But the poison —"

"Poison? What are you talking about?"

Jake shook her head. She understood why he didn't understand. He'd confused her for Keith. The cover-up wasn't about water. The scam revolved around the special districts that Keith had been writing about. Mr. Waters had been using all that idle money to quietly buy up farmland — land he was getting on the cheap because no one else had any hope of building anything on it. The Mayor was the key, not just to the money, but to the elimination of the STOP laws. The two were in cahoots.

"This is all about the districts," Jake said.

"Districts," Mr. Waters said. "Bah."

Voters had created them, albeit with the best intentions. Each special district was promoted and approved independently, all to attack specific troubles. Bugs. Parks. Cemeteries. Ironic as it now seemed, Mr. Waters said he'd spent hundreds of thousands in efforts to defeat each vote, all to no avail. Despite being told no new tax was a good tax, the property owners who pioneered Waters End had an eagerness to solve problems themselves, whether it was making sure the grass got mowed in the city's only cemetery, or ensuring the abatement of insects that infested the old man-made lake — the one Mr. Waters drained to get his way, then paved over to build the town. Once each problem was solved and out of sight, the issue went out of everyone else's mind. Tax dollars continued to be collected and the districts continued to function despite their lack of purpose. The Mayor had kept it all hush-hush by reappointing the same board members year after year after year. The Mayor had been in Calvin Waters' pocket all that time.

"Government's no better than a hobo that goes begging with a pocketful of booze money," Mr. Waters said. "Did you know the state is still collecting taxes for roadside emergency phones when everybody carries a mobile?"

Jake rocked forward in anticipation of a dizzy spell. Much as it was a relief to realize her lie was a lie — that the drinking water was safe — this new truth threw her off balance. *Keith. Keith. Keith.* It had been Keith all along. His stories about special districts instigated the worry that drove The Mayor and Mr. Waters to the point of intervention. They sought to silence Keith, not her. This time she was the accessory. *One simple step.* If only Keith had taken one simple step beyond the numbers published in a budget and looked closer. If only he'd inquired about the actual balance in each account he could have saved the day. Jake always took the time to look. Not Keith. Keith was to blame. Keith was the reason she was in this mess. What was fair was no longer fair. Her legs trembled as she dug her heels into the grass.

"Destroyer … creator … God," Mr. Waters said. "They're all the same. You cannot remake Eden without blasting everything to hell first."

"You're not God," she said.

"I didn't ask them to name that place after me. I never sought fame. You can't spend it. You can't undo it. You get a little older and you'll start to realize what a burden a big name can be. You'll warn your kids about it. You'll see."

Jake heaved a sigh. "I don't have kids."

"I don't either," he said. "Not anymore."

Jake wrung the steering wheel as she sat in the Corolla with the windows up and the engine off. She breathed deep the dry heat and watched the men loiter in the doorway of the market. Each one looked to be a portrait of self-destruction — bag-wrapped bottles in their hands, sunburnt bruises for faces, and bare feet so black Jake mistook them for shoes. She told herself self-destruction was accidental, that deep down each of these men clung to wishes for a ready-made life complete with a job, a house, a wife and kids. They had to be homeless by mistake, not because their lives had slipped into some predetermined slot. Life couldn't be merely a patchwork of predetermined paths mapped out in holy Highlighter ink.

She pulled Maggie's number from her purse and dialed.

Jake didn't bother to say hello, but launched right into what she needed to know. "Maggie, tell me about your worst time … the worst time ever. What'd you do?"

Maggie's voice was bright and free of hesitation, the rumble of clothes dryers and washers so loud that Jake could hear them in the background. "I got into debt," Maggie said. "Baking wasn't going so good. I got a job. But taxes, gasoline, groceries … *Eee*. It got worse. I bought things I didn't need, just to feel good, just to feel like I was able to do what I wasn't able to do. Credit cards. Record clubs. *Mija*, don't never get jumped into no record club. *Cholos* in the hood got better chances of getting out of gangs than you got of getting out of the record clubs on TV."

Jake struggled to conceal her impatience as she waited for Maggie to finish. "But what did you do?" Jake begged. "How did you make it right?"

"America, *Mija*. I filed bankruptcy and started over."

Jake wiped her sweaty forehead and took a deep breath, her car completely cleansed of the years-old scent of spilled college coffee and fries. "But, didn't you feel like a failure?" she asked. "What was it all worth if you gave it all up?"

"*Mija*, troubles are like *masa*. You squeeze 'em on this end, they blow up bigger over there. Why so serious? Is this about this morning?"

"Dead end," Jake told her.

"No such thing as 'dead ends,' *Mija*. In the suburbs they're cul-de-sacs. All the best people live on the cul-de-sac."

Jake took the the high road back to Reseda, rode the ridge line along Mulholland Drive past the securely gated homes of the unknown rich. She'd sought it out as a way around, an alternative to the freeway traffic, her patience too thin to sit still. Nonetheless, she ended up sitting stuck, bumper to bumper through five cycles of the light at Beverly Glen Boulevard. She pulled the reissued checks from her purse as she waited and stared blankly at that name — Mr. J. LaMotta. How many people had he been? How many would she be?

She rolled down her window as a horn blasted two cars away.

"Whole goddamn city," another driver shouted. "Place is too broke to fix. All they do is move the fucking problem. Tear it up here, screw it up there. Tear the whole mother up. Somebody oughta tear … this mother … up!"

Once Jake was beyond the bounds of Van Nuys, she turned into an overlook and cut the engine. She snatched her purse and her cell phone and got out.

She leaned back against the front grill of the Corolla and looked down at the sprawling San Fernando Valley just inches from her toes, over the cliff and down. Her gaze swept from the paisley-like pattern of cul-de-sacs on the brink of Sherman Oaks to the double-stitched seam of the Ventura Freeway to the massive blanket of straight streets, rooftops, treetops and fields across the valley floor. She bounced herself off the hood and inched nearer the verge, further convinced of her need to either give in and abide by the choices she'd made, or to give up and self-destruct. A warm evening breeze blew up the back of her neck and she shut her eyes. Gravel fell away ahead of her toes, its chatter like the slow splash of waves at low tide. She swallowed hard and made her decision.

"For the best," she said and dialed Buckwalter's desk phone.

She skipped the introduction and jumped to an insistence of complete anonymity. "Not for attribution," she said. "Background only. Only you're to know where this information came from. Got it?"

He agreed and she proceeded to play the phone like an instrument, running the whole deal down as the sun set, the connection so clear she could hear the scratch of Buckwalter's pen.

"Special districts," she said. "Shills ... Hollow shells ... Stolen assets ... The Mayor ... Burton Brand ... Calvin O. Waters —"

"*The* Calvin Waters?"

Apparently Buckwalter hadn't considered it either.

"A private guy," Jake said. "Doesn't like attention."

"Well, he's got mine," Buckwalter replied.

Jake explained where to go, what to seek and the precise language to include in any written request for public records.

"Actual bank records," she repeated. "Budget numbers are a sham. You have to get certified bank documents."

She dictated every name and number she'd memorized from the company directory, and capped her pitch with the journalistic equivalent of a hearty *amen*.

"Follow the money," she said.

"You know what will happen if all this is true," Buckwalter told her. "Why do this for me? What's in it for you?"

Doubt was healthy. Skepticism was good.

"This isn't about you," Jake said. "It's not about me either. They shouldn't get away with it."

Buckwalter sounded ebullient as he laughed her off the line. He called her "a changed woman" and almost seemed to lament her departure. "We're not so different, you and I. But, it's not just us."

Jake left it at that. She hung up without a goodbye and fished Rusty Tirzah's card out of her purse.

It was time to buy a house.

————————

Keith froze with the cell phone in his hand as Jake shuffled into the living room looking as though she was still half asleep.

"What are you doing up?" he asked, his broken toe taped, but still throbbing.

Jake dropped to the carpet, legs crossed, elbows on her knees and fists to her chin. "I couldn't sleep," she said, her voice soft and sweet. "You calling to tell him? It's like eight in the morning where he's at."

Keith clapped the phone closed and raised his foot to rest it on the coffee table.

"What'd you do?" she said and pointed to the white tape on his toe.

"Broke it," he said.

"Again?"

He shook the phone at her. "Can I get a little privacy so I can call my father?"

Jake stretched her arms and groaned through a grin. "Of course," she said. "I'll go shower. Rusty's going to bring the bid by for you to sign at nine."

A twinge shot up the side of Keith's foot. Having Jake in the room only made the pain worse, that and the thought of buying a house with Maxine all ready to drop a bomb in the paper. He had to stop her. He dialed again.

"Why do you even have to be here?" he asked Jake. "Just go up and get the mail in Waters End. We're supposed to get paid. We're going to need that money."

Jake pulled her bag from beneath the coffee table, removed the envelope with the reissued paychecks and tossed them into his lap. "They came yesterday," she said.

There were two checks for a total of $16,000. "What the fuck?" Keith said. "Why didn't you put this in the bank."

"Forgot," she said, and tossed her hair back. "I was networking, like you said I should. I had one lunch. One coffee after that. Then I got caught in traffic and … that's when I decided. That's why I called. I couldn't wait to —"

Keith gripped each end of the checks between his fingertips, bent them inward, then snapped them straight, again and again.

"You're still OK with it?" she asked. "The cat agreement, and all? I know you hated that paneling, but Charlie and Clara dropped the price so much for us and it feels like a —"

She'd explained it enough already, had kept him on the phone for half an hour the afternoon before, going on and on about making everything right again, all while she was supposed to be bringing him dinner. Her attitude had changed entirely in a single day. The money. It had to be the money that set her straight. Sixteen thousand dollars. More than Keith's father had paid for his house. The old man had never held that much money all at once.

"Yeah, yeah," he told her.

He had to agree. She'd given him no choice. She'd already given him everything he wanted, even asked him to take control. She'd claimed to understand how difficult it had been to hold up his end. She'd said this was the first of many ways she intended to make amends. She'd insisted Keith take all the credit, put the house in his name and claim the title "breadwinner." The suggestion to call his father was brilliant. It was eight o'clock where his father was, but that wasn't who Keith was calling. Not yet anyway. First he had to stop Maxine from putting Jake's water story into print. He'd been trying to reach her for eleven hours straight.

"I want to do what's fair," Jake murmured as she wound her wedding finger tight with a stray hair.

"Finally!" Keith said and glared.

"Honey, I want this to be about you," she told him. "All of this is happening all because of you. But I didn't mean it to upset you so much you couldn't sleep."

"I'm fine. Leave me alone. It's my foot. It hurts."

"Let's get it looked at then. Let me drive you."

He pulled himself up and hobbled on his heels to the kitchen. "I know how to take care of it," he said. "I've done this before."

Police Apprehend Open-House Hoods After Long Hunt

By Bobby Fuchs
Pendulum Staff Writer

Waters End Police say the Sunday arrest of a husband and wife in the Waters End community of Bernin Ridge brings to an end a string of more than 25 brazen burglaries that have plagued area open houses since spring.

The couple, identified as Ricky and Ophelia Nicksen of Yorba Linda, allegedly stole cash, jewelry, medication, and small electronics while walking through Sunday open houses. Police say the pair posed as house hunters and took turns distracting realty agents while the other one ransacked closets, cupboards and drawers.

"We've been warning our members about these people for months," said Fulton Gilby, chairman of the Realty Enterprisers Association of Waters End. "The home-buying experience is built on trust and they took advantage of that. We're very pleased to hear they're off the street."

Please turn to page A15

CHAPTER 14 – BUBBLE TEA

At first glance, it looked like Maxine had a dagger.

She held it straight up, the slight silver blade reflecting light from its drastic point down to the black something that lay atop her fist like an elaborate handle guard. Whatever the hell it was it made Keith hesitate as he hobbled across the boba tea parlor, still reliant on a cane four weeks after the fracture.

Maxine had taken a seat in the back, at one of several small, orange tables. The place was full, mostly with blonde trophy moms, all pushing sport-utility strollers tricked out with plastic bumpers and UV-blocking mesh. Maxine looked out of place, though her hair appeared blonder than before, her roots no longer as obvious as they'd been during lunch at Yo Mahmah.

"Candy," she chirped as Keith tossed a copy of *The Pendulum* on the table and hooked his cane to the chair back.

"You suck 'boba,'" she said. "They call it 'boba.'"

Keith drew back as Maxine shoved a tall, paper cup at him. The red straw stuck so far out the plastic lid that it nearly poked him in the eye.

"Try it," she said.

He pushed the cup back. "Hell no. It's not even noon and … You don't even know what it is."

"It's boba," she said and gnashed the chewy candy balls faster.

When she thrust the hand with the dagger at him his hands went to cover his face, only to find it was a pen, a silver Cross pen tied with a bow of black ribbon at the hilt.

"It's for you, Kiki," Maxine said and wagged the shaft up and down. "For today. Your big day. You can both use it."

"It's me," Keith said. "Only me."

"But, how can Jake not —"

"We'd never have gotten this far if it was up to her. I'm putting the house in my name. We agreed on it."

"Marriage," Maxine said. "A constant negotiation."

She sucked her straw and sat back, watching Keith twirl the pen between his fingers. "Whatever it is, I love it," she said.

"Marriage? You love marriage?"

"No, silly. Boba."

Keith twisted to look at the line forming at the register, then tested the pen on his copy of the newspaper, blacking out the teeth of two mug shots on the front page.

"You won't believe how many things they make you sign," Maxine told him. "You're gonna need your energy, Kiki. There's like ninety pages. No kidding. Closing is a big deal."

"Yeah, well … How pissed was *Fuck*walter when you told him?"

"Kinda," she said. "Maybe. Who cares? I got a better one now, so he's been mostly quiet all month. He's more excited about this one. I told you it would be OK."

"Just like that? He didn't ask why you wanted to dump the story? You weren't supposed to tell him why. You didn't tell him why, did you?"

"Like he'd believe it anyway. Like anyone thinks Jake would lie about —"

Keith hissed to shush her. "Between you and me," he said. "Just between us."

"Don't be silly," she said. "I told you. Don't worry. He doesn't care. He's editing the other story now anyway. He's forgotten all about the water thing."

"What other story?"

TJ SULLIVAN

"It's big."

"Anything I should —"

"Don't be mad," she whispered and cocked her eyes back and forth.

"Mad about what?"

"About the story. It's *your* story, but bigger. Really bigger."

"I don't have a story."

"Your tax series," she explained. "I found … It's about … There's something you must have overlooked and —"

Keith laughed so loud it woke up the baby behind him, making it bawl and heave. "You found something more about the special districts thing? Seriously? Have at it. Whatever. Good for you."

Maxine slurped the last two balls from her cup and winked. "I'll deliver," she said, chewing as she spoke. "I'll be your papergirl. But, between now and Sunday, it's between you and me. You can't even tell Jake. Especially not her."

Something rough and vaguely sharp on the side of the pen caught Keith's fingernail as he absently twirled it. It was a line of engraving — the day's date and the words "house sweet house."

He snorted and turned his face up to Maxine. "It's 'home sweet home,'" he said.

"Nuh uh," she corrected. "A cardboard box can be a home. But your first house … That's the whole dream thingy."

———————

Rusty Tirzah pointed out the tremor in Keith's right hand as he scribbled his signature on the last of the 78 pages in the stack.

"Exciting, isn't it?" she said and pulled open her bottom desk drawer. "You're officially a homeowner."

"A *house* owner," Keith said and snickered. "All of it. *Mine.*"

She handed him a set of keys labeled for the front and back doors, the garage, the pool-equipment shed, and a padlock, which Charlie had used to secure the chain that held the water heater in place. "You have to keep those things secure in case of earthquakes," she said.

She reached again into the drawer and pulled out a bottle of Brut champagne and a can of Merrick gourmet "California Roll" cat food. "From me to you and that loving wife of yours," Rusty said. "You're oh so truly —"

Keith wrinkled the skin on his nose in anticipation of what she was about to say.

"— blessed by God."

He erupted.

"Blessed?" he shouted. "God didn't have a thing to do with this. Me! I did this. God? Fate? Luck? Where was all of that the last five years when everyone was telling me 'no?'"

Rusty straightened the stack of closing documents and bound it with a rubber band. "Of course," she said. "Of course. I only meant to —"

"Get your goddamn lawn sign out of my yard by Friday. I don't want my movers tripped up by that thing. The truck's booked for Saturday."

He jabbed his cane into the floor as he strode to the door, then stopped and returned to retrieve the silver pen. He brandished it in his free hand as he bounded back to the exit.

Rusty rushed around and ahead of him and held the door open. "Careful," she said and nodded to the pen sticking point-first out his fist. "The last thing you want is to fall on that."

EXCLUSIVE:
Mayor, Developer Conspired to Bilk Local Farmers

By Maxine Lugner
Pendulum Staff Writer

An investigation by *The Pendulum* has revealed that Waters End Mayor Chick Nimbus and other officials illegally loaned more than $60 million in surplus tax revenue to a Los Angeles developer, who used it to buy up local farmland.

Anonymous sources say the covert loans made it possible to conceal the identity of the man purchasing the land because the transactions were recorded in the names of shell companies. However, records indicate all the shell companies were owned by Waters End founder and namesake Calvin O. Waters.

Insiders say the scheme was part of an elaborate effort to devalue local farmland by promoting the passage of open-space protections. Once the discounted purchases of that land were completed this year, Nimbus then pushed for the rescission of the open-space protections, and Waters proposed construction of 23,000 new homes on the land.

Please turn to page A16

CHAPTER 15 – FIXER-UPPER

The cat saw trouble before Jake did.

First the purring stopped, then its eyes shot to the open window, to the sky and the flash of whatever went soaring through the sunlight above the lawn out front. The cat's neck swooped and its ears went back. Jake stopped unpacking to have a look of her own — the day after moving day and still so much left to put away. Her eyes darted from the cat to the flash of light, then traced the trajectory of the object back to the fingers of a newspaper carrier in a pickup, his brown arm still straight out the window. Even without her eyeglasses Jake could see well enough to tell that the carrier's face was turned toward the house. The pickup continued to coast, but the driver's body seemed frozen, as though overcome by the kind of paralysis that follows sudden, uncorrectable mistakes. Jake could tell that his throw was off-kilter, the paper's arc too high to hit the front porch mat that welcomed visitors to what used to be Clara's and Charlie's "loverly home." It hit the glass folded end first. The smack was dead-solid-perfect, so precise that it penetrated the lowest little pane beside the door with a sound like a clap of applause. At least, that's how it sounded to Jake in the bedroom.

A loud crash came from the living room a heartbeat later, then a curse so loud it echoed off the house across the street. There was a sloppy splash and more cursing. It was Keith. Jake sighed in response to the clamor and turned her attention back to the pickup as it continued to coast quietly by. A second later it lurched and whined quickly down the block. *Smart move.* The cat took off, too. It launched off its patch of compressed carpet beneath the window, bombed between Jake's knees and around the boxes, then raced toward the source of the commotion.

Keith exploded with another angry shout before Jake made it into the hallway.

"Fucking cat! No!" he yelled.

He was brandishing his walking cane like a club when Jake caught up. The cat had passed him already, its wet footprints leading on into the kitchen.

"She's just scared," Jake said calmly.

Keith was standing beside the front door, dressed in his purple, terry bathrobe, barefoot except for the bandage on his broken toe — four weeks since he started taping it and still in too much pain to help Jake with the move. Broken window glass and the shattered remnants of a ceramic mug lay all around him in a puddle of steaming coffee. The white gauze was soaked brown by it.

"Well," Jake said and laughed. "I guess you found the coffeemaker."

"This is your fault," he said.

Jake soaked up the blame and smiled sweetly. "You wouldn't have wanted to drink that stuff anyway," she said. "We've had that can of Folgers since Idaho."

She reached to help him hop around the mess, but he shooed her hands away and poked the rubber-capped end of his cane at the Sunday edition of *The Pendulum*, which lay folded-end first, halfway through the lowest pane to the left of the door.

"Why'd you order that fucking thing?" he spit.

Jake raised her shoulders in a half-hearted shrug and sighed. "It's probably Clara's and Charlie's. I'll cancel it Monday, once we get the phones hooked up."

"No, no. Do it today. On your cell. And get those boxes out too."

"I told you I would," she said and patted her hips for her cell phone, the only thing in the pockets of the JUICY sweatpants she'd yet to return to Bernie. "A promise is a promise."

"Yeah, you and your promises," he grumbled.

Jake turned to walk back toward the bedroom with her phone in her hand, but Keith stopped her with a flurry of finger snaps. "Get that fixed today too," he said and wagged his cane at the broken window. "AC is leaking out. It looks like hell to the neighbors. And, some burglar's gonna —"

"Nobody wants what we —" Jake said and stopped. "I'll turn off the AC. I got the bedroom window open anyway."

Jake glanced at the living room — the ratty blue futon couch with an unfinished wood frame; the television so old it had no remote control; and the wrought-iron coffee table so unwieldy that the movers had dropped and cracked the custom glass top. By most people's standards, the place looked like it had already been looted of the good stuff. She and Keith had one bookshelf and seven books, all reference guides that Keith had pilfered from the newsrooms in both Hailey, Idaho, and Waters End — a thesaurus, a dictionary, an out-dated AP Stylebook, and four successive editions of the Places Rated Almanac. The spare bedroom across from the master had a pressed-wood desk they'd purchased at a garage sale, and a purple iMac Jake got for $50 when the Waters End School District upgraded its equipment three years before. Other than that there was only the one bed and the boxes, and most of those were filled with old newspaper clippings and notebooks. It was all they owned. It was nothing.

"What about the cat?" Keith said. "Fucking tragedy that would be, first day in the house and the cat escapes out a busted window. And I'll be the one who gets it. I signed the papers taking responsibility for the thing. I'll be the one who gets fucked."

Jake bent to inspect the damage and winced at an ache on both sides of her lower back. She'd taken on too much. Even with the assistance of the movers, there'd been no end to the bending for four days in a row. She'd put every box together, packed and taped them closed too. Now, she had to undo it all, all by herself.

She wiggled the newspaper the rest of the way through the jagged hole in the window and let it fall flat to the puddle of coffee. The splash sent her scooting back in her flip-flops. A smattering of brown spots appeared up the front of her sweatpants.

"No way, no how," Jake said as she pinched and wiggled one of the blades of broken glass that remained lodged inside the window frame. "Bunny couldn't fit. She wouldn't even try."

"You'd be surprised," Keith told her. "Cats can slither out of some tight shit."

"It's not like she's blind, or stupid," Jake insisted. "She'll see the glass."

Keith laughed and pointed his cane toward the street out front. "Animals run in front of cars all the time," he said. "They see those too. Roadkill happens."

Jake picked the newspaper off the floor and folded it to match the rectangular shape of the broken pane.

"Cats got instincts," she said and tucked the paper tightly into the window frame, covering the hole.

"They're afraid of water," Keith replied. "What good are the instincts of an animal that's afraid of water?"

Jake stepped back to review her repair job and laughed. "Now the only holes left are the ones in the stories," she said.

Jake gave the master bedroom one last look before moving to unpack the kitchen. All the boxes of clothing and shoes had been emptied, collapsed and stacked against the hallway wall. Four more rooms left to go. Nothing would remain in cardboard at sundown, provided Keith kept out of her way. It's why she'd sent him to the store for essentials — butter, cheese, jelly, mustard, ketchup, salt and pepper … She'd let him think it was his idea. The house was so quiet with him gone. Not even the cat disturbed her.

"Bunny?" she called softly. "Bunny girl, where you at?"

Jake scooted to the living room first, to be sure the front door was shut and the newspaper patch still in place. She found the den empty, the sliding doors to the backyard closed. Her search ended back in the master bedroom, beneath the bed. The cat had slunk into the shadows, partially hidden by a pair of Keith's trousers. Jake guessed they'd been dragged. Bunny was licking the fabric, her tiny tongue making the littlest sound of a scrape.

Jake crouched on her hands and knees, her forehead mashed into the carpet. "You want him to punt you?" she whispered and gently tugged the pant leg.

The cat took it for play, batted with both paws, snagging the fabric and holding so fast the whole of her body slid along as Jake pulled slowly.

"You're not supposed to have claws," she whispered. "What's so irresistible about *him* anyway? Can't you see how mean he is to you?"

The spot the cat had been licking looked shiny and nearly transparent once Jake had it out in the light. Her first thought was a skin-thin patch of melted candle wax, but it didn't crumble when bent. She rubbed it with her fingers, then folded it over and scrubbed it into itself. She scratched at it with what little bit of nails she had left, which made her suddenly self-conscious about her hands. Her hands. She dropped to her elbows on the carpet and sat back to look at them. She knew she'd been biting her nails, but it wasn't until that moment that she realized she'd been *biting* her nails. She'd never been one of *those* women before. Another pinch of pain shot up both sides of her lower back as she pushed herself off the carpet and moved to the edge of the bed. She returned her attention to the front of the pants, gave it a sniff and looked down at the cat.

"That's … I don't know. Fishy?" she said. "These should have been in the wash before I packed."

She gave the pockets the usual frisk for ballpoints and cash. The first pocket had the feel of money inside, though it turned out to be nothing but a crinkled receipt, the ink barely legible but for the date and the name — "Yo Mahmah Sushi."

"This should be in the tax-receipt box," Jake said.

The back pocket had something too, more spongy than soft. For whatever reason, before she saw what it was, she thought of something Keith had said a month before.

You don't fuck anything, including me —

A foil-and-plastic packet sprung open across her palm as she opened her fist — "Trojan … Ribbed for her pleasure."

Promises … Promises.

Keith returned from the First Harvest Grocery at eleven o'clock and immediately released a fresh batch of curses in the kitchen. Jake took her time responding from the spare bedroom at the other end of the house as he declared her cupboard arrangement "utterly unworkable."

The plates were where the bowls ought to be, and the bowls had been put on a shelf better suited to drinking glasses. Dishware cracked and cabinet doors banged, Keith's storm of emotion growing more intense with each outburst. The doorbell stopped them both before a single punch was thrown. Jake's legs seized up, both flip-flops flat, three feet apart. Keith went quiet too.

Jake pulled her cell phone from her pocket to double-check the time. Eleven o'clock.

It had to be a neighbor — a wine basket fluffed full of synthetic nesting material, maybe, or a plant from the supermarket. Charlie and Clara were the last of their kind on the block, the only couple for miles who'd have even considered carting over a warm chicken casserole in a covered piece of CorningWare, or a home-baked marble cake cast in a copper Bundt mold. The new suburbanites were a new breed of snoop, the sort who came bearing easy, store-bought alibis. By the second ding of the doorbell, Jake was back in the bedroom staring out the cat's favorite window toward the backside of Maxine Lugner, that bumble-bee yellow blouse and those black spandex tights too distinctive to belong to anyone else. Maxine pushed the button a third time and held it extra long. The cat was at Jake's feet, ringing round her ankles.

That woman!

That woman's mouth opened as soon as Keith let her in. That woman's voice sounded as shrill as the doorbell. "Oh my goodness!" that woman said, loud enough for the neighbors to hear. "Just look at how wonderful a little fixer you got."

Jake peeked around the bedroom doorway to spy, still so sure of the trouble *that woman* represented.

"Of course, we're talking extreme makeover," Maxine said and clunked her clogs on the flooring. "Is this real linoleum?"

The clogs went quiet on the carpet as Maxine twirled further into the living room, a platter balanced up on one hand. She actually slapped the wall, as if to test its structural soundness. Jake was twenty feet away, down the hall, without her eyeglasses, but she could still detect Maxine's shape, that figure that lingered like an everlasting bruise.

That woman was trouble.

Jake seethed as she slunk back into the master bedroom and fumbled through the closet. She zipped hangars across the rod, pulled out a blouse, then a pair of jeans, then a skirt, then a dress. *That woman*! Jake had to change clothes, couldn't let that woman see her in sweatpants and a baby tee. But even as she slipped her slender thumbs into the waistband she knew she couldn't do it. She couldn't let herself change a thing for *that woman*.

"Did you see it?" Maxine said to Keith.

"What?" he hissed. "Have you gone insane? Why are you here?"

"A promise is a promise," she said. "I'm your papergirl. I told you. Today's the day."

"Papergirl?" Keith snapped and jerked his cane at the broken window. "Did you do that?"

Maxine shuffled to the door and stooped to pull the paper from its place inside the window frame. "Why's this all mashed in here?" she said. "What's all this gunk all over my —"

Keith shouted: "What are you doing? Why are you here?"

Maxine dropped the paper, its pages flapping in the breeze blowing through the open door. "My story, Kiki," she said. "Mommy has extra copies in the car. I can't carry *everything*. Look! I made lemon bars. Sweet and sour, just for you."

Keith snapped his eyes to Jake as she started down the hall from the bedroom still dressed in the sweats.

Maxine, apparently oblivious to Jake's approach, snatched the red napkin off the plate of lemon bars and thrust it under Keith's nose. "It's a twofer," she said. "Part housewarming gift, and part apology for the sushi thing at —"

Keith whipped his focus away from Jake and cut Maxine short. "What story?"

"You didn't read it?" Maxine said. "Can you believe Nimbus actually tried to get me not to write it? First, he offers me a shady job working for some rich friend of his. Then, he says you'd be hurt by it. *As if.* Fletch says Nimbus will be popular in jail with a name like Chick. Isn't that funny? I never thought of that. Chick. Like a girl."

A blush ran up the back of Keith's neck. "Jail?" he said. "You ... you promised you wouldn't do that! We agreed. You —"

Maxine waved him off. "No silly. Not my water story ... But, Fletch really does want that one too I'm afraid. I need more sources, Kiki. It's too thin with just Burton Brand. And —"

Jake stomped hard enough to make the floor shake. "*My* water story?" she shouted. "Burton Brand?"

Maxine's arms flew open, the plate of lemon bars still balanced on her right hand. Her eyes ran up Jake's frame, from the flip-flops to the ponytail and down again. "Jake!" she exclaimed. "You look … kinda pretty without your glasses."

"*My* water story?" Jake repeated. "Burton Brand?"

A smirk snuck into the corners of Maxine's mouth as she looked from Keith to Jake and back. "You're not the only reporter in the world," Maxine said. "It's not like you own him."

Keith had somehow ended up with the plate of lemon bars as Maxine excused herself to fetch the extra copies of *The Pendulum* from her Land Rover. Jake blocked her way, bent across the doorway and bumped the seat of her JUICY sweatpants against Maxine's hip.

"I got a copy right here," Jake said as she plucked the coffee-stained edition up off the floor. The paper was dry.

The lead story stretched the width of the broadsheet as Jake snapped it open and skimmed the lead. She read aloud from the third paragraph:

> *"Insiders say the scheme was part of an elaborate effort to devalue local farmland by —"*

Jake clapped her flip-flop to the floor. "Insiders?" she said. "What insiders?"

"I'm a reporter," Maxine replied. "I can't reveal sources."

"Sources? What do you mean 'sources?'"

Maxine bucked up both her chins. "How do you think I got where I am?"

"You?" Jake said and stopped to breathe. "You got this whole thing from —"

Maxine reached toward Jake's left shoulder, but didn't quite touch it. "This is because of the baby, isn't it?" Maxine said. "Your hormones are all knotted up and —"

Cigarette cellophane crackled out of Maxine's purse as she removed a Bic lighter and a bent Dunhill.

"I probably shouldn't," she said and put the filter between her lips. "I mean, not with the baby."

"There's no baby!" Jake said.

"Oh, you are so pregnant," Maxine said and sparked the lighter.

"You're totally showing and everything. New mamas always do sweatpants. It helps hide your lil' pudge."

She puffed a plume of smoke into the cottage cheese of the ceiling.

The paper was wide open in Keith's hands as his head bobbed down the jump page. "We're screwed," he muttered. "Fucked."

Another flip-flop slapped the linoleum. "What did he tell you?" Jake demanded of Maxine.

More smoke spewed out of Maxine's mouth. "Stan's actually jealous," she said. "But, he'll move east with me if I get the Pulitzer. We already sold the house. It's a bad time to own anyway and —"

Jake stripped the paper from Keith's hands. "Tell me what you did," she said.

Maxine sputtered with a shush. "He didn't give me a thing. I found Burton on my own. He admitted he was your source. It's not like you're the boss of him."

Keith's feet remained planted beneath both shoulders as Jake stopped an inch away from his chin. "What does Burton Brand have to do with any of it?" she hissed. "He's in a coma."

"Careful," Keith said. "We're *both* in this now."

Maxine laughed and puffed. "Your hormones are way, way out there," she said. "Outer space. The Twilight Zone."

An electrical charge seemed to linger in the air as pages of the newspaper separated in the breeze, each sheet floating independent of the other, their movement mirrored by the layers of cigarette smoke above. Jake broke it all apart, walked through the clouds and the pages, right up into Maxine's face.

"Did he tell you Burton Brand was my source?" she said. "Didn't you think how impossible that was? Burton Brand is in a coma … The story was … He was *my* husband. This isn't about your —"

"Yep, hormones," Maxine said. "Honey, Burton is not your husband. Just slow down and breathe."

Jake balled her fingers and prepared to confront Keith with the condom and the receipt and the stain, but as she tried to put it all together in her head, the reason behind it all came apart. She didn't want to figure it out. She didn't care. She couldn't even hold her fist together. As she stood there thinking, one hand up and her lips parted to speak, the ground began to sway, then shake. Jake chased her sense of balance into the center of the room, stepping into the plate of lemon bars and out of her flip-flops. Then the room dropped and tossed her to the carpet, limp as a doll. She tried to roar, but had no air. Her first thought was *earthquake*.

Jake's eyes were closed, but her ears filled in the blanks. She felt Maxine stumble, pictured those meaty, spandex-clad thighs bouncing as they reeled through the kitchen archway. There was a thud that had to be Keith's shoulder hitting the wall. Then came the tinny tones, which she surmised were car alarms tripped by the tremor. She tried to stand but dropped back. A muffled crash made her flinch for fear it was the bookcase. A metallic tinkle suggested silverware spilling out the kitchen drawers. A boom inferred the refrigerator had fallen to its side. A foggy halo of light hung above as her eyelids parted to confirm the eventual calm. A warm breeze blew through the door and dried the tears at the corners of her eyes.

The shag tickled between her fingers as she gripped it and brought her legs together to stand, finding the cushy softness of the cat purring between her knees.

Maxine bent down, her face a stale breath away from Jake's. "Did your water break?" she asked.

The cigarette was gone from Maxine's fingers, but the smoke smelled stronger, sharper and oddly pleasant, like campfire kindling.

"What the fuck?" Keith said and paced as Jake stood up. "Another spell?"

The walls and ceiling were both intact. The bookshelf was upright. The sound of the refrigerator compressor in the kitchen confirmed it hadn't fallen. Jake felt her chest, her heart throbbing at twice its regular pace. The tinny tones she'd heard were now coming from her pocket. It was her cell phone. She left it to ring and put her arms out for balance.

"Lay down," Maxine said. "Best you can do is lay down."

Keith jacked his thumb at Maxine. "She's crazy," he said to Jake. "You know that."

"It's over," Jake said, the cat curling around her ankles in a figure eight, nuzzling its head across her bare toes.

"No way," Keith said. "We'll sue them. The Mayor will sue them. We'll —"

"*We?*" Jake said. "There's no *we*."

She shoved her hands into the pockets of her sweats and looked hard into Keith's eyes — nothing but the flicker of orange light, a dying flame. Her head was still fuzzy. She opened her fists and let the restaurant receipt and condom packet drop to the floor.

The flames were real.

Newspaper pages were billowing and burning in the far corner of the room, surfing on a current of air blowing through the open door. Maxine's cigarette was the start, its filter resting at the point of a V-shaped ash-and-ember shadow on the carpet, right beside the flip-flops that had slipped from Jake's feet. Within seconds the boxes were caught up in what was becoming a conflagration, the flames sending smoky licks of soot up the walls. Bunny leapt from between Jake's legs and to the open door. Maxine and Keith jumped too, in the other direction, to beat at the flames, which only made them burn bigger. Jake went after the cat, but stopped. Who was she to make it stay? What was left?

Jake curled her toes around the bump of weather stripping across the threshold as she watched the cat bounce away up the street. She pulled apart her ponytail and took hold of the doorjamb, pinching it between her fingers and thumbs. She rocked back and bolted. She ran first to the sidewalk, then across the cool swatch of grass in the tree lawn. Her arms cranked as she sprung barefoot on the warm asphalt past the corner and beyond the open-house arrows tacked to palm trees at the end of the next block. When a young couple in an old car crested the hill, she refused to yield, running faster instead, running right at them until they pulled to the curb to make way.

Jake ran to the field at the end of the street, then kept running through that too. She followed the same boundless path as the cat until the cat disappeared, then she ran some more, crushing nasturtiums and ice plants with her bare feet. She stuck out her jaw and felt her heart adjust, the burning pain in her lungs going comfortably numb after awhile. The sway of her shoulders matched her hips, forward and back in a dance so enjoyable she could swear she heard music. It was her cell phone singing out the pocket of her sweats. She slowed to a walk and pulled it out.

Jake laughed so hard at the readout she had to stop. *Undetermined.* If anything, this caller was determined.

She considered the chance that it could be Keith, but answered anyway, too winded to say "hello," able only to mutter an indistinct "huh."

She pressed the receiver tight to her ear and strained to focus on the silhouettes of carpenters and craftsmen in a half-finished house, 300 feet or so ahead of where she stood in the field. Each body mirrored the other, the heads all topped with helmets, the hips all bound by back supports and tool belts. Jake found joy in seeing them so busy on a Sunday, all working as a unit across beams and down ladders.

The phone receiver echoed Jake's heavy breathing as her attention returned to it. She waited to listen rather than talk. Whoever was at the other end was breathing just as heavily, the sound somehow soothing, like the distant whoosh of ocean surf, or traffic at midday. She gripped the phone with both hands, cupped one palm over the mouthpiece and the other around her ear. Something lay behind the breathing, a tapping, or a thwacking, a constant ticking of some sort. It grew stronger the longer she listened. The clicks and clacks became absolute as she wiped the sweaty corners of her eyes. Mixers and fans. It had to be the mixers and fans at the bakery, the sound of home — Española.

Jake's throat swelled as she tried to talk, but managed only a garbled rasp of single syllables.

"Ma," she said and stretched her neck. "I … mom? It's you, isn't it? It's been you all this time. It's —"

"*Mija*? *Mija*, you there?"

The voice was not her mother's.

"It's Maggie, *Mija*. Can you hear me?"

Jake began to walk again, drifting closer to the construction site, the shapes no longer in the skeleton, but together on the ground, all lined between two delivery vans. Their clothing began to come into focus. Most wore plaid shirts, though a few looked to be in uniforms.

"Maggie?"

"I'm on Manny's cell. At the well pump. Such a racket. I can barely hear. It's back, *Mija*. The water came back. Water. *Agua*. We have our water back!"

Jake squinted at the symbols painted on the sides of the vans, their color and contour both familiar and foreboding. Suddenly the workers appeared less like a team united in purpose and more like prisoners joined at the hip. They remained in a line, their heads down and their hands drawn behind their backs. A dog barked and bounced on its front legs, its leash taut. It was pulling a man in uniform behind it. They were

200 feet away from Jake, but moving closer every second. She doubled her pace and headed right for them. It was *La Migra*.

"Water, *Mija*," Maggie said. "The water's all we —"

Jake interrupted. "Maggie?" she said. "I think I'm going to need a favor."

"Anything, *Mija*," Maggie told her. "Did you see the paper? The story, *Mija*. They did your story. The Mayor is sure for jail. You did —"

"Maggie, if I needed a ride in a few days, do you think Manny would pick me up?"

"Anywhere, *Mija*. He says he'll take you anywhere you want to go. Anywhere."

"Not *take* me," Jake said. "Pick me up."

Jake kept walking as she spoke, closing the gap between her and the officer and the dog to less than a hundred feet. The officer pulled off his sunglasses and drew back on the leash, pounding his boot heels into the dirt, stirring up clouds of dust while slowing his approach. His whole body shook with each forceful step, the ring of keys on his left hip jingling, his firm breasts bouncing. *Breasts? Bouncing breasts?* The officer was female. A woman, though just barely. Jake was close enough to see that now — the sunburnt pillows of baby fat in the young woman's cheeks, her shiny black hair cut schoolboy short, her arms so small-boned she double-wrapped her wrist with the leash handle. The officer's freehand shot forward, like a cop signaling an order to stop, then, with one deft movement, she slipped the same hand down and back to her hip, the center of her pink palm balanced on the butt of her holstered handgun. The dog stopped barking, but continued to strain at the chain around its neck, two syrupy strings of saliva dangling from its jowls. Jake eased off and slowed to a stroll.

Maggie's voice buzzed out the phone. "*Mija*, what you gonna do?"

"I'll call from Tijuana," Jake said in a low voice. "It'll probably take a couple days."

Whatever Maggie's response, Jake didn't wait to hear it. She dropped the phone in a patch of flowering weeds and put both hands up so high that her T-shirt rode above the waistband of her JUICY sweatpants. She continued forward, her hands still raised, the grit of the field between her toes and the warmth of the sun on her tiny brown wink of a belly button.

"No ID," she said. "No ID."

ACKNOWLEDGMENTS

There are many people to acknowledge and thank, but none more important than you. You not only found this book, but you're actually reading the acknowledgments. Thank you.

I hope you'll read the next one, and the one after that too.

— TJ Sullivan

TJ Sullivan

TJ Sullivan was born and raised in the City of Detroit. A graduate of the University of Kentucky, he began his journalism career as the Ketchum, Idaho, bureau chief of the *Wood River Journal*, which has since closed. He covered horse racing, prep sports, public schools and city hall for the *Santa Fe New Mexican*, and was the statehouse reporter for *The Albuquerque Tribune*, which has since closed. TJ's investigative reporting and feature writing for the *Ventura County (CA) Star* received many awards, including top honors from the Society of Professional Journalists (SPJ), the Associated Press News Executives Council, The American Association of Sunday and Feature Editors, Best of the West, the California Newspaper Publishers Association and the Los Angeles Press Club. He's also been commissioned a Kentucky Colonel, the highest honor awarded by the Commonwealth of Kentucky. TJ has mentored and instructed student journalists at California State University, Northridge; the University of California, Los Angeles, *Daily Bruin*; and through SPJ's The Working Press intern program.

TJ is married and lives in LA.

Breinigsville, PA USA
14 November 2009
227573BV00003B/1/P

9 780615 325279